Thornton Sully

THE COURTESANS
OF GOD

Book One: The Prophecy of Che'Wan

Thornton Sully

THE COURTESANS OF GOD

Book One: The Prophecy of Che'Wan

A Word with You Press

Editors and Advocates for Fine Stories in the Digital Age

with offices and affiliates in the USA, the UK, Germany, Poland, and the Czech Republic

www.awordwithyoupress.com

also by Thornton Sully

The Boy with a Torn Hat
Almost Avalon
The Courtesans of God Book Two: Defiance
Fire in the Belly: How to write your novel with Purpose and Passion

Anthologies:

The Coffeeshop Chronicles: Oh, the Places I have Bean!
Kid Expressions 2012
Inside the Lines—Outside the Box
5×5: Keeping the Dream Aloft

"The most powerful weapon on earth is a spirit on fire."

Ferdinand Foch,
prevailing French general, WWI

www.awordwithyoupress.com

Sully, Thornton
The Courtesans of God
Book One: The Prophecy of Che'Wan

ISBN-13: 978-1-7365480-2-8

The Courtesans of God is published by:
A Word with You Press

For information please direct emails to:
thorn@awordwithyoupress.com or visit our website:
www.awordwithyoupress.com

Book cover and interior designed by Eszter Saródy

First Edition, November, 2022

Printed in the United States of America

10 9 8 7 6 5 4 3 2 1 22 23 24 25 26 27 28 29 30 31

Dedication

For Eszter

The only man who could love you more
is the man you are helping me to become.

Je t'aime.

A Disclaimer

I truly love multi-cultural Malaysia and am awed by the beautiful tenets of Islam, and the gentleness, wisdom and kindness of the faithful. While significant events regarding Catherine D'Cruz are real, the King of Malaysia was an invention, a part of the canvas necessary to paint Catherine's story. The first king was coronated on August 31, 1957, when Malaya gained independence from the British and became the Republic of Malaysia. The official title of its honorary head of state is *Yang di-Pertuan Agong*: "He who is made Lord." At the time our story takes place, *Tuanku* Abdul Rahman was elected by the Conference of Rulers. The honor of being the constitutional monarch is rotated every five years. In addition to being addressed as King, the title is also formally referred to as Supreme Head of the Federation (of 13 states) or Paramount Ruler. Neither the most honorable Tuanku Abdul Rahman nor members of his administration bear any resemblance physically or in thought or deed to the characters in the *Courtesans of God*.

Before you begin ...

Dear Reader,

Be not tempted to dismiss the chasm of history you are about to enter as pure fiction. Most events, as portrayed, were quite real. The story was leaked to me in small increments over the course of a long marriage to the woman you are about to meet, a young girl where her story begins.

I had my doubts; the horrors of her childhood and the manner in which Catherine D'Cruz survived were beyond my comprehension, as were the events that will follow in Book Two: *Defiance*. Almost 35 years ago I accompanied Catherine to Kuala Lumpur, where her story unfolds, and tracked down the Catholic convent/cum orphanage where the Sisters failed to crush her spirit, after tremendous efforts to do so.

In Book One: *The Prohecy of Che'Wan*, you'll venture into the cellar to meet Maggie, a deformed and mentally deficient orphan denied the company of others, for fear of that her condition might be contagious. I knew all about Maggie, and her part in Catherine's story. When we located the convent, it had caught up with modern times, and no longer offered itself as an orphanage, but Maggie was never able to fend for herself or function beyond the walls of the convent, so she remained (no longer in the damp catacombs of the cellar) and was cared for in a more loving manner than during Catherine's confinement there in the late 50's and early 60's. We were welcomed by the nuns, and Catherine pointed to where scenes of her story were played out, scenes I accurately portray in what follows.

As we wandered through the halls, a curious woman in her late 30's ambled into our path. There was mutual recognition, despite the passage of time, and Maggie and Catherine melted into each other in a loving, sisterly embrace. After witnessing that, all the other pieces fell into place for me, became credible, and Catherine's story incubated, here retold, at last.

Thank you for joining us.

Thornton Sully,

author, and one of the many lovers of the Courtesan of God

The Courtesans of God

Book One

The Prophecy of Che'Wan

"Catherine. This much I *promise*
you. I *will* see you again ...
In seven-years-time, you will
find your way to the temple,
and I *will* see you again."

Premonition

No one knew for certain how old the woman really was. Those who had quietly seen their own hair turning gray could only recall from distant childhoods that she had always been as old as they themselves were now becoming.

She slept on a low bed made of straw, and silk, and clouds, and she slept very soundly until she felt the breath of Bendahara, the tiger, blow hot across her cheeks and brow. He had padded through the halls of the temple to find her, to join her.

"Your breath," she said. With her eyes still closed she reached up to push away the tiger's chin, but he was persistent, and would not let her rise until that chin of his was properly scratched.

"All right, all right," she said, with pretended anger. "Only, don't drool."

Bendahara turned his chin this way and that to make certain she got all the spots that itched, and then, feeling more content, he stretched out alongside her bed, and waited.

The old woman sat up and took one of the green leaves from the clay pot beside the bed and slipped it into the side of her cheek. Night-to-day, sleep-to-wakefulness, even, life-to-death; these were transitions that required dignity and she was not going to rush any of these events.

It was a while, then, before she stood.

Barefoot, she ambled through the archway that opened to her private garden, where the morning sun was illuminating the ferns and warming her favorite spot. "Are you coming?"

Bendahara followed at her heels and watched as she ascended the stone with some effort. Bendahara leapt up beside her with no effort at all. The broad, flat granite had been worn smooth over the centuries by the old woman and those who came before her. The sun quickly penetrated her thin, white tunic, entered her shoulders, and rejuvenated her blood. She sat, lotus-like, as she did each morning, and invited the tiger to rest his head in the hollow of her lap. She scratched behind his ears and adored the fire in his perfect, golden eyes.

The old woman began to feel the power flow from the leaf that was softening in her toothless jaw.

When the tiger had fallen asleep, his head heavy in her lap, she tuned her own breathing to the rhythm of his primordial purr, and she entered the dream-sleep of meditation. There she gossiped freely with her younger selves.

Before the trance evaporated, before Che' Wan approached her with a cup of warm, green tea and kissed her brow, it was they, the blissful inhabitants of dream-sleep, who on this morning foretold the coming of the young girl who would sit upon this very stone, and release her, at last, from all worldly obligations.

"Is it you?" she whispered, her faint smile savoring the words as they passed her lips. "I've waited so long."

Chapter One

In the Year of the Monkey in the heart of the tropics on the morning of a perpetual, centuries-old summer, God thickened the river with mud to slow the advance of time. Up the slope from his labors and unnoticed even by God, a nimble girl of seven hoisted herself through the branches of the tallest tree in the yard of the Madrigal plantation.

The uppermost branches swayed with the uncertainty of her weight, slight though it was. She could feel the muscle of the meranti tree tighten and flex, and the leaves tremble, as if they feared her weight might prove too much for the bough. She focused on remembered words: *When you start at the trunk of the tree,* her mother had told her, *you must be strong, like a caterpillar. But when you reach the top, you are light, your grip is soft. You are a butterfly.*

She could feel her mother urging her upwards. Whatever was pawing its way through the valley beyond the high wall that kept intruders out and the raw jungle at bay could only be seen from the branches where the birds nested. She had never dared to come so high, at least, not without her mother. *If only she could see me,* thought Catherine. Now, she had only to wait.

Every few moments, with her legs locked around the limb on which she sat, she twisted around and parted the leaves behind her, and looked down upon the house, its zinc roof slowly being eaten by the morning sun. Her grandmother's presence was very strong, and her rocking chair on the veranda, though vacant and still, faced the tree and gathered information. The house itself was as quiet as the summer heat, as listless as a snake with a goat in its belly. *She sleeps,* thought Catherine. Her grandmother had already caught her once earlier in the week climbing the tree and offered the perfect threat: "Girl. I'll burn it down if I catch you up there again."

Not this tree, Catherine swore. *Not ever. This tree belongs to my mother, and it will be standing here, I will be here, when, someday, she returns for me.*

Before the violence had changed everything, sometimes, when Gran'ma had gone to market, Catherine's mother would slip off her sandals and sarong and her high-collared blouse—everything, in fact, that civilized society had deemed proper—and leave it in a heap while she would climb the very branch that Catherine herself now straddled. When Catherine was an infant, her mother would sling her over her shoulders in a straw kit until she was old enough to grasp the branches herself. Cooking, cleaning, or tending to the needs of men—these would be the dubious skills that others would force upon her, but her mother taught her how to climb her way to the heavens, akin to the gift of flight. Miri, as her mother was called, would cradle Catherine in the comfort of the branches, and comb and braid her hair. For time measured only by the passing of clouds she would tell her daughter stories of the far-off land of Borneo, across the South China Sea, stories of hunting and of the Great War, stories of her tribe and the British soldier who fell into their *kampong* from the sky, clinging to the net of a captured cloud, scattering the goats and children, bargaining, offering Western cigarettes and money for each Japanese head Miri's father delivered. And, without any trace of sadness, Miri would tell the story of how she stole Catherine's father from the Japanese as the war drew to a close, and how that brought her here. That was Catherine's favorite story, and she often begged her mother to tell it over and over again. Not only did the telling let her feel herself heir to her mother's bravery, she could imagine her father as the Malay soldier, young and bold, and not the man with the bent back, who smoked too much, who drank too much, who cursed his own mother under his breath and did her bidding.

"Your mother lies," her grandmother would say. "It's all rubbish." Catherine would nod in agreement and say nothing, schooled in the consequences of contradicting her, but she hung upon her mother's every word and believed. Gran'ma also said the stories that Miri told offended God, especially the ones about how babies were made. Catherine failed to understand why, but, of course, she never asked her grandmother to explain. She only knew the stories angered her, the powerful Sarafina Madrigal D'Cruz, who spat on the roots of the tree whenever Miri went aloft, beyond her jurisdiction.

"Get down here and put on your clothes." Sarafina would scowl at her daughter-in-law from the ground below, bludgeoning her with modesty. "Heathen."

When Catherine's mother would saunter through the house in only a loincloth, oblivious to her own half-nudity or the turmoil it provoked as she paraded past the open bedrooms of the men under the roof, the grandmother would march stiffly after her with a brassiere in her hand, like a halter for a half-wild animal. Catherine would watch from behind the divan as her bewildered mother complied, and dressed, only to be defiant the very next day and be scolded all over again. And then one morning, the bare skin of *that jungle woman*, as Catherine's grandmother called her, was sufficiently scarred with the accumulation of shame that she began routinely to dress in the manner of a civilized housewife and did so until the day that left blood on the carpet.

But in this tree Catherine's mother felt no shame, and felt no obligations to Sarafina, mother of her husband and matriarch of the family. This tree was her sanctuary, and within the embrace of its branches Miri would shade her daughter from the blazing heat of Sarafina's wrath as best she could. She would stroke her skin and tell her all she knew of the world she had left behind for the captivity of privilege. Though a full two years had passed since Catherine had even seen her mother, the memory of her touch was renewed every time the tree invited her aloft, and for this—the scent, the shadow, the silhouette of her mother's spirit—no risk was too great.

Now, she looked back in the direction of the river and could see startled birds rising in panic along the trail. She was right; there *was* something there. Elders of late, particularly *Pak* Sarkia, the village headman, looked at her sternly, as if to silence her, when she spoke of the body of things before they actually appeared, or events before they unfolded.

She worked her way down through the branches, concealed by the thin veil of leaves. *It must be the whore coming,* she speculated. This moment might be her best chance to find out for sure, while her grandmother took her morning nap, and while Kamille, the amah, tended to the younger children of the household and hung the laundry in the back yard. This, too, she had seen over the zinc roof of the house. Two plump children chased butterflies around the grass. These were the well-fed children of the *good* mother, Auntie Joyce, sister of Catherine's father. Catherine's own brother and sister, spawn of that ungrateful jungle woman, followed Kamille with a basket of wet clothes, unaware their sister spied upon them from the tree.

A week earlier Catherine had made her usual forbidden foray into the pantry adjacent the kitchen to steal food for herself and Fin and Beni, her siblings. She had become their protector since their mother fled. As if she knew that day would be coming, Miri tutored her daughter in the art of stealth, teaching her just how much food she could smuggle without it being noticed as missing. Neither mother nor daughter were ever caught. But there could always be a first time. Catherine caught her breath when the groaning of the rocking chair on the veranda stopped, and, when she heard the rasp of hinges to the screen door of the kitchen, she dropped behind the coarse gunny-sacks of rice, making herself small. Sarafina Madrigal D'Cruz lumbered into the kitchen, with the ever-obedient Kamille on her heels, returned from market with fresh food and fresher gossip.

"And what is the talk, today, Kamille?" she began passively, as Kamille put down her wares on the table in the center of the room. Sarafina's back was to her servant, and she opened a drawer where an arsenal of her sharpest knives lay at her disposal.

"The elders, Ma'am. They got a letter tied with a yellow ribbon." A shank of goat's meat, though wrapped in butcher paper, was drawing the first flies.

"*Yellow?* Are you sure?" Sarafina stiffened, her fingers choking the handle of a cleaver. She had yet to turn to face Kamille.

"Yes, Ma'am. Yellow, I'm sure."

"Do you know what it said?"

"Yes, Ma'am. Everyone knows. Che'Wan is coming here, to Sentul."

Sarafina spun in place, stabbing the air as she spoke. "That's rubbish. She robbed this village the last cycle. What, has it been seven years already? She never comes to the same place twice."

Kamille flinched, shocked by the proximity of the blade to her face. "But it's true. Pak Sarkia has called for a meeting tonight after prayer. Everyone is excited. Everyone was talking about it. They ..."

"She's going to bring trouble with her. You'll see."

"I'm sorry. I ..."

"Sorry no cure. You think I don't know what she does?"

"Yes, Ma'am, I mean, no I ..."

"Never you mind. She's got no business coming here again." From her hiding place, Catherine saw each word her grandmother spoke flame briefly, and then turn gray and black, and fall like dead embers.

"But Ma'am, she's a *Disappearing One*." The strength in Kamille's voice trailed off as she realized, too late, that she was falling from her matron's good graces so early in the day.

"Che' Wan is a witch. You tell them *that*." It was more than a complaint—it was an order—and she expected Kamille to carry it out.

The ashes of ugly words settled on the food on the table, and Catherine lost all appetite. Kamille took a step backwards and covered her mouth and coughed unavoidably. Sarafina set down the cleaver momentarily and unraveled the butcher paper. She slapped down the slab of meat and pinioned it to the chopping block and took up the knife again. "And another thing ... I forbid you to mention that woman's name in this house." She sliced the air with the knife, and the blade dripped red before it ever touched the meat immobilized beneath her grip. For reasons she never bothered to explain to herself, Sarafina was suspicious, even contemptuous, of any occurrence within her fiefdom that she herself did not germinate. And Che' Wan was a *woman*. A man might be forgiven for being so important. Kamille was almost out the back door. "And as for Catherine, you keep that runt of the litter away from that whore."

... In the full week that had passed, nothing more had been said about the matter, but Catherine could think of nothing else. Now, the "runt of the litter" had shimmied down from the tree and sprinted across the yard and was halfway down the grassy slope before colliding into a barricade of horror; she had left the iron gate open. Breathless, she pivoted to charge back up the hill to swing it closed before Sarafina could discover her granddaughter had defied her once again, but in that same moment, Catherine heard a faint brass gong beckoning her to the river.

It was irresistible.

On the dawn of that same morning, fifty kilometers away and on the fringe of Kuala Lumpur, the city that took its name from the River of Mud, the sky was still the soft gray of pewter, and the faithful had not yet been called to prayer.

"Wake up, Zainuddin. This is the day," whispered Che' Wan. The boy to whom she had spoken was half asleep as she brushed his hair and dressed him, and she held his hand as she led him through the corridors and out a service entrance to where her driver was warming the Mercedes. Two women bowed as Che' Wan approached, and they ushered the boy into the front seat and opened the rear door for Che' Wan. They sat on either side of her without speaking. Che' Wan motioned for Safir, her driver and protector, to begin. "The Ancient One does not come to help you choose?" asked Safir.

"She does," she replied, "but only in spirit."

"Oh, I see. I hear she has not been well."

Che' Wan avoided truthful comment. She loved the old man but knew he was prone to gossip. "The *Yang Kuno* will out-live us all."

The dark spiral of descending road uncoiled before them like a cobra and leveled out when they passed the guardhouse at the South Gate. The highway was vacant, but for them. In the distance, beneath a thin line of silver, the horizon was still dark and cool, asleep. Occasional shop-houses clung to the side of the road, sometimes in clusters, but they became fewer in number as they motored on, and the scent of pineapples began to flow through the open windows of the car. Half-hidden service roads crisscrossed the fields and highway.

"That way," she pointed.

The snake-skin pavement turned to gravel, as if molting.

The fields were waist-high with pineapples just as the *mata hari*, the "eye of the day," began its unfailing ritual of warmth and ascent. The road they followed slithered into the obscurity of the tall grass and the first stand of trees, and shortly thereafter they reached the river. Here the road narrowed and was lacerated by the ruts of ox carts. The undergrowth to the left and right of the road grew tall and thick, and waited hungrily for the first opportunity to devour the trail altogether.

Safir gentled the car to a halt and glanced in the rear-view mirror at the woman seated between her two attendants. He had served her half his life, from the time she was a child, and he did not like disappointing her. This was the first time she had made an outing in months, and he felt personally liable for the narrowing of the road, still so far from their destination. He cleared his throat of old age and prepared his apology. He turned over his shoulder. "Forgive me, *Puan*, we can go no further. Are you certain this is the way? It's been a long time." He waited plaintively for a response.

"Oh yes. I'm quite sure." She gave no other reassurance and instructed him to turn off the motor. The river could be felt, even seen, less than twenty yards away though still partially obscured by undergrowth and a prevailing curtain of vines that dangled from the canopy above. She closed her eyes and visualized the bridge to Sentul, which she was certain was not far ahead. She whispered to the boy in the front seat next to Safir, "Zainuddin? Have you fallen asleep?"

"No, *Ibu*, I didn't fall asleep even once." Safir, who knew differently, smiled at the woman in the rear-view mirror.

"Zainuddin?"

"Yes, Ibu?"

"Do you know the legend of Sha'anni Kalizar?"

"The eagle?"

"More than an eagle ... a *garruda*, an eagle with the heart of a human and the spirit of a healer, like us. Have I told you the story?"

"No, but the Yang Kuno has told me."

"And what did she say?"

"She said Sha'anni Kalizar saved a whole village from fire once, a long time ago. Is it true?"

"Yes. Yes, it's true. Long before I was born."

"And she said the garruda protects the virtuous."

"Yes. This is also true, but did she tell you Sha'anni Kalizar makes her nest here, in Sentul?"

"No, Ibu."

"Cleanse your thoughts of everything, and fill your heart with clear, blue sky. Sha'anni Kalizar has not fluttered a wing nor drawn a breath in seven years, but, today, that will change." Then she added, "But only if you prepare yourself for her."

"Yes, Ibu. I understand."

They were well shaded and comfortable, and Che' Wan was fully confident that the impasse on the trail had been anticipated. She was seldom wrong about anything, and it was only a matter of time (*all* things, were a matter of time) before their patience bore fruit. She touched Zainuddin on the shoulder. "There. Can you feel it?"

"Feel what, Ibu?"

"The wind."

The air was still.

Zainuddin closed his eyes in concentration. "Yes. I can. What can it be?"

"Sha'anni Kalizar. She comes for us."

Zainuddin opened his eyes and stared through the windscreen of the limousine. In the near distance and above the grass he saw the wings of the garruda, just as Che' Wan had said it would be, and he heard the sharp *ping* of a brass gong. The underbrush was as tall as a full-grown man. That, and the curve in the road, obscured the approach of those who had come under the shadow of the great bird to escort them the rest of the way, and obscured also the cubicle the bird carried in its clutch.

Pak Sarkia was the first to emerge from the trail before them. He bore five hundred years of dignity and bowed crisply. Without looking backwards, he motioned two of the boys behind him to clear space adjacent to the limousine. As one of them reached to his belt to unsheathe his *parang*, the other stopped him with a curtly whispered "*Tidak*." and then glanced furtively to see if they had been noticed. Mercifully the old man's gaze was still fixed on the limousine.

... But Pak Sarkia *had* seen, in the reflection of the highly polished grillwork of the car. Later, privately, he would corner the boy. "I only meant to clear the brush." the astonished boy would say in his own defense, only to see the jaw of the old man tighten.

"It is a *weapon*. You *never* draw a blade in the presence of a court priestess. When I was a boy, you would have been *killed* for that, British law be damned. How could you not have known?" ...

The two young Malays, both on the tenuous cusp of manhood, bent down the grass and trod it flat. The earlier admonitions of Pak Sarkia echoed in their heads ... "and you must *never* have your back to the priestess."

Zainuddin was indifferent to their labors. He could not keep his eyes from Sha'anni Kalizar, who hovered above them all until the boys had prepared the nest. The ornate cubicle within her talons was shouldered by four of the strongest Malays from the kampong. Her wings were fixed in perpetual flight.

"*Ibu*. She's made of *wood*."

She let the boy think through what he had said before responding. "Are you *certain*?" To some, the garruda was only a wood carving, and lifeless. To others, the teak was a masquerade, encapsulating a living spirit within.

"Bless the ground, Noor," said Che' Wan to the woman on her left.

Sha'anni Kalizar glided gently to descent and offered Che' Wan passage within the coach she carried.

Zainuddin stared life into the carving and was certain he had seen the bird blink.

A woman with twisted fingers and crooked legs shuffled her way forward, a bundle of banana leaves cradled in her arms like a sleeping infant. One by one, she arranged an overlapping pattern of the broad leaves upon the trampled grass, laying a carpet for the priestess. She bore no part of Pak Sarkia's tension or the fear of the young boys who had cleared the path. Her age placed her well beyond that. She held one of the leaves up to the light. The filigree of each leaf, the capillaries through which flowed water, time, and life, were clearly embroidered by the nimble hand of God. She took the time to think this thought and felt the better for it. The old, unhurried woman admired her work for a moment, pleased with her carpet, though she knew it was unnecessary. Everyone knew that when Che' Wan walked, her feet never touched the ground. The old woman bowed and removed herself.

Che' Wan stepped from the Mercedes and came forward. The sunlight had found a breach, as if for her, in the canopy above. She stood before the village elders and their youthful kin in radiant bloom, gowned completely in white except for the yellow band on the cuff of her tunic. She bowed sparingly to those assembled before her—a slight, dignified nod—a detached acknowledgment by one who is revered to those who are reverent.

She lifted her head to gaze a moment upon the garruda. The wings of Sha'anni Kalizar eclipsed the sun, and her fanned tail feathers shaded the cubicle below, which she continued to hold firmly. Che' Wan bent down to kiss the cheek of Zainuddin, who had stepped beside her. "Is she only wood?" she asked him.

Zainuddin studied once more the silhouette against the morning sky, before answering. "Just now, when I closed my eyes, I saw her blink." Then the boy tugged on Che' Wan's sleeve, drawing her close enough to whisper. "Someone watches us. Up ahead."

"Yes. I know."

Noor took the boy's hand. Che' Wan's other attendant, Sita, held open the light, silk curtains of the carriage, which were opaque with a fringe of yellow ribbon, the color of the sun, the color of healing. The carriage itself, a cabin, really, consisted of a high-backed throne carved in teak, generously golden with age, with two posts and a rail in front of the seat to support a cabin top and the weight of the garruda. It was similar though smaller than the confessional of a church, but it was airy and open, with no possibility for a stagnant sin to fester. Che' Wan bowed to Sha'anni Kalizar, whose talons were integral to the roof, and stepped inside.

At this the men who had carried the chair from the village bent down to take the poles on which it was suspended. As they stood erect with their burden, each man was unmistakably aware that it was lighter now than it was when it had been empty. Was it the excitement of the moment? Had Che' Wan made them stronger? Or were the legends true? They were bursting to speak to one another, but it would have to wait.

Pak Sarkia took his place at the fore of the procession. His grandson handed him a small, brass gong, which he struck once, and with his first step forward their pious march had become a parade. He struck the gong every now and then, as he had done coming from the village, and the sound scattered monkeys and birds, and it drove uninvited jungle spirits intent on mischief from the path. But it did not seem to drive away the young girl hidden in the grass, out of breath and spellbound.

Nor did the sharp sound of the brass distract Che' Wan, who listened to the wordless beauty of the countryside, and closed her eyes as it spoke to her. She could see it growing. It was the *image* of the same jungle, the same path, of years earlier. But it was not the same jungle. Each leaf, each blade of tall grass, was only the replication of generations past. And the river—the same course, the same movement—but not the same river, filled and flowing now with a different season of rains. She saw not the transient body of things, but the spirit within. She, too, was only a replication of an earlier self who had known this trail seven years ago. She felt herself lifted by the wings of a motionless garruda, carved from a fallen tree, and she hovered over memories visible only from the sky above.

Che' Wan, who could hear the trunk of a tree outgrowing its bark, turned her attention to the faint rustling of reeds and grass up ahead. From the higher vantage point of her carriage, she could see a child cowering out of everyone else's sight. She perceived that the girl had been running hard—she could hear it in her breathing, though the girl muffled her breath in her forearm and stayed low to the ground. Her head was pounding and Che' Wan could feel the pulse in the air.

Catherine realized she was too close to the path, and was terrified as Pak Sarkia passed by her, followed by a dozen others. *They must be in a trance not to see me,* she thought. Then she felt a shadow overhead and heard the beating of the broad wings and felt the ripple as Sha'anni Kalizar fanned the grass. In the talons of the garruda she saw the one that she was forbidden to see, though her features were made indistinct by the cloud of silk curtains draped over the coach. *The witch,* shuddered Catherine. *The whore. Whatever that is, it must be worse than a witch,* she thought, remembering the rage in her grandmother's voice when she spoke the word.

She stiffened in the grass and watched a boy her own age follow behind Sha'anni Kalizar. He wore a white tunic with gold embroidery, and rather than wearing a sarong he wore loose fitting trousers, also white. A Pan flute made from the tips of river reeds laced together hung upon his chest like a medallion. The only boys Catherine had ever seen were from the kampong, and he was not like them. He was well-groomed, even elegant, and though his black hair grew down to his shoulders, unusual for a boy, he did not seem to be at all girlish. He did not look her way as he passed, obeying Che' Wan's telepathic message to him.

Catherine dug her fingers into the dirt until the last of the elders in the procession had passed. No one, she was certain, had noticed her, and she took some comfort in that. She stood, parted the brush, and followed them at a distance, like a cat that wants the company of humans, but only if the door is left ajar for an unfettered retreat.

"Just a moment," said the high priestess, as the path they had followed had reached the flowing water and the bridge to kampong. The entourage came to a halt. "Pak Sarkia," asked Che' Wan, "is this a clean bridge?"

His heart stopped.

The monsoon flood several years before had uprooted the bridge, leaving nothing. The present bridge, though weathered, was clearly not the one upon which they had trod seven years ago. This had escaped Pak Sarkia, but not Che' Wan.

"Yes ...Yes, it is," he said with relief.

Until recently, and even now in some of the more remote villages, when a bridge was built there would be the coincidental disappearance of a young girl. Speculations would be feigned in public discussion and private gossip. She was lost in the jungle or taken by a crocodile up the river. Search parties discovered nothing. But the men who would hunt for her would be conspicuously silent, since they were privy to the truth from the beginning. What choice did they have? The more malicious of the river spirits considered a bridge as trespass and could be appeased in but one way.

After a few weeks, there would be a wake with an empty coffin, and a small basket into which mourners would place money to help the family immobilized by tragedy. The poor surrendered their entire fortunes. Even the well-to-do gave something. The real fate of the girl was never acknowledged, not even privately between the parents. They were admired for the way they endured their grief and played their part, and for the beauty of their sacrifice. Everyone knew the head of their daughter was pinioned beneath the first piling.

"You must be certain, *Tuan*, that the bridge is clean. If it is not so, by the time I am halfway across I will be of no value to you, or anyone."

"Yes, Puan. I understand. I myself sunk the first piling."

To cross a bridge polluted by violence would condone the misguided ritual, and Che' Wan would have no part of it. Had she remained oblivious and begun the crossing, she would have felt herself choking on the blood of the deed anyway, as it contaminated her spirit, rendering her almost powerless, subjecting her to the punishing forces of human gravity ... but Che' Wan trusted the word of the *tuan kepala*, the village headman, that the bridge was pure.

"Well, then," she said firmly, "let's not disappoint all those people on the other side."

"Yes, Puan." His vigor soared again, uplifted by the current of Che' Wan's approval. He struck the gong once again and, as his step touched the first plank of the bridge, the air blossomed with applause from the far side of the river.

Sha'anni Kalizar swept her way forward and scanned the crowd that awaited them. The virtuous could ride upon her wings, but evil beings, whether flesh or spirit, would scatter at the garruda's approach. She could ferret out the deceitful with her black sapphire eyes that only the pure of heart could gaze upon. Invisible demons panicked and fled to the sound of the piercing cry that only they could hear, discharged from the breast of Sha'anni Kalizar.

After seven years of stillness, she had spontaneously awakened this summer morning to retrieve her mistress and was now proudly returning to display the gift she ferried beneath her.

Among these people, Sha'anni Kalizar had earned her place shortly after the turn of the century. Late one night, when everyone had been asleep, she was heard screaming from her perch in the mosque moments before flame was visible or smoke detectable. A few who had been children then remembered how the urgent warning of the garruda mobilized a water brigade that kept the fire from spreading.

Those same children were now the elders who walked behind Sha'anni Kalizar and could see the truth that others were too young to perceive: it was the garruda who carried the sacred one across the river. The bearers carried only the throne on which she sat.

The slender reeds in the shadow of the bridge stood shoulder-to-shoulder in random clusters until the last in the entourage had crossed. At this, the slight girl who had been watching everything emerged from the invisibility the reeds afforded her. The long and open bridge provided no such security, and she scampered across quickly, as Sha'anni Kalizar and Che' Wan were absorbed upon the banks of the kampong. The villagers parted for them and bowed as they passed, like broad leaves bending in a gentle rain. Catherine slipped in behind them before the crowd closed the gap to the trail they had opened, and she followed Che' Wan through the village towards the mosque.

So, this is what Kamille had been talking about, thought Catherine. *It's true.* Seven days prior to this moment a runner had been sent with a written message to Pak Sarkia, informing him of Che' Wan's intended arrival. No explanation was given;

it was well understood what a visit from the high priestess from the Palace of the King implied.

Preparations were immediate and intense. She had chosen Sentul for a second time. This baffled Pak Sarkia. What would cause her to deviate from tradition? And where was the Ancient One, the Yang Kuno? He kept this to himself and focused on the task before him. A second time. The honor was of unimaginable proportions.

Though pineapples had just come in season, Pak Sarkia culled almost half the men from the fields, this with the begrudging consent of Sarafina Madrigal D'Cruz. Those who stayed with the harvest shared their wages with those chosen to renovate the kampong and prepare for the arrival of Che' Wan. It had been her blessing of the village alone that had allowed them to be spared so much of the agony that befell the rest of the Malay Peninsula during the War.

Silt that had made the drainage ditches stagnant was dredged, and goats were set free to feed on the random patches of weeds throughout the kampong. The mosque was hastily repainted, and the sand in the square it bordered was raked in symmetrical patterns where a ceremonial tent was erected. The ground was blessed, and the sky itself was washed with prayer. Were Che' Wan to see anything impure or perceive anything imperfect through any of her many senses, she could become tainted, and any blessing that she might offer to the village would have no power or magic.

The women began planning the menu and sent their children to gather the herbs and roots that needed several days to prepare and ferment. Mothers would look judiciously at the children of appropriate age, and in the evenings, after prayer, would rehearse with them the dance of their ancestors as the men provided soft-as-rain gamelan music late into the night.

A slight limp disappeared from Pak Sarkia's step that week, as the challenge to prepare made him youthful. But he could not inspire everyone.

There were the old Chinese families, that owned the stores, the Indian family, that owned a truck, and, of course, the Madrigals, the family that burned candles for Jesus and owned the rubber tree and pineapple plantations.

The Chinese believed—and it was confirmed by none other than Sarafina Madrigal D'Cruz herself—that the garruda could see into their houses and come to life at the bidding of Che' Wan, to swoop through their doors to steal their children. "You let that wooden bird of hers into your house, it will pluck your children from their beds and carry them to a cave in the mountains." She offered evidence. "The white tops of the mountains? That's the bleaching bones of the children it eats. The real reason Che' Wan comes ... is to feed her pet."

Because Sarafina spoke so fearlessly, the fearful believed her every word. The superstitious prepared for Che' Wan with a traditional defense against evil; they wired pieces of broken mirror to their closed doors so that the garruda would see no children within, would see only its hideous self. A rusted nail was put upon every windowsill to impale its spirit should it try to gain entry.

The Indian family worked very hard to express no opinion at all.

But among the Malays no effort was spared to groom the more refined children who might pass under the eye of Che' Wan. Their posture, their speech, their mannerisms, suddenly were scrutinized by every adult in Sentul. The children she had recruited seven years earlier were children no more, and it was time to regenerate. Every seven years it had been thus, as far back as anyone could remember, but never twice from the same village, never such favoritism.

So little time to prepare for all this. Who would ever have thought that she would return? For the entire week parents secretly speculated which children might find favor with Che' Wan and have the chance to become what only she could make of them, vessels of healing ... and of pleasure.

On this day Che' Wan would decide whose lives she would change forever, the ones she would patiently tutor, preening wings as yet untried, teaching them to dance, to heal others, to shape the desires of the flesh into the flight of birds, to become the courtesans of God, and to be so light of spirit they would leave no footprint as they walked the ground, transforming them into the intermediaries of the spirit world who could evaporate at will into the future or the past—*Bida Devi*— the Disappearing Ones.

And perhaps, in this crop of children, she would find the one so strong of spirit but so unfettered by the gravity of the world that the old woman in the temple could at last be free to explore the pleasure of her own death. It was for this Che' Wan had come.

Sha'anni Kalizar surveyed the crowd as she glided across the bridge and saw only goodness. On a hilltop not far away, Sarafina Madrigal D'Cruz awakened from her morning nap, stepped onto the veranda, and saw only that the gate had been left open.

Chapter Two

In the fore of the mosque was a treeless quadrant formed by Chinese houses whose parlors served as shops for the entire village. Each of the merchants stocked the same wares—rice, coffee, batik, lamp oil, a few simple household utensils—almost nothing that cost more than a day's wages. Each merchant had their own following, and, since they all sold the same things, it was the quality of gossip a shop disseminated that created loyalty among customers. Catherine, as always, avoided passing the shop of Ephram Lim, who always saved the finest batik and best gossip for Sarafina Madrigal D'Cruz. Ephram was Sarafina's most devoted spy.

The square itself pulsated on market days, or on warm, rainless evenings when neighbors would bring out their woven mats to sit together for the *wayang kulit*, the puppet show of mythical heroes whose shadow images were cast upon a taut sheet by the glow of a fire behind the puppet master. "Blasphemy," Sarafina would say. Catherine was forbidden to attend, and never missed a performance.

Now the square was filled, shoulder-to-shoulder, and in the crush of so many people Catherine was separated from the view of the garruda. She climbed on top of a covered rain barrel next to one of the shops and held the downspout from the gutter to balance herself, and from here she saw not only the garruda but also a huge tent, gay and colorful, erected for the day's activities. The whispered name "Sha'anni Kalizar" was passed from one believer to another, as reverently as bread is passed at a table.

The garruda was lowered to the sand, like porcelain. At this the men made themselves small as they did when they prayed, the humbling union of brow to earth, and the women retreated discreetly to the obscurity of the fringes. Suddenly the cabin beneath the wings was visible, though no one dared to look. The silk veil that protected Che' Wan from their stares of the imperfect was about to be parted.

Catherine pressed herself against the wall, becoming shadow, as the witch in her grandmother's warning stepped from her throne and took the hand of the boy who had followed directly behind her. Catherine held her hand over her mouth to keep from saying out loud, "*Allah*. She's *beautiful.*"

Pak Sarkia, having been released of the obligations to protocol by Che Wan when she first arrived on the jungle trail, stood and nodded to the *muezzin*, the caller of prayer, to enter the tent and invoke a blessing. Islam had groomed the heart and intellect of the Malays for centuries, now, conforming the population the way the banks restricted the waters of the river. But as well-defined as the current might be, independent eddies formed contrary to the flow, and were part of the same river. Absolute faith in Mohammed's god, and absolute faith in a spirit world, the world of Che' Wan and the Bida Dewi, contained no hypocrisy for the village of Sentul.

Che' Wan entered the purified tent, where she could converse and engage with others without her purity being compromised. A platform dappled with the petals of flowers awaited her. She ascended the three steps, followed by Zainuddin and then Sita and Noor. Che' Wan sat upon the mats, facing the open flap to the tent, and Noor and Sita sat behind her, available to hear a private word or to do her bidding. Zainuddin sat by her side.

"You may enter."

Pak Sarkia bowed and came in, followed by musicians who did the same. "*Selemat pagi*," she said. Good morning, and she smiled. A few of them were reluctant to smile back and turned their heads shyly, ashamed that poverty and age had left them almost toothless. Her smile was so perfect. They each carried an instrument of their own construction and gathered themselves in the corner of the tent. They were eager to offer music. They arranged themselves on the mats, cradled their instruments, and waited for Pak Sarkia's direction.

With the sharp ping of the small brass gong Pak Sarkia dispersed the same spirits he had scattered from the jungle path, for it was likely they were mustering their courage at the open flap to the tent.

Noor vacated the stage to stand by the entrance. She motioned for the awaiting mothers and children who had come for this moment and purified them with a few drops of water from a vial she had filled from the spring water of the temple. As soon as they were blessed, the auditions began.

Pak Sarkia gestured to the old men, and soon music began to fill the tent as gently as rain evaporating from banana leaves on a hot August morning. With chimes and with drums, with brass and with bamboo, with flute and with humming, a mother gingerly cast her daughter free to the open space before the priestess, and the child began to dance. Barefoot, moving slowly upon woven mats, her hips swaying ever so gently, the fingers of her hands courting one another, all in rhythm to the humble gamelan music that had coaxed her spirit to reveal itself.

Che' Wan studied the link between mother and daughter. The child's unsure eyes dashed sporadically towards the mother for approval.

"Come, child." The music had stopped. "You dance very well." The girl and the mother approached the priestess.

"Thank you, Puan."

"And such poise in one so young." Che' Wan said this to the mother, but with just enough intensity that she could be heard by the others waiting patiently along the perimeter of the tent. "I … shall think on it." Che' Wan then lowered her head to the mother, a gesture of humility that would spare the mother of any loss of face she might have for her daughter being rejected.

The next child stood, danced, was interviewed politely and then returned to her place, followed by another. "Let me hear you walk," she would say to one child. "Let me see you speak," she would say to another. She was looking for lyric in both step and voice. So progressed the morning, and two girls and a young boy would soon sleep in the temple of the Bida Dewi, within the citadel of the king. Still, Che' Wan had hoped for more. She closed her eyes for a moment, to listen to what the old woman in the temple was saying to her.

Zainuddin, with aristocratic poise, stood from his velvet cushion and put his hand upon Che' Wan's shoulder while she sat. He quietly advised her, "Ibu, the one who was hiding by the trail."

"Yes. I've been watching her." She opened her eyes.

For some time, the girl had been standing just outside the tent, peeking through the smallest of holes in the fabric. Each time she heard the music start, she herself began to dance. The morning sun was behind her, and her shadow became the silhouette that intrigued the young boy within the tent. Zainuddin whispered once more, "She moves like the wayang kulit. She dances with her own shadow."

"Yes … she certainly does."

Only then did Pak Sarkia discover the presence of the girl, and he stumbled outside to shoo her away.

"Pak Sarkia." He stopped and bowed when he heard the voice of Che' Wan. "That girl. Show her in."

The village elder swallowed hard. "Yes, Puan."

Outside the tent he looked sternly at Catherine, holding her in place with his stare. She readied herself to bolt and run. "The priestess would like you to enter."

"Priestess?"

"Yes. Of course. The *Seri Jaya*. The Highest One. Che' Wan."

"I thought she was a witch."

"Hold your tongue." Pak Sarkia was beside himself and looked over his shoulder to see if they might be overheard. "Just ... get inside ... keep your head bowed, and don't say *anything*."

She stood straight up, gathered her long, tangled hair and tossed it out of the way behind her, and did her best to make herself bigger than she was before making her entrance. She was wearing only a singlet and short pants, a tomboy. Mud from the banks of the river was the only color of her wardrobe.

"Noor. Bless the child."

Noor produced the vial with water from the temple and anointed the girl's forehead. "She has been purified, Puan."

"Good ... come forward, child."

Catherine did as she was told and stepped forward meagerly. She glanced back at Pak Sarkia for a moment, and felt small and defenseless, and prepared for her punishment. She paused and then, willfully, as if to say "I have done *nothing* wrong" to the old man, she took a deep breath that inflated her, and threw back her shoulders. When she turned her head towards the stage, she looked the priestess straight in the eyes. Before Che' Wan could speak, the little girl who stood before her said, "Why, you're not *at all* ugly."

"What?"

Pak Sarkia rushed forward.

"No, no. Let her be ... Well, thank you. Now, what do you mean, I'm 'not at all ugly'?"

"No. In fact, you're quite beautiful, for a witch."

"*Pardon me*, Puan." Sarkia could not contain himself. "May I have a private word?"

Che' Wan motioned him forward. He lowered his voice. "This one. She's from the Madrigal plantation."

"A servant's child?"

"Oh, no. The granddaughter of Sarafina Madrigal D'Cruz herself. Puan ... she is not even *Muslim*."

"And the mother? What of the mother?"

"Oh ..." Pak Sarkia lowered his head and voice even further. "She was a bad woman. She made a lot of trouble. She is *Iban*. Borneo. A jungle woman. Her father was even a chief. He took heads."

"Where is she now, the girl's mother?"

"No one knows. Singapore, maybe. No one knows."

"Not back to her own people?"

"She can't go back. She *left* them. They'll kill her."

Che' Wan understood. Even the daughter of a chief could not desert a tribe with impunity. She must have left them without consent. Che' Wan herself was from Borneo, and had even lived among the Ibans, as a child, before she heard the whisper of an old woman calling to her from across the South China Sea, the old woman who even now was meditating in her garden with the morning sun on her shoulders, visualizing the events of the day.

"Thank you, Pak." She looked thoughtfully at the girl before her and dismissed Pak Sarkia with a soft wave of her hand.

The water that Noor had run down the girl's forehead had washed off enough mud to reveal a small scab in the center of the brow, a childhood scrape that meant nothing. But upon Che' Wan's brow, beneath a moonstone that dangled from a tiara, was the diamond shaped scar that was branded upon her the day she became Bida Dewi.

"Come closer, girl."

Catherine obliged. Here was a small girl, a little undernourished but remarkably self-assured. There was the usual array of scratches upon the knees and elbows so common to a child that age, but Che' Wan was able to discern also, upon Catherine's forearm, a pattern of deep purple crescents that can only be made by the fingernails of an angry adult.

"Tell me. How old are you?"

"Seven."

The number of completion, thought Che' Wan.

"And when were you born?"

"In the Year of the Tiger. My mother told me."

"And where is your mother, now?"

Catherine lowered her eyes, and remembered the day her mother ....

"You've got her spirit in you, don't you?"

"Yes. I do." At this Catherine lifted her head again, defiantly proud of the mother condemned by so many.

"Girl, do you like to dance?"

"My *name* is Catherine."

"Oh. Forgive me. Catherine. Do you like to dance?"

"Yes. I do."

"Then, dance for me ... Catherine."

Pak Sarkia, though an elder, was not yet old enough to be amused. He rolled his eyes, looked at the musicians, and had them play. The child began to dance. She had seen the other girls, their moves, their rhythm, but had never been tutored, as had they. It didn't seem to bother her. She invented movement and was completely oblivious to anyone's scrutiny. She enjoyed herself. While she danced, Che' Wan thought, *this is a good sign, how the girl replied about her age*. She could have given a numerical answer. She could have said '1950'. *I wonder if by instinct she knows that time is more than linear measurement, more than beads on a string? What else does she know of what cannot be seen?*

"She dances very well," commented Sita.

"She does indeed." *1950 is the halfway point of the century*, thought Che' Wan. *The pinnacle that divides what has been and what will be.* And, she thought, born in the same chasm of time as Zainuddin, who will someday need a mate. This could not be by chance. She had seen enough. She raised her hand and the music stopped. "Come here, Catherine. Let me take a closer look at you." She took the girl's hands and looked at the raw knuckles and muddy nails. Almost at once, when their flesh connected, she could hear a voice from the temple urging her. "*This one.*"

The girl had a high, intelligent forehead, and that scar. It must be more than coincidence. She stared into the girl's deep and trusting eyes, reading her history, trying to read her future. "*This one.*" She heard the voice again and answered out loud. "Yes. I know." She began to imagine what her little urchin would look like with a bath and could hardly wait to run a comb through her hair.

And then, knowing what she would find, she turned the girl's hand in her own, and examined the lines of her palm. There it was. Unmistakable. A perfect square. The sign of a healer. The sign of a high priestess. She kissed the girl's open palm. "Look, Catherine."

She traced the square for her. "Do you know what this means?"

"No."

"It means you're special." Che' Wan showed Catherine her own palm, with the identical marking.

Catherine looked at the similarities. "Am I a witch?"

Che' Wan laughed and kissed the girl on the forehead.

A runner was sent to the Madrigal estate, with a brief note tied with a yellow ribbon.

Chapter Three

Sarafina rocked slowly and deliberately in the shade of the zinc roof that flared over the veranda. She fanned herself and stared at the open gate half hidden by the huge meranti tree that was somehow an accomplice to her many misfortunes, when the out-of-breath messenger arrived, and stuttered the news that Catherine had found her way into the center of things again. He handed Sarafina the note, which she did not open.

"The high priestess herself comes to barter for the girl's future," he concluded, and he was suddenly embarrassed by his own unshared enthusiasm. Kamille offered him water, thanked him on behalf of Sarafina, and suggested that he leave. Sarafina had not said a word through all of this but continued to rock. When the coolie was gone, Sarafina stood and leaned on the banister. She muttered a few things to Kamille, orders. Kamille took the rocking chair into the house, and un-scrolled finely woven mats in its place. *That tree has got to come down,* and soon, thought Sarafina to herself. She tossed the letter into the bin to the side of the door.

Kamille brought out a low serving table on which she centered a bowl of rose water and a tray of beetle nuts. "Will there be anything else, Puan?"

"No." She didn't bother to turn and face her servant. "Just see that Beni and Fin stay in their room ... Put them down for their afternoon nap." Beni and Fin, unlike their sister, Catherine, were too young to have a will of their own and were no threat to Sarafina.

"Yes, Puan."

"*Those* two, at least, you should be able to manage," she said, taking a quick slice at Kamille for letting Catherine stray that morning. Kamille lowered her head and disappeared into the house, taking the bin with her without being told.

Sarafina sat down on the mats and helped herself to some beetle-nuts. She leaned against the side of the house, and folded her legs beneath her, lotus-style. The heat had made even the air lethargic, like a snake that had just fed, and it crawled into the shade of the veranda where Sarafina fanned herself and waited. Time itself stepped more slowly than usual in deference to the heat, and then it stopped altogether, stirring again only when the first few members of Che' Wan's delegation made their way through the gate. Sarafina watched as Che' Wan instructed her people to wait in the grove between the house and the gate before she proceeded to the veranda. Sarafina revealed no expression when she saw the hand of her insolent granddaughter in that of the priestess. As Che' Wan approached, Sarafina got to her feet, making it appear to be an effort, as if her joints ached, and she bowed more deeply than a woman of her status might be expected to do in the presence of her guest.

"Welcome. Welcome," she said, bowing again as she spoke. "It is a pleasure to meet you at last. A pleasure," and she gestured for Che' Wan to join her on the veranda. The priestess was taken aback—Sarafina's mouth was bright red, and Che' Wan thought the woman was bleeding from within. Che' Wan glanced at the table, at the shelled beetle-nuts, and quickly understood. Years of chewing the beetle-nut had permanently stained Sarafina's mouth and left her looking carnivorous. Che' Wan could feel a slight shudder in the young girl whose hand she still held.

Che' Wan nodded and stepped up on the porch. As Sarafina bowed one last time Che' Wan got a good look at her shoulders. They seemed too powerful for a woman whose station in life made heavy labor an option rather than a necessity, and a crucifix dangled from a rather muscular neck. Her black hair, beginning to streak with the white mutiny of aging, was gathered behind her head in a loose bun, and held in place with a modest silver pin, like a slender, curved dagger. When she lifted her head, even her smile was muscular. Sarafina directed her guest to a cushion, and she herself, with embarrassing modesty, sat opposite her on no cushion at all.

"The pleasure is mine to be here, Puan," said Che' Wan, without passion.

"Have you had your tea, my dear?"

"Oh, no, I haven't. That would be fine, thank you."

"Kamille? Would you please?" she called over her shoulder. She knew Kamille would be just inside the door.

As tea brewed Che' Wan inquired about the harvest, and about the children, and made the customary remarks about the small rose garden to the left and right of the steps to the veranda. It was only when tea was set before them that Che' Wan got to the heart of the matter. "Madam D'Cruz, I have come to ask your consent to take Catherine back with me today, to live in the temple."

Sarafina feigned surprise. "*My* granddaughter?"

"Yes. Your granddaughter." Che' Wan stopped herself from reaching for her teacup, angered at Sarafina's pretended humility. Catherine wanted to speak, wanted to warn Che' Wan, but knew she could say nothing.

"Madam D'Cruz," continued Che' Wan, "if you let me have Catherine, and let me take her with me to our temple, I can do things for her that this village never can. What is there for her here? And with no mother?"

"I do more for the girl than the mother ever could," said Sarafina, abrasively.

"Indeed, you *do*," replied Che' Wan, seizing the initiative. "And here is a chance to do even *more*."

Sarafina hid her mouth behind her teacup.

"Puan," continued Che' Wan, "if you allow me to take her, I will love her as I would my own daughter. *I* will be her *ibu*, her mother. I will teach her not only *our* ways, but the ways of the West, as well. I will have her reading English, and Sanskrit, if you like. I will teach her the ways of the dancer, and of the healer. I will bri ..."

"*I myself* am a healer. Ask anyone. Ask them all. It is *me* they come to, when they are sick, or their bones are broke. Ask them. I can teach her these things."

But will you? thought Che' Wan. *There is deceit here.*

But this much was true. Sarafina Madrigal D'Cruz was the *bomoh*, the medicine woman for Sentul. Pak Sarkia had told Che' Wan stories about her before she left the tent that afternoon. When herbs and ointment failed, Sarafina would invoke the darker spirits, bargaining with them on behalf of those she would heal. Those she succeeded in curing were as intimidated by Sarafina as they were by the spirits she claimed had caused their illness, but they spread word of her power, and became indebted, indentured to her. She accumulated their souls and kept them in an opaque vial by her humidor.

Sarafina noticed that the priestess had yet to sip her tea, the gesture of acceptance. She decided to call her on it. "Your tea, my dear?"

"It's still quite hot." Che' Wan felt no obligation to be sincere.

Sarafina stared past Che' Wan's shoulder. The entourage that had accompanied her to the house sat beneath the rambutan and mango trees, and that damned meranti tree in the island made by the circular drive. "Tell me," she said. "Who's the boy? Your son?"

"That is Zainuddin. No. I am not his birth mother, but I am like an ibu to him."

"Really? And what sort of things do you teach *him* to do in the temple?"

"I teach him to *do* nothing. I teach him to *be* everything." Che' Wan would not be baited. "He's very special, like your granddaughter."

Sarafina took another sip from her tea. *Too hot indeed*, she said to herself. "And what about ... the *church*." Sarafina, in the tradition of the Madrigals, was Catholic, and even gave money when Sister Masselin would come from the convent to visit from time to time.

"If she is meant to be Catholic, if she is meant to be as ... you are ... it will reveal itself, over time. I won't interfere with that."

Sarafina fondled the crucifix that dangled from her neck. *What a blasphemous notion*, she thought, *but of no importance*. "My dear, I don't think Catholic girls are meant to do *all* the things you intend to teach her. I've heard what goes on in your .... *temple*."

Catherine had maneuvered to the relative obscurity of the doorway, behind Kamille, who had quietly returned from the nursery. How many times Catherine recalled her grandmother threatening to get rid of her. Now if only she would. Che' Wan could feel the girl pleading.

"I am only thinking of the girl, you see," said Madam D'Cruz. "I only want what is best for her."

You have never wanted what was best for the girl. This Che' Wan said to Sarafina without moving her lips or making a sound, and Sarafina heard each word.

"But tell me this, would you?" asked Sarafina politely. "Is it true the king actually sends a tithe each month, to the mothers of the children you take with you?"

Very cautiously, Che' Wan asked, "Would you expect a tithe from the king?"

"The girl is very special, very dear to me."

Not once have you referred to Catherine by name, thought Che' Wan. *Why is she only 'the girl'? No wonder Catherine had been so insistent back in the tent that she be called by her true name.*

Sarafina looked behind Kamille's shoulder and motioned Catherine to approach. She took her by the elbow and pulled her down to sit in her lap. "She is not like the other girls," she explained, "the ones in the *kampong*, poor things. She is worth ... so much more." She reached behind her, taking possession of Catherine's forearm.

Che' Wan understood and looked sadly at Catherine. Her grandmother would never give her consent to leave. She merely wanted to see what the royal temple would offer for her. "Madam D'Cruz, it is true that a tithe is given, but it is a very small sum, certainly to a woman with your means. And it is freely given, as the children are freely given. We do not buy children." She paused, further angered that Catherine's welfare had very little to do with Sarafina's motives, Sarafina, who sipped genteelly from her teacup and waited for her guest to continue. "And, yes, I agree. She is very, very special, more than either of us may know. I can understand why you would not want to part with her."

Suddenly Catherine blurted out, "Gran'ma, let me go with her."

"I only want what is best for you." Rage tightened the muscles of Sarafina's face, and her nails dug ever so slightly into Catherine's skin.

"*Please*. Let her take me."

"It all right, Catherine," said Che' Wan, who did not want to antagonize Sarafina at Catherine's expense. Sarafina stiffened as she felt her façade being undermined by the child on her lap.

"Come, daughter," said Che' Wan quietly, as she stood. "Walk me to the gate."

Catherine freed herself from her grandmother and clung to Che' Wan the way a child awakening from a bad dream clings to a pillow in the dark.

"Thank you for your hospitality," said Che' Wan. "Please consider my proposal for Catherine." She stepped down from the veranda and began walking the long drive with Catherine's hand in her own. Her people in the grove had already headed off when they first inhaled the air contaminated by the volcanic ash of Sarafina's meanness that wafted their way.

"I ... shall think on it," said Sarafina, smiling as she watched them go. The simmering teacup, untouched by the priestess, said nothing, glared into silence by the admonishing glance from the woman leaning on the balustrade.

Halfway to the gate and without breaking stride, Che' Wan spoke. "Don't cry, Catherine. Be *strong*. It is your first lesson. Be strong."

Yes, thought Catherine. *I can be strong. I can be strong for Che' Wan*. Still, she felt all hope vanishing as they approached the gate. They stopped, and Che' Wan watched for a moment as Sarafina turned into smoke and flame on the veranda and continued to smile politely.

"Catherine. This much I *promise* you. I *will* see you again." She bent down and wrapped her arms around the girl who was already so adoring of her. Catherine's memories of her real mother were vague but somehow awakened, memories so different from what her grandmother told her was true. "In seven-years-time, you will find your way to the temple, and I *will* see you again."

Che' Wan stood. "Be strong," she said, but this time empathically. She closed her eyes and inhaled the scent of the fragile little girl who still clung to her. The essence of that breath she would not expel until she was within the temple, transporting the seed of Catherine's spirit to safety. She peeled the child away from herself and held her at arm's length, memorizing the face. "Goodbye, Catherine. I *will* see you again." She passed through the gate without looking back, having done what she could to empower Catherine to fend for herself.

Catherine turned to see her grandmother leaning over the rail of the veranda, posing, but she could hear even from fifty yards the old woman's teeth grinding together. She dashed out the gate before she could be called and ran to the pineapple fields where her grandmother would never follow.

That girl, thought Sarafina. *She is just like her mother, that jungle woman.*

Kamille knew enough to remove the mats at once and return the rocker. Her matron no longer needed the pretense of humility. Sarafina let her weight drop in the chair. "Kamille," she barked, "bring me my cigars."

In a moment Kamille produced the humidor and matches and set them on the low table. From years of service, she knew that this was to be a private moment, and she disappeared to the kitchen.

Sarafina opened the humidor, scrutinized the selection, and circumcised her choice. She sucked in the first few drafts of gray smoke, and in a few moments, all seemed to be right with the world again. Rocking and smoking, she persuaded herself that she had gotten the better of the encounter with the priestess. *Healer indeed.* She would deal with her granddaughter's insolence, in time. The girl had to come home, eventually. There was always the tree, though from years spent crippling her own children she knew the threat of punishment was often more tortuous and of more value than the punishment itself.

This cigar, she thought, *this fine cigar. What a pleasure it is. A pleasure.*

Her composure had returned.

She was noticing that the guavas in the small grove in front of the house were overly ripe, and either rotting on the tree or on the ground. She could not remember which of her servants to berate for this neglect, but any servant would do, really, a quick expression of authority. That tall coolie under the straw hat now entering the gate. He ... but it was no coolie, evident only as he lifted his hat and waved towards the house.

It was William, her husband, returned early from the fields.

And now Sarafina smiled in earnest. William she truly loved and felt almost girlish in his presence. He was the one man that she truly respected. The only person with whom she could enjoy a good smoke. She inhaled once more as he approached. She held her breath, and in the smoke dungeon of her lungs she suffocated all thoughts of Che' Wan and Catherine ... and that despicable mother of Catherine's— that *jungle woman*.

Chapter Four

A conspiracy of vines was all that anchored the highest branches of the trees to the denser jungle far below, or the trees would surely have grown past the soft silver clouds of Borneo and into heaven itself. It was well known that from these very branches God made his first descent to walk the earth and explore all that he had made.

Before she had ever known of Sarafina Madrigal D'Cruz, or even that there was a world other than her own, that *jungle* woman had seen fourteen years pass, and much of it from these tall trees. On this particular morning she had made a nest for herself thirty feet above the damp floor of the rain forest, in the rungs of God's own ladder.

Beneath her the undergrowth glistened, as sunlight evaporated the morning offering of rain. The vapor lifted from each leaf like cool, lazy smoke, and carried with it the sweet smell of deep brown earth mingled with the scent of animal and the bloom of hyacinth. A thousand butterflies floated in the air like falling petals of flowers in a light breeze, drifting on the breath of God. A thin trail bent its way past the trunk of the tree, formed by the convergence of two opposing slopes. The girl could detect all movement below from this vantage point, and yet, from below, to anyone looking up, she appeared to be only a part of the spiral of branches, a leaf against the sky.

On the rain-worn stub of a broken branch she hung her kit, a pliant basket laced to a wooden harness, on which was strapped her blowpipe and quiver of darts, ready in an instant to take down her prey of choice. The spear of which she was so proud and with which she was so precociously adept lay cradled in her lap, and her parang dangled at her side in a sheath made from the hide of an animal she herself had killed and butchered.

She reached into the basket and pulled out yet another ripe mango, and leaned forward, oblivious to the height, to keep the first bite from spurting on her bare breast, just washed clean and still beading with drops of fresh rain. She sucked the pulp and tossed the seed, and gathered her long black hair behind her, in a swirl, a cushion, and laid her head against a crotch in the branches. One leg dangled lazily and the other propped her firmly into place—her place—in the branches, in the jungle, in the world.

And the world was hers. She was quite content to daydream from her nest, and as far as she could see was the land of her people. She wondered if the mountain beyond the valley was really gray, for green was the natural color of the world. The distant pinnacles were white, no doubt the broken shells from the rookery of eagles. Someday she would journey for a closer look, but for now her father forbade her from hunting outside their valley, or from approaching the settlement of Miri where the river replenished the sea.

Her father, Jon the Poet, was quite proud of her. He had long ago conceded that she had a man's spirit, and rather than discouraging her boyish tendencies, instead tutored her in the ways of the hunter. She could throw a spear as far and as passionately as any man, and it had long been taken for granted that when Miri, named for the village forbidden to her, went hunting, she would return with the weight of a kill upon her shoulders to divide among her tribe.

She loved to hunt, and she loved to race her *perahu* along the faster currents of the river, banking at the eddies and coves where she tended the nets that invariably snared fish for her. To the endless list of her adventures, she had recently added the startling pleasure that young men provided, and it was this that fancified her dreams high in her loft. She pursued and conquered them in spite of their pretended shyness. She loved the way they would touch her skin, and she loved the feel of their manhood pressed deep into her youthful and powerful hips, and she loved the flirtations and teasing.

It was not quite mid-day, though time had little significance for her. Her valley was so abundant with game that she could stay out almost until the blush of sunset and still be assured that she would find something worthy of a kill on the way back to her kampong. Indeed, she had passed up an opportunity to take down a small boar, because she had come across it so early in her outing. Had she killed it she would have been compelled to return prematurely, before she had her fill of adventure, for the squeal of the dying boar would attract a leopard, or even a tiger, the other predators who shared hunting privileges with the Iban in the valley.

But in recent years there were others, uninvited others, who stalked the same hunting grounds. The girl in the branches of the meranti tree sensed before she heard, and she heard before she saw, a column of soldiers grunting and stumbling their way up the trail beneath her. This was not the first time she had seen the Japanese, though none had ever seen her.

She and her brothers had twice entertained themselves by lighting fire to their makeshift encampments, and watched them panic to put the fires out, which was always too late, leaving them to sleep the night in the rain. Her brother had even taken a head, which he proudly presented to his father.

As a *Dayak*, a native, she would be a rare prize to the Japanese, who captured indigenous people to use as guides in this unfamiliar territory. But the Dayaks would usually permit themselves to be captured, and then 'guide' their captors into thick, wet jungle, only to escape and leave them stranded. It was great sport.

Several years earlier Miri and her brothers were awed by the sight of a British paratrooper floating down to their village on the strings of a cloud, with a bold proposition for their father, whose reputation was well-known even in the civilized town at the delta.

Money.

Money could be used on market days in Miri to trade for a vast array of goods the Dayaks could not make for themselves. The soldier had brought samples. Chocolate. Pocketknives. Knit shirts. Tin cups. Cigarettes.

And money would be theirs on a regular basis at the rate of ten *ringgit* for each Japanese head they delivered.

It was an easy bargain. The Ibans, a more prominent race of Dayaks, had no love for the Japanese, who slaughtered people indiscriminately and with no explicable ritual, and they burned countless acres of jungle if rumored to contain even a handful of British or Malayan soldiers. The taking of heads was already a tradition of the tribe, a trophy of the combat that occasionally flared into ritualized skirmishes with bordering clans. The British soldier shook the hand of Jon the Poet and drank from his cup, and the Japanese became the Iban's prey of choice.

And the prey of choice, to Miri's amusement, was now clustered beneath her tree, smoking cigarettes, and blowing smoke into the beleaguered faces of recently captured Malayan Regulars.

Miri counted perhaps two dozen prisoners, bound to each other neck-to-neck with coarse rope, like the beads of a necklace, and their hands were tied behind them at their wrist and elbows. Some of the prisoners looked very worn and barely able to walk. Fortunately for them the Japanese were far from adept at hiking a jungle trail, and even if unfettered by their train of prisoners they would have made slow progress. A few of the prisoners, with nervous rifles trained at their backs, were given parangs to hack away the fresh growth that choked the trail.

Miri turned herself into bark and to branch and was confident she could not be seen against the mid-day sun. The Japanese rarely looked skyward anyway. Their work was on the ground. There were only five of them, and so many prisoners to watch. *Only five*, thought Miri, *as many as I have darts in my quiver.*

Most of the prisoners had any initiative to escape beaten out of them, but some of them seemed to be alert, and scanning for opportunities. One soldier, taller than the others and toward the end of the column, looked up and detected movement against the sky. For an absurd moment he remembered being spellbound by the shadow puppets as a boy in his home in Sentul, back in Malaya. He had the good sense to drop his head before he was seen staring, and when he discreetly looked for a second time, the silhouette against the sky had vanished.

A Japanese soldier flicked the stub of his cigarette and stood to relieve himself on a prisoner squatting in exhaustion. *This must have been the cue*, thought Miri, *that their rest was over*, for in a moment the other Japanese stood, prodded the prisoners, and the column moved on.

The girl in the trees, still in the trees, decided to forgo the pleasures of the hunt in favor of following the contingent of prisoners. At the very least she could entertain herself by inventing new ways to annoy the Japanese. She could see no harm, either, in permitting herself to be seen by the soldier who had seen her silhouette. She anticipated their course, and would place herself strategically ahead of them, revealing herself covertly to the tall prisoner who intrigued her by the way he carried himself, bound though he was, like the others. There was a tint of maroon to his skin, distinguishing him from most of the Malays she had seen in her life whose skin was more like a muddy river. His hair was closely cropped, his forehead high, and his jaws and cheeks rather angular. Miri smiled to herself when she realized she found him handsome. She admired his head.

The Japanese insisted on frequent stops, for their training had never fully prepared them for the rigors of packing through the thick Borneo jungle, and their skin had no natural immunity to mosquitoes. It was rather early in the day, then, that they found a patch of ground open enough to suggest a clearing for a campsite. Miri was stunned—her tall prisoner was untied and given a parang. She could hear a guard grunting a few words that sounded like Malay and could see him gesturing with his rifle. The soldier understood and began to cut down the bamboo stalks and swath of banana leaves needed to make shelter.

Here is your chance, thought Miri. *Take it. Do it now. A quick thrust and then into the jungle. You will lose them so quickly and I will find you.*

Her heart raced as she wanted to think for him, to act for him, to put her thoughts and her cunning into his spirit, but she could only watch in frustrated silence as the tall one obeyed his captor and made shelter for the Japanese. They confiscated the parang when he had finished, and tied him once again to the others, who huddled at the edge of the clearing. Darkness and rain were slow in coming. Eric Madrigal D'Cruz, the tall prisoner with the handsome face, wondered if he was still being watched.

It had been two or three hours since he had last seen the jungle woman. At first, he could ascribe no motive to her behavior, but then a parasitic thought fed upon him. She was not following *them*. She was following *him*. He was being stalked. He knew of the Ibans. He knew what they did.

Before the night blackened completely Eric could see most of his companions were dozing off. Exhaustion and pain had done this to them. He, too, wished that he could sleep, but the events of the day still churned in his head. He had been conscripted along with his brother Joseph, just months before, hastily trained, and in Sarawak on the island of Borneo for less than two weeks. Indeed, it was on one of their very first patrols earlier in the day that they were captured along with six or eight others, including two British officers.

They were just disembarking from their motor launch a few miles upriver from the settlement, not really alert, thinking that any contact with the enemy would occur deeper in the jungle. They were wrong. The Japanese were waiting for them. As the last of the Malayans stepped off the skiff, the Japanese simply stood up in force from the cover of the thick underbrush along the banks of the river.

With all the weapons trained upon them, and with only a few yards between themselves and the river and absolutely no cover, they surrendered without a shot being fired. Their radio was tossed in the river and their launch was scuttled. They were quickly marshaled over a small hill where they joined other prisoners taken days earlier to the east. It was clear that their comrades had already been 'interrogated' and were suffering badly from the ordeal.

Eric listened as a fellow soldier with a swollen eye and scabbed forehead quietly told him that they were being marched inland to a secluded internment camp. It was a holding tank, he said. When the camp reached its capacity, they would in all likelihood be marching again, this time down to the sea. All of them had heard about the railroad in Burma, and the Japanese obsession to complete it, and the rumor was they had been spared to work the line.

The Japanese were anxious to get away from the river. The area was thickening with guerrilla units of British and even Australians. And, earlier in the week, the Japanese had found the remains of one of their own soldiers, badly mauled and partially eaten, the work first of predator and then of scavenger. The head, vacant from the shoulders, had clearly been severed with a knife.

That very day a soldier guarding the rear as they marched simply vanished. The disappearance was so effectively accomplished that the prisoners continued to march for almost half a mile before they even realized he was missing. It was after that incident that the prisoners were linked together, with the coarse hemp that sanded raw their shoulders and throat.

Rumors of Iban headhunters worked to the advantage of the freshly captured prisoners, sparing them from interrogation on the spot, while in such dangerous territory. But interrogation would surely come, and soon, while whatever information they might possess was equally fresh …

Eric tried unsuccessfully to will himself to sleep. The woman who followed them was surely Iban. She *had* to be stalking him. Still, he was confused. He was certain he had seen her smile at him. He tried to reassure himself. It had been several hours since he had last seen her.

The sun stopped falling when it reached the tops of the trees, the network of branch and leaf too finely woven to let it drop any further, and there it remained like a golden egg in a nest, fading as indigo crept silently into the abdicated sky, and shy stars began to reveal themselves above the treetops. The first rain of evening washed any traces of light still trapped beneath the canopy, and the world became very, very dark, a private blackness known only in the jungle of Borneo.

Exhaustion had infected everyone and was more potent even than fear. The prisoners fell together in the open, oblivious to the light blanket of rain falling upon their shoulders. A single guard stationed himself beneath a large miranti tree, while others of his kind slept in the small shelter Eric had made for them. The sentry examined the sky and adjusted his cap, which was slightly torn at the brim. Much of the rain was deflected by the contorting branches above him.

To the sentry's way of thinking, they had made good progress during the day, and it was highly unlikely that the British would attack at night. They would be helpless to navigate, assuming they even had word yet that they had lost a patrol. The British would do the sensible thing and wait until morning to follow, for although the jungle was difficult by day, it was absolutely horrifying at night to those unaccustomed to its power.

But the Ibans ... that was another matter. The sentry adjusted his cap again, nervously. There was no way of telling if they were still in Iban territory, and very little was known of their ways. They were told that Ibans had a natural prohibition against killing by night, that the soul of their victim could escape in the darkness. But it was an unreliable rumor, extracted by torture from a Dayak. The uncertainty kept the sentry awake, and a battalion of mosquitoes kept him alert. With his bayonet he provoked the small fire to flame and smoke—the flame by which to see his prisoners, the smoke to keep the mosquitoes at bay.

The prisoners were certainly less of a threat than the mosquitoes. Cinched together as they were, one could not move without starting a chain reaction that would rile them all. No one dared move, even if they fell from the branches of sleep into wakefulness. The sentry reasoned that the narrow trail that led back to their point of origin would be impossible to follow at night. To submit to the wilderness alone would be almost certain death, and he was sure there were no heroes in the lot. Any will power that may have survived their interrogation would certainly have been suffocated by the stifling trek through the jungle.

The rain let up, just a bit, and the sentry re-stationed himself at the bottleneck to the trail, a demonstration of cunning, he thought, if by chance one of his own sleeping comrades should awaken and check on him. He squatted on his haunches and could see that all his prisoners were asleep but for one, who was staring at him with terror in his eyes. The sentry congratulated himself on inspiring the appropriate fear, and smiled sardonically as he lit another cigarette.

Smiling, too, was the daring Iban girl who stood erect not three feet behind him. She had never left, and from over the shoulders of the sentry she gestured to the spellbound prisoner to keep silent.

Eric closed his eyes and swallowed hard, afraid he would give her away. He opened his eyes and was equally startled to find the girl had vanished once again, just as the sentry inched his way backwards to lean against the accommodating tree. The night was an hour deeper into darkness when Eric felt the hands of the invisible one upon his spine, slipping like a bead of rain down a leaf to his hips, where his hands were bound. A small pocketknife, courtesy of the dozing guard not fifteen feet before them, was taking tiny slices at the coarse hemp, and in a few moments his hands were free, and blood surged through his aching wrists once again.

He could feel reassuring hands ease their way between the back of his neck and the loop of rope that sand-papered across his skin and left it burning, and in a moment, the jungle woman cut him free of the noose. He kept his eyes straight forward, on the sentry, and all the while Joseph slept with his head on Eric's lap. The Iban girl cut Joseph free, too, without his even knowing it, complying to the subtle but urgent gestures from the man she had chosen to rescue. Eric awakened his brother cautiously, certain they would break the fragile sleep of the guard.

But it was an elusive mosquito that woke the guard, who abruptly slapped his cheek to kill the tiny predator. At this, the guard convinced himself that he had not really been sleeping at all. He stood, and stretched, and a cursory glance to the clustered shadow of prisoners told him that all was in order.

He stoked the fire once again and fueled it with a few small branches peeled free of wet bark, before returning to the relative comfort beneath the tree. It would not be until daylight that he would discover that there were two fewer prisoners in his charge.

Upon soil that had never been dry or even felt the sun, Miri, Eric and Joseph slithered off into the insatiable darkness. More time had passed than distance, but Miri sensed that it was safe to sit up and confer, if only in whispers. The language of the Ibans was like Malay, though heavily salted, and the girl even spoke a few words of English she had stolen on forbidden adventures into the delta settlement on market days.

Her instructions were basic, terse. Be silent ... follow me ... do as I do. They could stand now, the camp was half an hour behind them, and Miri led them for another half an hour through trailless underbrush. Very little distance had actually been covered, for no light had been trapped under the canopy at sunset by which to maneuver, and the moon, obligated to glow for heaven, spared little of itself for the world beneath the treetops.

"We're lost," Joseph whispered to his older brother. Miri turned around, dumbfounded that they would leave a trail of words hanging on the leaves for anyone to follow. She put her hand over his mouth, until he understood, and then she turned and stepped into the first water pooled under branch and vine, a swamp.

Their clumsy escape route had left a trail so obvious to her Ibanese thinking that even the Japanese could follow it. The swamp would put an end to that, or at least slow them down. She doubted that the Japanese, who needed shelter from rain and even oil against mosquitoes would willingly immerse themselves in these wretched waters.

It was well past midnight, Eric reckoned. *How can she see in this darkness?* he thought. Apparently, she knew what she was doing and was never more than an arm's length ahead of him, and his brother never more than an arm's length behind. No one spoke, but they all shared the same thought, now. Snakes.

They were chest-deep in black water, each agonizing step sucked them into the mud. Only the network of overhanging branches kept them from sinking into death, and they pulled themselves forward. Each branch in the harness above them seemed too delicate to support their weight. They would hold one branch firmly, while testing the next, and their progress was very slow. Eric groped in the darkness above him, guided only by the sound of the woman ahead of him. His fingers located a looping branch and as he shifted his weight the branch contracted within his grasp, when he felt it slither, not really a branch at all. He released his grip and started to struggle and sink, but Miri had reached the incline at the bank of the swamp and was able to seize his wrist while she stood in shallow water.

"Aeihh." In the darkness and panic Eric thought her grip was the jaw of the snake, and he flailed at the water. Miri held tight and threw herself towards the bank before losing her grip, but her momentum put Eric into shallow water and Joseph managed to pull himself ashore by reeds bent down in his brother's confused struggle.

Miri threw herself upon Eric to stop his thrashing, but it felt to him only like the snake was pulling him down. Miri backed off and let him play it out, angry at the noise he made. "*Hush.*"

In the darkness Eric scrambled for the sound of the voice. He could make out the form of Joseph and the girl, and fell towards them. "*A snake.*"

"Yes, I know," said Miri. There was no point in explaining. Eric was panting and she let him catch his breath before she spoke again. "Stay here. I'll be back for you." Eric was on his back and raised himself just enough to nod, and Miri slipped back into the swamp and was gone.

"My God." said Joseph. "Who *is* she."

"I have no idea, but she was following us all afternoon."

"She won't *leave* us here, do you think?"

"I should think not. She went through bloody hell to get us out of there."

"*Eric.* She must be *Iban.*"

"Of *course* she is. What do you think."

"*Head hunters.*"

"I'd rather take my chances with her than with those Japanese buggers. She *saved* us, didn't she?"

"Yes ... but for what?"

"All I know is we're dead men if she doesn't come back. *I* can't get us out of here, even in daylight." Eric was right.

"Where do you think she went?" asked Joseph, his eyes scanning the darkness for any hint of movement.

"She had a kit with her earlier, and a spear, I think. She must have stashed it somewhere." And on this score, Eric was also right. In about twenty minutes Miri returned, having covered the ground that had taken the three of them together over an hour. She had retrieved her backpack and weapons, and the two soldiers stood as she approached, almost as if standing for review.

"We've got to find higher ground," she said, clearly the one in command, her language halting but not her intent. She led them away from the swamp, and the ground became firmer under foot. Mercifully, they passed under a waterfall, which washed them of the bad waters of the swamp that left them wanting to peel off their own skin. Taller trees thinned out, and a thin sliver of moon guided them up an escarpment. They reached its peak—at least a hundred feet, reckoned Eric—and pivoted to see below them the dew of the moon, the damp, silver glowing mist, conceal all but the tallest of trees.

Rain showered briefly and stopped, and in the interlude between perils Eric had his first moment to study the courageous girl who had freed him. She was clothed only in a beaded loincloth, and she was not only brave, but beautiful. A hint of moonlight revealed that. Her shoulders were smooth and round, and her hair, long and wet from waterfall and rain, clung to her skin and concealed her breast. Joseph was watching her also, staring really, and when Eric noticed this, he himself turned away, uneasy.

His skin still itched. He scratched his forearm and then by moonlight he could see the new horror. He had picked up a swath of leeches from the swamp, they all had. He began to slap and dig indiscriminately, and Joseph did the same. Miri tried to stop them, but they were oblivious to her.

She turned to her kit and shot a word at them like a dart from a blowpipe. "*Stop.*"

For a moment they were stunned, and in that moment to their amazement she pulled out a tin canister, something made by a *machine*, in which she kept dry a small block of salt, bargained from the Chinese in Miri. She broke off a small chunk and ground it with the butt of her parang on a flat rock, and she sprinkled a few granules to a leech on Eric's forearm. The leech instantly retracted its slimy barb and fell writhing to the ground.

Miri broke off another chunk of salt and handed it to Joseph, but she attended to Eric herself, curious to feel his skin and reward herself for her audacity. She pulled his wet shirt over his shoulders, and his lanky form glistened in the moonlight. He was thin, but muscular. She drew her hair behind her head and bent down to unlace his boots, and Eric was immobilized. No woman had ever done that.

Joseph struggled with his own boots and undid his trousers. Leeches were everywhere. Eric was still unable to move as Miri undid his buttons and tugged at the leggings to his pants. He huddled over in his nakedness and crossed his arms over his manhood. Then Miri worked salt over most of his body and gave him a crushed handful—to treat his more private parts.

Not until all the leeches had dis-engorged Eric did Miri tend to herself, and then, as an afterthought, she handed him some salt and turned her back and gestured for him to salt the leeches beyond her reach, as she had done for him. Moonlight and raindrops had transformed beautiful bronze skin into beautiful silver skin, the skin he had been invited to touch. He felt himself drawn to her, and quickly diverted himself, with words.

"I ... am Eric," he began tentatively. "Eric Madrigal D'Cruz, and this is my brother, Joseph."

"I am Miri," she said unhesitatingly, "daughter of Jon the Poet." She assumed that everyone had heard of her legendary father.

"I am ... we *are* ... very pleased to make your acquaintance." He was halfway through his formal introduction before he realized how silly he sounded. The woman had just saved their lives.

"Do they know we're gone?" Joseph asked of her.

"They were all asleep," she said.

"I think the Sergeant Major saw us," said Eric, "but our people would hide it as long as they could." Eric could see by her alert responses that she understood English, though she spoke it with hesitation. She clarified herself at times with a word from her own language, so close to Malay. He also became aware that she let her eyes wonder freely, everywhere, and he was suddenly quite conscious of his nakedness. He turned as properly as he could, stood up and pulled on his trousers, cueing his brother to do the same. The girl seemed either quite at ease with her own near nakedness or oblivious to the impact it had on the two young soldiers from the Malay Peninsula.

Their escape was a scant three hours old, and they incredibly had covered only half a mile. Miri permitted no more talk, and as soon as their boots were laced, they proceeded down the backside of the escarpment, to the fringe of thick vegetation once more. Miri insisted, once more, that they crawl beneath the underbrush, rather than trampling it and drawing attention to their trail. After about fifty yards she deemed it safe to stand. They were under the trees again, the canopy so dense that even the sickle shaped moon could not slice its way through. But the jungle itself seemed iridescent, magical, glowing from within.

The brush twisted itself together in every direction, and Miri handed her pack and spear to Joseph and Eric, freeing her to clear a path with her parang. Eric's admiration for her grew when he shouldered her pack. *This is heavy*, he thought, and how she managed to be so nimble and quick through the brush and trees and still carry all her gear amazed him.

"Forgive me," she said, when she first raised her blade.

"What?"

She looked at him and realized that he probably did not understand. "At night, the spirit of the jungle climbs up through the roots of the trees and grass to hunt. It will bleed if it's still in the leaves … but I have to do this." She let fall the blade and made passageway for them. For this sacrilege the monkeys who until then had been sleeping in their harness of vines and branches scolded her, and birds made flight to inform the gods. And if, by chance, the gods were uninterested in the news, the Japanese would surely know in what direction to begin their inevitable pursuit.

The trio had not gone far before Miri realized that this would not do. She could not remember ever needing to chop a path for herself. On her own she could slip through the jungle like a stream, disturbing nothing, stopped by nothing. But it was different with these two behind her. The monkeys above would not stop screaming insults, and Miri brought everything to a halt at the base of a rotund *banquiri* tree, and waited for the silence of the tree dwellers, who seemed to be on every branch, on every tree, but mysteriously vacant from this tree alone.

She gazed upward and slapped the trunk a few times with the flat side of her parang.

"What is she about?" whispered Joseph, not wishing to break her concentration.

"Damned if I know," said Eric, speaking no louder than necessary.

Miri slipped her parang back in its scabbard and began an effortless ascent. She was soon out of sight.

"Gone up to get a bearing, I should think," said Joseph.

"In *this* darkness?" Still, he could think of no other reason for her to make the climb. *She's an animal*, he thought. Maybe she sees in the dark. A few minutes passed.

"I'd sell my soul for a cigarette about now," said Joseph.

And a beer, mused Eric, but before the thought became words, he heard the snapping of the branches above him. Something heavy was falling fast, and he and his brother hit the ground and shielded their heads, just as the convulsing body of a python at least fifteen feet long fell between them, followed instantly by its neatly severed head, the size of a husked coconut.

In a few minutes Miri was on the ground again. Her parang was in its scabbard and she casually informed them "We sleep up there tonight."

"In *that* tree," whined Joseph. "You're not getting me up there."

"Do what she says."

"No. I'll take my chances on the ground." The dead snake had stopped twisting.

Eric took the first branch with a little help from Miri. "Don't be stupid. Get up here."

Joseph was resolute. *Stubborn*, thought Eric. *He will die*, thought Miri, but she turned her attention to Eric, and led him higher into the tree. It was quite safe. There was room for them to sit together on a huge branch halfway up the tree. "How did you know about the snake?"

"No monkeys in the tree. Has to be a snake. I see him when I slap the tree and he moves his head against the moon."

Amazing woman, thought Eric. Her thigh was pressed against his own as they sat.

"Come," she said. "A little more high." She had found a hollow in the trunk on her first climb, deep enough for her to stash Eric. She wedged him into place with her spear, to keep him from falling forward in his sleep, before she herself climbed higher.

She had much to think about, as she hung her pack on the stub of a broken branch and found a limb that faced the direction by which they had come, by which the Japanese *would* come. She was angry at herself for having made so much noise, though the night had absorbed much of the sound. And then there was the dead snake at the base of the tree. It could not be long before the scavengers would come in, and, in turn, the predators. But her two soldiers needed light to make their way, and maybe even sleep, and she had no choice but to wait for dawn. *The tall one is so handsome*, she thought. *My father will be so proud. I hope he lets him live. For a little while, at least.*

She draped herself over the limb, like a tiger, and settled down for the evening, ending the day as it had begun, nesting in the rungs of God's own ladder.

Chapter Five

Joseph had not slept at all, fear and mosquitoes gnawing upon him as he curled up in the knuckled roots of the trunk. He imagined every sound he heard was the footfall of a Japanese soldier, or the growl of a tiger, and the patter of rain was the hiss of a snake.

And yet he did not hear at four in the morning that jungle woman make her descent, pass lightly over him, and make her way back to the escarpment that stood between them and the Japanese. The blue-black sky was beginning to age gray, though darkness still prowled in obscurity beneath the canopy.

Miri concealed herself between two boulders near the peak, and watched for signs from the Japanese camp, distant and below her. What's *wrong* with them, she thought, to be sleeping so late? She had planned to remain until she could see if they were being pursued, and she waited for a tell-tale flight of birds or panic in the upper branches as monkeys scattered. But when the color that had gone to ground during the night began returning to the tops of the trees, turning the gray to green, Miri decided it was best to waste no more time.

She returned to find that Joseph had at last fallen asleep. "Good morning, sir," said Miri, thinking to impress him with her best English. Joseph snapped from his sleep as if caught in sin, at once fearful and alert.

"Oh, good morning." It was the first time he had heard the woman speak other than in a whisper.

Miri spent little time with him—her mind was on the younger brother still aloft. She scaled the tree to retrieve her pack and her spear, and to see how Eric had fared during the night. She brushed termites from his skin, and this awakened him. She helped him down.

"Are you thirsty?"

"Yes. Terribly."

They huddled on the ground, the three of them, and from the pack that seemed to contain all the wonders of the world Miri pulled out a segment of bamboo, stoppered at one end and containing fresh water. She held it to their lips, rationing out just a sip for each of them. Joseph said nothing, but noticed that she seemed to show a bit of favoritism towards his brother. It angered him, but like the prick of a mosquito it did not really irritate him until a few moments after the sting.

Miri pulled out another bamboo stalk the length of her forearm, and this one she chopped in two lengthwise. It had been filled with dry rice and even a few herbs, saturated with water and laid at the edge of a fire to boil and steam from within. The meal was rounded off with a cooked yam from her village—these things intended as her lunch the day before.

Time, the muscle that ripples from the shoulder of God, was flexing once more, pulling them away from this place. They were on the move again, this time with light blossoming everywhere, showing them the way. They had not gone far before they came across a run slightly worn by wild boar. *Perfect*, thought Miri, *it leads in the right direction.* The traveling was easy, and they made good time. Rain and sun shared the same sky, and multiple rainbows arched and throbbed with color.

As they worked their way into higher country the underbrush thinned out, and streams, several of them, moved swiftly enough to be free of algae and mosquitoes. Miri replenished her bamboo canteen, and allowed her wards the luxury of bathing a few moments. Still, she was cautious. Each stream provided a new opportunity to obscure their trail. The prudent daughter of Jon the Poet had them wade alternately upstream or downstream before making any imprint on the opposite bank. She continued to believe that the Japanese could follow a trail, but as the day wore on, she allowed that it was possible that they either lacked the skill or inclination to do so. But the day was not over, nor their escape complete.

Eric himself began to doubt that they were being followed. He and his brother were neither white nor officers, and therefore too insignificant to bother with, he reasoned. On the other hand, the Japanese could be exploding with humiliation, and driven to vengeance. He thought of the convoluted course by which they had come. They can't possibly find us. No one could. Even so, fear had lit bonfires to his logic, and he could not reassure himself by mid-day, when Miri sat them down to rest in a stand of trees. A more subtle fear began to stalk Eric and displaced his thoughts about the Japanese. The course they were taking, if his sense of direction still functioned, led them deeper into the interior, further from the coast and security of his regiment. "We rest here," Miri said. But where was 'here'?

As she had so often, Miri went aloft once more, this time to gather fruit, rambutans and mangoes. At times she would shift from one tree to the next without coming down. Eric and Joseph followed beneath her to catch what she would drop.

She spied a durian, her favorite fruit, and with a quick chop of her parang it fell. Eric was so tired that for a moment he poised to catch that, too, nearly forgetting that durian were heavy and spiked. It hit the ground at his feet and hardly rolled.

Miri dropped to the ground to join them for a while. They were high enough up the slopes to see the entire valley. They sat close together, facing each other, their knees almost touching. Even as they picked at the small mound of fruit between them, Miri was watchful, her eyes roving the valley below. But she did notice how tired the brothers were, and she noticed also, much to her amusement, that the boys kept staring at her breasts, and this puzzled her greatly.

Eric remembered when their mother caught him along with his brother spying once on their sister, Joyce, while bathing herself in her room. Their mother beat them severely, and then, to make certain they would never do it again, she beat their sister, too, with a rattan cane that left welts that stayed for weeks. Although Joyce had been oblivious to their voyeurism, Sarafina reasoned that no doubt their sister deserved the beating, too, for feeling impulses just barely beyond her reach on the adult side of childhood.

The event had left all three of them certain they were going to hell. But Sarafina Madrigal D'Cruz was not here to beat them now, and the sweet juice of a ripe mango was dripping down the perfect breast of a girl who was *not* their sister, and each move she made brought them agony.

Joseph squirmed behind his brother, hiding the evidence of his thoughts, and Eric raised his knees to his chest as they sat. Miri tossed her hair behind her head and stretched her arms towards the sky as if yawning, just to see the boys react. She thought to herself, as she had thought earlier, *I hope my father does not kill you.* She had a wonderful smile.

She patted the ground, once. "*Tidor di sini.*" Sleep here. She herself had no intention of sleeping, and chose a tree. Her ascent was swift and nimble, and once aloft she made herself as comfortable as she had been the day before, when she had waited passively for the appearance of her prey of choice.

Sunlight warmed her body, and she felt very good indeed. It was not until late afternoon that she came down from her tower, satisfied at last that they had not been followed. She had seen a flock of birds sporadically take flight in the distance, but there was no pattern to their eruptions, which were more likely provoked by a tiger or other cat. It had been several hours since she had seen any outburst at all.

She dropped lightly to the ground. Her two soldiers—boys, really—not much older than she was, were as deeply lost in their sleep as they were in the jungle. She was absolutely fascinated with them, and it was some time before she chose to wake them.

She took a leaf with a long stem and landed it like a mosquito under Eric's chin, and let it dance a moment, pulling it away as he swiped at it in his sleep. Again, she tickled his chin and, once again, in a stupor he brushed it away. She played with him for some time, this way, happily amused.

She liked his features. He was so unlike the men from her tribe, or even the Malays who lived at the delta. And he was tall. He was very, very tall. Much more so than his brother. He was as tall as the British soldier who fell to earth tugging on the strings to his own cloud. And he was so handsome. She slid her hand under his singlet and felt the hard muscle of his chest, firm even as he slept. He did not stir. She allowed her hand to linger long enough to absorb his warmth, and she dipped her face to feel his breath upon her brow, and to fill her nostrils with his scent.

Her curiosity, for the moment, had been satisfied, and she withdrew her hand. Then she shook him abruptly by the shoulder, startling him into wakefulness. "It's time to move."

It took the boys a few moments to realize where they were and recall the exhausting horror of the last twenty-four hours. How could this woman seem so calm and indifferent to it all?

They took a bit of water before standing and stretching, and Miri shouldered her pack and pulled her spear from the ground. She started to walk, almost marching, and did not bother to look back to see if the boys were following. *Of course they will follow*, she thought, *what choice do they have?* She picked up the pace.

The boys fell in behind her. The quickness of her step amplified their fear. She was jogging now, as if on a hunt, and oblivious to all else. "Ask her." insisted Joseph. "Ask her now."

"Miri, wait," shouted Eric, who needed no urging from his brother. "We need to talk."

All the immediate dangers—the Japanese, the snakes, the darkness—were behind them now, gone, but in that void a more subtle dagger slipped from its sheath. Where *were* they? Where were they going? Nothing they had seen even remotely suggested the coast or the way they had come with the Japanese after they had been captured.

"Miri, Miri ... wait."

But Miri remained indifferent to them, demanding they keep pace with her.

"MIRI. WHERE ARE WE GOING?"

At this she stopped and turned on the small rise, now ten yards ahead of the boys struggling to overtake her. As they caught up with her, as they caught their breath, she pointed proudly with her spear. "There."

They had slept the last four hours a mere two hundred yards from the village of Jon the Poet, the man who slid his blade upon a whetting stone as he waited for the return of his long overdue daughter.

Chapter Six

The first to be relieved by Miri's appearance was the milk goat. It trotted happily to her side and conveyed its annoyance at the two young boys who had been "hunting" it all day long as it rambled freely about the village in search of discarded vegetables.

"Miri. Be careful." The smaller of the two boys raised his spear. "It's a tiger."

Miri looked sympathetically at the trusting goat. "*Ayuh.* I never see a tiger with a bell around its neck."

"We put it there to warn everybody when she comes."

"Good idea. Hey, you think maybe she want to eat these two?"

"Maybe. They look pretty skinny."

"I know," said Miri. She looked over her shoulder to see Joseph and Eric making half-hearted attempts to smile bravely at her two cousins, Abo and Atai.

"Why you don't come back last night? Everybody looking for you," said Abo.

"... And your papa plenty mad."

"I was hunting," said Miri, her voice playful. "Just look what I caught."

Caught, thought Eric. *My god.*

The two boys, whose combined ages could be counted on two hands, raised their pointed wooden sticks with mock valor. Forgotten was the "tiger" that trotted ahead on the widening path, no doubt causing panic within the village.

"Prisoners," concluded Atai.

"Yes. Of course."

At this, Abo, the ferocious four-year-old, took up position in the rear. He knew all about prisoners. A quick jab to the buttocks would keep them in line. Miri started up again, while the other little warrior ran ahead. Miri's arrival was already sending ripples down the long corridor, that bloomed of ripening vegetables brightly lit with sunshine.

Their current settlement was on the fringe of the highlands, and crops did quite well. Higher from the valley floor, her tribe had a very slight breeze to keep them cool, and an abundance of streams in which to bathe and catch fish, and the underbrush did not have the stifling density as it did further down the slopes. This was home, and it was not at all unpleasant.

With Atai proudly dancing and skipping in the lead, and Abo dutifully bringing up the rear, Miri and her two finds marched through patches of yams and sweet potatoes, neatly fenced off to keep out the goats and small, wild deer that were so abundant on the slopes. Chickens scattered in every direction as they marched, and butterflies and swarms of fluttering children joined the entourage. Squarely ahead of them at the end of the clearing Eric could see the only structure, the long house held in the sky by a network of a hundred stilts.

By now, everyone knew that Miri had returned. When dusk had arrived the night before, and Miri had not sauntered in, a few of the elders had begun to take notice. And when the dusk caved in to the weight of the black night and she still had not shown, no one could invent a believable explanation for her delay. They worried about her, as one. The entire kampong had been sleepless, and at dawn Miri's father had sent out the trackers.

And now the women and the men made fragile with age who had been stooped in the gardens stood as Miri approached, with that cocky walk of hers, and they followed behind her. Two Malayan Regulars. This had the makings of a very good story.

The commotion could be felt all the way to the long house, and a few of the dogs, then all of the dogs, began to bark. The veranda began to fill from the many doors that faced the approach. Thirty or forty people had come outside to investigate the noise. A young girl who had been running ahead of them was calling "Papa, Papa!" and she ran up the steps, skipping two at a time, and scampered across the veranda and disappeared through a doorway in the center of the house.

Miri's moment of triumph, one of so many, youthful triumphs, was upon her. She walked forward in as manly a way as she knew, strutting and swaggering, making herself bigger with each step. She brought her entourage to a halt in the open space ten yards from the long house, and planted the butt of her spear in the ground. She did not speak—no one spoke—but she growled once at the dogs that inched towards her prisoners, and the barking stopped. Then, in the void, she called, "Papa."

She had an audience on the veranda above her now, all leaning on the rail for a better look. *What has that girl done now,* they thought.

"Papa. Come look." He knew, of course, that she was waiting. *I will keep her waiting just a moment longer,* her father thought to himself. From the private shadows of his room, he could see her, and he exhaled deeply, expelling the worry that had been feasting on him through the night and mid-morning.

"Papa."

Still, he hesitated. *Let her see that I am not overly anxious about her late return,* he thought. He eyed the two limp soldiers standing weakly behind her. He stepped to the threshold of his door, in the direct center of a row of at least a dozen doors, and all eyes were now upon *him*.

Eric nudged his brother and whispered. They couldn't make out his face. Half-a-dozen wind chimes dangled and spun in the slight breeze, hung from the beam that supported the roof, obscuring the man about to make his entrance.

Eric watched the hypnotic sway of the wind chimes, lulling his exhausted senses. Then it occurred to him—the chimes were soundless. He squinted in the bright sunlight, and stared up into the dark shade of the veranda for some time before he could focus ...

... Not wind chimes at al ...

("Oh my God ... Joseph.")

("Yes. I see them, too.")

Jon the Poet stepped through the narrow opening of his room, taking his place, the place of a chief, among those crowding the banister. He suppressed a smile. His favorite daughter had returned unharmed. He leaned forward on the rail, gripping it with two very powerful hands, the natural conclusion to his very muscular arms. Making room for his vast shoulders, he delicately slid the tether on the rail above him, on which hung not a wind chime, but a head shriveled to the size of a man's fist. "Where have you been?" he bellowed, convincing everyone of his wrath except the one he intended to scold.

"Hunting, of course." She stood her ground. Miri could see him studying her soldiers.

It was an easy situation for Jon the Poet to assess, and he didn't really need an explanation from her. The soldiers would be in her company only if she had stolen them from the Japanese, and she would have taken the long way home to avoid being followed.

"You better come up inside," he said, begrudgingly.

Miri smiled to herself. She had been forgiven.

Jon the Poet pivoted and entered his quarters without waiting for her or looking back. He grinned when he stepped inside, and no one could see. Safe. *And with two soldiers in tow.*

Miri looked over her shoulder at the two brothers. "Come on," she said, without much passion. Eric could feel in his heart that this was not an instruction, but an order. He did not comply; he obeyed. Old women and young girls poked and tugged at him as he and his brother trod up the steps behind the jungle woman and into the den of Jon the Poet and his many children.

His quarters were no different from any of the others, in spite of his exalted position. The floor was made of loosely fitted planks of either ulin or banquiri, two very durable woods but hard to cut. Several layers of woven mats spread upon the fairly level floor, and they could be conveniently rolled aside for housecleaning, which consisted of sweeping dust and leftovers from the afternoon meals through the cavities in the floor to the pigs corralled directly beneath the dwelling. It was terribly efficient. A hole in the corner served the same function for human waste.

The floors were strong enough to support a slab of flat stone in a corner, on which a flame, small but constant, squatted on its haunches beneath a slowly boiling kettle suspended from a tripod. Jon the Poet had already assumed his place in the opposing corner of the room and took up his pipe when his daughter entered. Joseph and Eric still had the notion that the woman might somehow be their protector and stepped in behind her to avoid the inquisitive stings of the tribe that had swarmed upon them like mosquitoes. Several small children wormed their way through the crowd and entered the chamber without invitation. The smallest boy nestled by Jon the Poet, his father, who stroked him lovingly.

"Well ..." he began, "it looks like you have had quite an adventure." He started his pipe.

Miri relieved herself of her pack and set it down before her and sat down. She tugged at Joseph and Eric to sit as well, and before she began her tale a middle-aged woman entered with an urn and tin cups. She had taken it upon herself to cook and help raise the children Jon the Poet had sired after his wife died. She smiled at him as she knelt down and ladled out a serving to her chief. He took a sip without taking his eyes off the two bewildered strangers.

"Have some of this," said the man with the pipe, and the power. He didn't bother to ask his daughter if they could understand dialect.

"Thank you, sir," said Eric, who had been handed a cup. He sipped, as did Joseph. It was like swallowing hot daggers, and Jon the Poet was amused as he saw their faces boil.

Miri began her tale. It seemed so unremarkable to her that she embellished her heroics to hold her father's full attention. She kept him spellbound. Everyone crowded outside the door to hear, stood flesh against flesh, parting only to let in more children. Miri was talking too rapidly for Eric to understand every word, and he began to feel the brew he had swallowed confiscating whatever was left of his senses. He was oblivious to his cup being filled a second time. And a third.

"Stand."

It took a moment for Eric to realize that he was being addressed. He had no idea that Miri, who had finished her tale, had just surrendered his fate and that of his brother to Jon the Poet. The chief wanted a good look at them. Eric stood and faced him. Burnt air filled the room and the chief continued to make smoke with his pipe. Joseph also stood, but Eric realized that Jon the Poet was more interested in him. He had always drawn more attention, even as a boy, for being so tall. He did his best to stand rigidly, as if at attention. No one, including Jon the Poet, had ever seen anyone stand that way. It was so strange. It seemed so unnatural.

Eric's gaze slipped through the smoke, and he inadvertently stared at the Iban sitting cross-legged on the floor in front of him. Deep purple tattoos rippled across dark brown skin when he moved, each tattoo documenting an important event in his life. And, by this measure, Jon the Poet was a very important man.

As a young man he had been well-loved and respected, even by those outside his clan, for his beautiful singing voice and his way with words. He could mimic almost any bird that sang, and he entertained everyone at night with ballads from their own mythology, half-spoken and half-sung. He was so disarming that he was often chosen to arbitrate disputes within families or among quarreling friends. He would sing the solutions to their disagreements, invoking the spirit of the animals or birds whose voice he had assimilated, so that his judgments were very well respected. Song, music, was the tongue of God.

One day, long ago, his clan, the Melanau, had a disagreement with a neighboring Iban tribe regarding hunting territory. Each of the tribes did their best to respect the territory of others and would not trespass. But one hunter had pursued a boar, a large male, for almost half a day, following a trail of hoof prints and droppings.

The boar had entered Melanau territory, but it seemed reasonable to the hunter that since the trail originated within his own tribe's domain, he could rightfully pursue it. And this he did.

He found his boar, dead. Jon the Poet was extracting a dart from its hide as he approached.

The hunter insisted the boar was his. Jon the Poet diplomatically informed him that he himself was meant to have the boar, and in his narrative of song and story he explained how in a dream the night before he was visited by a hornbill, who had promised him a successful hunt if he would follow in the morning. The bird materialized that dawn and led him to the place of the kill and instructed him to wait for the inevitable arrival of the boar.

The errant hunter listened passively to the story, but continued to insist that the boar was his, that it had strayed falsely into Melanau land. It was the fault of the boar, not his.

Jon the Poet listened to his explanation, and repeated his own claim, to the hunter who was becoming increasingly agitated and rude.

After hearing Jon the Poet's best song, sung in his best voice, with his best intentions, the hunter could not agree that the freshly killed boar belonged to anyone but him.

And so, Jon the Poet, with his best song, sung in his best voice, explained that his best intention was now to kill the hunter, which he did reluctantly, but promptly. He returned to his village with the boar, and with his first head, the wind chime that swung on the veranda outside his door. In a few weeks' time he was declared chief, without much ceremony but with general goodwill. His first tattoo immortalized his courage soon afterward ...

Eric began to totter from the concoction of fear and fatigue and very strong drink.

"And what shall I do with you?" mused Jon the Poet out loud, though he had already decided.

Eric was stunned. Jon the Poet spoke English. A man with a child on his lap, and with a passion to kill. *So civil*, thought Eric. *And he's going to kill us.*

"*Do* with us?" His wits momentarily returned. "My people will reward you for saving us." He felt suddenly hopeful.

"Yes. I suppose they would." He stood and went to his window, and plucked a cluster of rambutans from a branch that brushed up against the longhouse. He tossed it to Eric who almost caught it, and walked over to stir the flame-scorched cauldron. "But what have they got that I do not have?"

The last thing Eric remembered before passing out was a head that oozed to the surface of the cauldron stirred by Jon the Poet, who hummed himself a tune.

Chapter Seven

"Where's my brother?" Eric was flat on his back, the floor hard beneath him and the features of the room a-blur. The woman, the girl, towered over him, tall as a tree.

"He sleeps."

The words fell from her lips, gaining momentum as they dropped like coconuts upon his head. "Oh, my God ... what was that drink?"

"Jus' our drink," she said, concealing her amusement.

Eric rolled his throbbing head to get a bearing. He was no longer in the quarters of Jon the Poet, but stems and leaves, so close to an open window, told him he was still aloft in the longhouse. The sky was the soft black of midnight. "How long have you been standing there?"

"Not long." It had been two hours.

Eric managed to prop himself up on his elbows, and at that moment Miri sat down on the floor by him. An infant flame illuminated the room from a corner, and smelled of pitch. Miri gestured to an urn and a ladle she had brought, and Eric looked at them suspiciously. "Water," she assured him.

"Thank God for that."

She knelt beside him on the floor and encouraged him to let himself fall into the cradle of her lap. She held the ladle to his lips and helped him swallow. Then she set the ladle down and he slipped her cool hands upon his forehead. He could feel her moving, slightly, under his weight. Desire began to growl and murmur in his chest, as it had the night before, when her bare skin was wet and silver in the moonlight. He recalled that moment vividly now. He closed his eyes and saw himself, standing on the escarpment near her, wanting to touch her. And then he heard his mother speak his name, and the vision collapsed.

Miri opened her hands, broad and surprisingly smooth for a woman so coarse, and let her palms drift upon Eric's breast. She felt his muscles stiffen, and watched his eyes clamp down, as if shutting something out. She stopped stroking him, content to cup her hands over his chest to capture his warmth. She grazed, by accident, over his nipple, and felt its texture change to her touch, becoming firm and almost rough, like the skin of a lychee.

In the darkness of his own creation, Eric saw only his mother. Her unavoidable face was aflame and she tested a rattan cane against the air, assuring herself of its swiftness and sting. He remembered that beating, often. The skin had taken weeks to heal, and though he did not realize it at the time, his mother had forever fused shame to desire, like a scab on a wound, on that afternoon of boyhood curiosity so long ago at the family plantation in Sentul.

But the girl behind him, beneath him, knew nothing of this, and began again to coax the stiff muscles of his shoulders, and it felt desperately good to him. *This is wrong*, he thought. *This is wrong*. But at the moment Miri began to withdraw, as she sensed some struggle within him, he astonished himself by reaching up to capture her hand before the moment could escape. He pressed his hand upon hers, encouraging her to touch, and investigate.

He had been holding his breath, the way an animal does that hides in the brush. He at last exhaled, deeply, but only when he could no longer contain himself. He opened his eyes and his mother was gone, and in her place there was only Miri, who stroked him gently, who kissed him lightly, and who offered, without speaking, to let him do the same …

… When next he saw his mother's face, the black sky had become gray, and the gray sky had become blue. He could see her as she was, years before, with the furious cane in her hand and the outrage in her eyes, and he could see her now, standing at his feet with her dagger looks. But over the course of the night, she had lost her power to shame him, and he dismissed her from the room. Miri was nestled under his arm, asleep, and a thin sheet covered them both. Eric found himself wanting her to be awake, wanting to talk to her, wanting to profess love. He felt very pleased with himself.

Children ran past the door on the veranda. A few of them stopped and peeked in at them, before scampering off to the more important business of the day. Eric heard parangs slashing firewood in the trees behind him and could smell bananas frying from a room down the way. He waited patiently, then impatiently, for Miri to awaken.

Sparring butterflies entered the room through the window behind him and caught his attention. He could almost feel them fan the air with brilliant strokes of gold and purple. He wanted just then to awaken her, to show her how beautiful they were. They fluttered out and it was too late, but he could feel her begin to move. "Good morning," he whispered, hoping she would hear. She did not answer.

Please, be awake, he said to himself. *There is so much to say.*

Sunshine, warm and soothing, had chosen to enter, and investigate. It moved slowly over the sheet that covered them both and it grew stronger, as if pleased by what the two of them had done in the night and rewarding them with its comfort. Eric closed his eyes. It was all too good to be real.

"Good morning," she said, in her best English.

She *was* awake. His pulse quickened and his eyes flashed open.

The truth was, she had been awake for some time, but was content to lie in Eric's arms without speaking. With no intention to arouse or resume their passion, she let her hand graze and explore as she had the night before, and she kissed his flesh here and there before settling back down in the crook of his arm.

"Miri ... Miri?"

"Mmmn?"

"Miri? I ... I ... I've never done this before—with anyone."

"Done what?" She raised her head and was truly perplexed.

"*This.*"

"This?" She genuinely had no idea what he was talking about.

"Yes. Confound it. *This.* I've never made love to a woman before."

"Oh. That's terrible. Are there no women where you come from?"

"Well ... yes, only ... well ..." Then suddenly Eric realized the obvious. "You mean *you've* done this before."

Miri was dumbfounded. "Of course. I'm a *woman.*"

Eric, who a moment before was certain he had so much to say, said nothing. Miri settled back down in his arms and left him staring at the ceiling. She did not know his age, only that he was slightly older than herself, and she began to wonder how it could be that no woman had ever approached him. She lifted her head, suddenly very curious, and she straddled him where he lay, as if to break his stare upon the ceiling rafters. "But you're so *handsome?*"

What Eric did not know of the Melanau, and what Miri could not know of the rest of the world, was that the rules of courtship were reversed. Miri was astonished that no one had laid with such a handsome boy, and had no idea that sex implied some sort of obligation beyond the moment of pleasure. Eric, for his part, was unaware that in the culture of the Melanau, it was the men who remained aloof, and that the women were free to pursue and to bed whomever they fancied. And neither of them could realize that they were falling, not only in love, but also into this cavity of misunderstanding.

What they had done in the darkness, they did once again by sunlight, filling the room with the sounds of their pleasure, so immersed in each other that they were oblivious to the occasional stares and giggles of the curious who passed by the open door to the veranda. When they were done, they settled into each other's arms once again. *I have found my bride,* thought Eric. *I wonder if breakfast is ready,* thought Miri. They began to talk to each other.

"Miri?"

"Yes?"

"I was wondering ..." he found it hard to ask, but the question was slowly killing him. "I mean ... you've done this before. You would know."

"Know what?"

"Am I ... I mean ... was I ... was I as good at this, as the others?" He was too young to be embarrassed by the question.

"You are so strange, you, and your brother."

"What do you mean?"

"Last night, before I came in here, he asked me the same thing."

Chapter Eight

The days of first love had long since passed for Eric, fallen like a bird from the sky. In his lucid moments Eric blamed his mother, but in the delirium of loss, which was more constant, he blamed himself. It required less courage than blaming Sarafina. He became a prisoner of gravity, never to look skyward again.

"The sun will be up in an hour. I need one of you to go into the city." His mother's voice in the doorway ended a sleep devoid of dreams and passion. The bedroom, which for a brief period in its history had been ceded to Eric and Miri, was no longer a bridal suite. Eric now shared the room with Joseph, as he had as a boy.

Sarafina sniffed the air. "You boys haven't been drinking, have you?"

"No, Ma'am," they lied.

"There's bus fare on the table in the kitchen. Go and fetch Sister Masselin."

"I'll go," said Joseph, who saw a chance to get out of field work with their father, for half a day, at least.

"Good. See that you don't miss the bus." She understood his volunteerism.

"Yes, Ma'am."

Sarafina, who had a cup of hot tea in her hand, stepped onto the dark veranda and felt for her rocking chair. The escaping light from the doorway behind her glowed dim yellow against the cotton grayness of dawn. She maneuvered into her chair and rocked softly, her teacup steeping on the banister before her, cooling. Of late, she had often risen earlier than the duties of her household required, fixed her own tea and exercised her rocker in the obliqueness of dawn, until the features of the trees on both sides of the wall to the yard became distinct with light. She had not slept well in three months, ever since the unsettling visit from that sorceress, Che' Wan. She could not articulate why the encounter clawed at her from within as it did, but the feeling would not go away, even after beating Catherine who had brought it all about, and remained as insolent as ever. Sister Masselin, Sarafina reasoned, could help her sort things out. They always enjoyed each other's company.

They had known each other as girls, but it was after the fall of Singapore when the Japanese slaughtered all the Chinese in their march to Burma, that their alliance solidified. Sister Masselin had persuaded the Japanese that their interest would best be served by allowing the D'Cruz family to retain tenancy of their plantation, and even to pay them enough to manage the production of rubber, which the Japanese needed for their war effort. How Masselin did it baffled Sarafina, and why Masselin was even spared astounded her.

The Japanese could not know, of course, that money from the Madrigal side of the family dwarfed the income from rubber, and that the family would have survived the war quite comfortably without the subsidy. The tangible wealth, in the form of gold, jewels and raw pearls, had been secreted to the basement of the convent shortly after Singapore had been shelled and it became apparent no help would be coming from the south. Swiftly the Japanese would control the entire peninsula.

Sister Masselin had been rewarded for her initiative and loyalty, with money for the convent and a bit to tuck away for herself. And every time she received an invitation to leave the city to visit her old friend Sarafina, she knew she would return with an unsolicited donation. Usually a modest sum. A portion of it—the smaller portion—actually ended up in the poor box.

It was still dark when Joseph left that morning, awakened by his mother for the task only a few hours after he had staggered into bed. It was now nearly noon as he escorted Sister Masselin through the gate and up to the house where his mother awaited them. To his thinking he had completed his chore within a reasonable time, yet he could feel his mother's hands around his throat as he approached the veranda. His eyes must still be blood-shot, he thought, or maybe it was his breath. Or the bottle under the bed. Or Eric? It didn't much matter. His mother said nothing about it in the presence of the Sister, but he knew it would not be the last of it.

"Your father is in the fields," she said, coldly.

Joseph knew enough to take his leave. His head still throbbed punishment, and he hoped to catch up on some sleep in the pineapple fields before his father put him to work. He turned with his usual sense of shame and walked as briskly as he could manage down the long drive and out the gate that separated his mother's domain from that of his father. He shut the gate, a good boy.

"Masselin, my dear. How nice to see you. Won't you join me in some tea?" And though the words were the formal ones, that could be extended so easily to a stranger as well, they were quite genuine. It never occurred to Sarafina that Masselin was her only friend. Masselin had been a constant, long before Sarafina's wedding to William, or Masselin's wedding to Christ.

Masselin had been the daughter of very rich Chinese, and Sarafina the only daughter of the very rich Madrigals. Quite early on they realized that their wealth distinguished them from most of the other children with whom they went to school, in the very convent where Masselin had remained her entire life. That Masselin was Chinese was a defect that Sarafina benevolently overlooked.

Unlike Sister Masselin, Sarafina had left the convent when she was fourteen, her education having been deemed complete. She could read, she could write, and, to round out her education, she had been given the customary indoctrination about the evil nature of sex. She was able to survive the intended degradation in part because she was able to ignore it. According to her Philippine heritage, sex was the great equalizer. It allowed a woman to extract from a man what only a man could extract from the world—wealth and power. Sex might be something contemptuous, even vulgar, but it was an extremely valuable asset. In Sarafina's case, it was a superfluous asset. She did not need to marry William for his money, having plenty of her own.

In fact, William seemed indifferent to her wealth. This was due largely to the fact that he managed his own financial affairs and his modest inherited lands rather well as a young man. More importantly, he was a confident man who took his greatest pleasure in the simplest of things and in his own virtues. He could make things grow. He had the soul of a farmer and was capable of performing miracles with earth and with seed. He could therefore be neither intimidated nor seduced by wealth.

These things baffled, intrigued and infatuated Sarafina as a young lady, and impressed her father to the extent that he actually encouraged their flirtations.

Her father's approval, withheld since birth by disappointing him with her gender, made it possible for her to justify her attraction to William; she was doing it for her father.

Similarly, she could explain the intense pleasure of the marriage bed in altruistic terms, allowing her to keep her self-perception as a bastion of virtue. The pleasure, she reasoned, was but a reward for pleasing her husband, who was a godly man. *Her* pleasures were purely incidental to that. She did it for him. Never anything for herself.

But Masselin did not have Sarafina's agile mind to neutralize or explain away her hidden, evil desires to lay with a man, and puberty was a very frightening event for her. After much agony, and with killing humiliation, she discovered masturbation. It was a terrible secret for her to bear. And yet, each day in the convent, she could hardly wait for the night and its darkness, and the privacy under her single blanket in the dormitory when everyone else was asleep.

The conflict would not go away. The more she fought it, the greater seemed her pleasure at her own touch, followed by an even greater sense of shame the next day. It was an escalating cycle from which there seemed no escape.

But there *was* escape, and the pathway was cut as viciously as a parang slicing untrod jungle. Mother Superior.

Taking an unexpected shortcut through the dormitory one evening, Mother Superior heard the unmistakable murmur and saw the unforgivable motion of the young girl's form under the thin summer blanket, and she instantly and instinctively began to beat Masselin with unrestrained fury, waking everyone and leaving her bleeding and sobbing and at the mercy of her peers, who, of course, had no mercy.

She never really healed.

When the time at last had come for her to leave the convent, she begged indifferent parents to let her stay. She could bear her shame within the walls of the Convent of the Order of the Most Holy Infant Jesus. She could conceal her shame and budding breasts within the black cloak of a nun's habit. And she could atone for her shame with a lifetime of deprivation, and self-inflicted flagellation. Her parents gave their consent. Christ required no dowry.

Her spirit had passed through menopause ages ago, and now her body, rotting under her habit like compost, was finally purging her of desires that had tortured her most of her life.

She was glad for the chance to visit with Sarafina, and glad to escape, for a day at least, from the convent monotony that sucked the marrow from her bones.

Kamille brought out another chair and served tea. And the two old friends cracked open beetle-nut, sipped tea, and began to reassure themselves that all was right with the world. For Sarafina Madrigal D'Cruz, all was right for the world except for the presence of the granddaughter, who with each passing day more and more resembled that heathen who nearly took down the whole family. "Masselin?"

"Yes?"

"I wanted to talk to you about Catherine."

"Catherine? Go on."

"Yes. She's a wonderful girl but is lacking in moral education. What would you think ..."

... Joseph, in the meantime, had found an accommodating patch of grass far from the house but not yet within sight of where his father would be working. It was dry and thick, under a palm tree and just far enough from the path that he would be hidden from any of the men hired from the kampong on their way deeper into the fields to take their instructions from his father. He figured he would be good for a smoke and maybe an hour's sleep before his father would expect him back from Kuala Lumpur. *Bastard*, he thought. *Treats me no different than the coolies.*

Joseph had been gambling the night before with his brother. Eric seemed, though marginally, to be able to hold his liquor better than he and managed to accompany their father to the fields as they did every day during harvest. It did not seem fair that their father should have any more claim to the fields than the sons. He married into it, but the two brothers and their sister Joyce would inherit it all, just as their mother had done. It was theirs by blood.

At first Joseph had hardly noticed his young niece who had also sought a sanctuary of sorts in the vast anonymity of the cluster of palms along the trail to the pineapple fields. She seemed to be lost in conversation, but with whom? There was no one else around.

He put out his cigarette, extinguishing thoughts for the moment of life's injustices, and he focused his attention on the young girl not twenty yards away. He could not quite make out what she was saying. Her back was to him, and she was sitting quite comfortably in high, untended grass under a pineapple tree.

Joseph stood, checking the path behind him over his shoulder. There was no one coming in either direction, and it was a good quarter mile back to the house. What spontaneous good luck. He moved cautiously forward, taking a few steps and then halting, still baffled by the girl's conversation that sounded like the banter of two sisters. He half expected to see Fin, or perhaps a girl from the kampong in her company who was somehow obscured by the tall grass.

But there was no one.

He took a few more steps. The ground was very soft, and he was silent. He began to visualize his pleasure. His brother had long ago surrendered any claim that he might have had as Catherine's father, and Joseph had discovered, in increments, that he could do as he liked with Catherine, with impunity. Joseph's mother, to whom everyone was answerable, had never disguised her contempt for the girl, daughter of that outrageous jungle woman who made so much trouble for everyone. It freed his hand.

Joseph paused to give the situation a final assessment. He was now, perhaps, ten yards behind her. Her very real conversation with her very imaginary playmate came to an abrupt halt, as Catherine felt the presence of her uncle.

Catherine remained motionless, a low growl, barely audible, beginning to emanate from the tiny cavity of her chest.

She bristled at his approach.

She could sense the man, and his presence always aroused suspicion.

No matter, Joseph assured himself. *Catherine is of no consequence, and no one of any consequence would come to her aid.*

Or so thought Joseph Madrigal D'Cruz …

Chapter Nine

"JOSEPH." The voice of God cracked open the air like the skull of a coconut shattered with the swift chop of a parang. "Joseph, where have you been. You should have joined us an hour ago."

Joseph turned to see his towering father not five feet behind him. How unfair that his father should be so much taller and so much more powerful, and so unshakably entrenched in the prime of his life even at fifty years old.

"Yes, Father." Joseph bowed, hoping the gesture would pass for respect as he tried to conceal his rapidly vanishing erection. He made as quick an exit as he could, propelled by the wake of his father's wrath.

Catherine turned, having instantly forgotten the pending horror of just a moment before. She was not yet standing as her grandfather approached, and she shaded her brow and squinted to make out his silhouette against a noonday sun.

There He was. God. A halo to prove it. So tall and so much stronger than either of his disappointing sons, who seemed to have inherited none of his considerable virtues.

"Catherine?" he asked. "You are so far from the house?" He was genuinely perplexed.

Catherine said nothing. She wanted to explain that Grandma had told her to leave, but she knew he didn't like hearing about affairs of the household. He had long been comfortable with his arrangement with Sarafina. She would run the affairs of the house, manage the money, and see to the upbringing of the children, and he would make the plantation flourish.

… And indeed, he did. He was very stern in the fields, demanding as much of himself as he did of the coolies and of his sons, which was considerable. William would always be the first in the fields, and the last to leave, and those who had worked for him since the beginning had come to respect his strength and endurance. He, in turn, spoke to them and of them respectfully, and further defined the kind of man he was by fasting with them during the month of Ramadan, like a Muslim, though there was certainly no imperative for him to do so. He was so unlike the

British managers, who never got closer to the ground or the people who worked it than the saddle of their mount. He was too perfect, and it cost him his sons.

He couldn't remember when either of his sons, or his daughter, Joyce, for that matter, had ever looked him in the eye when they spoke even the simplest of things, like "good morning". He never understood their shame, or why they feared him.

But his granddaughter was another matter. Her audacity delighted him. One of his infrequent smiles found its way subtly upon his face, which was as smooth and as brown as tanned leather. William took another step forward, and his giant form now shaded his granddaughter completely, and she no longer needed to squint.

Quite impulsively Catherine reached up with her two arms, and her grandfather bent down, permitting Catherine to lock herself around his neck as he hoisted her effortlessly skyward, cradling her with his left arm, and allowing her the luxury of being carried back to the path that bisected the palms and tall grass.

He put her down gently and took her small and perpetually muddy fingers in the palm of his hand. "You like the feel of the dirt between your fingers, do you?"

Catherine didn't answer. Her grandmother always complained about how filthy she was when she returned from play.

"Come, child," William said. "Why don't we see how the fields are doing today."

They began their walk down the well-worn path, and after a while he hefted his granddaughter upon his shoulders, and gave her his broad, straw hat.

"As far as you can see, Catherine, this is our land." This was neither boast nor unintentional talk. He had begun quite recently and quite consciously to implant within her an awareness of her place in the world as his granddaughter. He visualized this little girl, lost and struggling to see from under the oversized hat, growing into her legacy, her birthright. He visualized the growth of all things.

In the distance, up ahead, Catherine could see the men from the kampong loading pineapples into a cart. She was much taller than anyone around her. High upon his shoulders, she could only imagine what it must be like to be this tall forever, like her grandfather.

In his casual, deep voice, William asked, "Who was that you were talking to, child?"

He did not ask questions the way Grandma did, who already knew the answers to everything she asked. ("Who *told* you to get so dirty? Who *told* you to interrupt ... who *told* you it was all right to go to the kampong?" ... "No one, Grandma. No one .... no one.")

But with Grandpa, it was different. He was not baiting her, waiting for an answer to correct.

High upon his shoulders, high upon the top of the world, she spread her arms like a bird in flight, a garruda, fearless and free. She decided that she could trust him with an answer. "Tippy," she said.

"Tippy, is it?" he said, gently. "Tell me. Are you the only one who can see her?"

She was a little startled with the observation but said quite proudly "Yes. I'm the only one she talks to."

"Oh ... I see."

"She comes to play with me sometimes, but only when she's very lonely or very afraid."

"Do *you* ever get lonely, or afraid?"

"No, Gran'pa. Only Tippy."

"Do you think I might meet her ... someday?"

"Maybe. But she's very shy."

And that was enough to satisfy William D'Cruz. This child, this girl, was certainly different.

It was a benign moment, typical for him. He was oblivious to the extent of Sarafina's dislike for the imp upon his shoulders, and if he was flawed at all, it was his blindness to his wife's darker side.

He put his grandchild down, snatching his hat from her before she jogged ahead. They approached a dozen of the harvesters, among them his two sons, who seemed to work extra hard at his approach, and had quickly spit out their half-smoked cigarettes. With them, at least, he had no delusions.

William leisurely inspected a cart nearing fullness and selected a pineapple to share with his granddaughter. His ever-present parang sliced it nicely on the back of the wagon, where he stopped to sit and exchange a few pleasantries with his men. Unlike his sons, they felt no shame in his presence, having worked diligently in his brief absence, and having a cart almost ready to pull down the road to show for it.

There was a brief rain, monkey rain. "*Monkey rain* sprinkles the world slightly and surprisingly," he told Catherine, "and makes you look up because you don't remember seeing any clouds. It falls even when the sun is shining, and when monkey rain is falling, it means somewhere close by there is a monkey wedding. It's very good luck. Sunshine, even while Life insists on raining upon you."

Catherine crouched under the wagon, leaving her grandfather to sit by himself and smoke a cigarette, indifferent to the slight monkey rain that pattered gently on the broad straw hat that covered his head and much of his shoulders.

The rain had stopped even before he had finished his cigarette. He was satisfied that the harvest was going well and informed his men he was going to inspect the fields that lay directly between them and the house, to see if it was ready for harvest as well, and almost as an afterthought he looked under the cart where Catherine was just finishing a last slice of pineapple.

"Come with me," he said, but it seemed to Catherine more like an invitation than an order, and she took his hand and followed him into the fields, saying goodbye to her father, who had hardly noticed her presence. She knew enough not to say goodbye to Uncle Joe, who had avoided looking at her at all while she had been but a few yards away. No matter, she thought. She was with her grandfather now, and no harm would come to her.

They meandered in the general direction of the house, and though it seemed like nothing more than a stroll to her, her grandfather knew what he was about. Where the grass was too high he would direct his men to clear it in the morning, and repair a drainage ditch that caught the surplus of water from the slightly cambered slopes.

There was nothing particularly adventurous about the walk, but it was nice to be in the presence of a man so obviously at peace with the world, and the only adult who demanded nothing of her.

"You can take another one home, if you like," he offered. "Let's pick out a ripe one."

Catherine pranced ahead to a bush directly in front of her, and suddenly froze. Coiled around the base of the plant was a cobra, startled out of its sleep, and it lifted and flared its hypnotic head, poised instantly to strike the girl who was motionless with fear not three feet before it. She had no breath to breathe.

More swiftly than anything she could ever remember, along her side came the strong and fearless arm of her grandfather, who, with a cobra's accuracy, grabbed just behind the head of the snake, and crushed it in the palm of his hand, pulling it free of the bush and snapping it like a bull whip against the ground in one incredible motion.

For good measure he chopped it in half and tossed it aside like a piece of rope too short to be of any use.

"Well," he said, "he's not going to take *our* pineapple." He cleaned his blade with a swipe upon the wet grass, and selected, as promised, a ripe pineapple for his young granddaughter.

She was stunned. It was not the near-death from the cobra, which must have been as big as her grandfather, but that he was so absolutely fearless, and now so seemingly indifferent to what had just happened. He assumed that the incident was over but could see that Catherine was still shaken by it.

"Catherine," he explained, in an attempt to reassure her, "you were never in any real danger. The snake was coiled *around* the bush. He could not have made a strike even if he wanted to."

It was not enough, and she was still trembling. "Someday, I'll teach you how to do it." Catherine steadied herself and paid attention. "You don't even have to be as quick as the snake. You just have to know when to strike." He did not know how else to comfort her, it having been so long since he had been afraid of anything.

But the most remarkable event of the day ... was that he found absolutely nothing remarkable *about* the event of the day. When the family sat down together at the table that evening, Catherine could not take her eyes off her grandfather. He made no mention of the snake over supper. It was not a matter of modesty.

He had simply forgotten it.

Chapter Ten

The following morning was market day, and Kamille was pleased to have her shopping duties fully restored, without the surveillance of her employer. Sarafina had accompanied her almost every Wednesday for two of the last three months, and while Sarafina was with her, Kamille seldom spoke to anyone, and her role had been reduced to that of a porter. At first, she thought that Sarafina made the walk down to the store of Ephram Lim to make certain that she got the best price for everything, and next she thought that Sarafina was investigating to see if the prices and the change Kamille returned to her tallied up, as if Kamille might be cheating her. But when this practice of personally going down the hill to shop continued up to the second month since Che' Wan had been to their kampong, Kamille began to suspect some other motive.

She thought about this in particular as she came up the drive and around to the back porch of the house. The screen door opened almost by itself, as Kamille sidestepped Catherine, who went racing from the kitchen with Beni and Fin frantically trying to keep up with her. Life, it seemed to Kamille, was returning to normal. Perhaps, she thought, even better than normal.

In the last three months there was a contagious sense of well-being, of importance and worth that permeated the entire kampong. Che' Wan had done that. The air itself even tasted different. Especially now that Sarafina allowed her to the kampong independently, the vapor of transcendence clung to Kamille like the scent of flowers.

But it was that scent that betrayed her.

Kamille was oblivious to the presence she had carried in with her as she unpacked her rattan basket on the kitchen table. She hummed pleasantly to herself, unaware that the essence of Che' Wan was now adrift in the house. It flowed quietly, gently, into the parlor where Sarafina was napping, and watched the rise and fall of her breathing. After some time had passed, it whispered, "Do no more harm to that child."

Sarafina was aroused by the voiceless whisper and got up noiselessly from her divan. She saw no one, saw nothing, but could hear Kamille milling about. As she stepped softly to the kitchen the scent and color of the presence that had awakened her intensified.

"And what is the talk *today*, Kamille?" she said pleasantly.

Kamille had not noticed Sarafina come from behind her, and was slightly startled. But she was startled not so much by the presence of her mistress, as by the sudden recognition that she had been shamelessly humming out loud. She put her fingers to her lips without thinking and felt even more alarmed that by so doing she drew attention to what might otherwise have gone unnoticed. She cleared her throat. "Ephram Lim is not well."

"*Again?*"

"One of her daughters, Anca, this time, is minding the store."

"Ephram Lim is getting old," judged Sarafina, with the very slightest hint of disgust.

"There is talk that Anca may take over running the store alltogether."

"I never really liked the old woman," pondered Sarafina, "but at least with her, you could bargain. The daughter is not like that. Very hard."

Kamille continued to unpack her basket. *Maybe she did not notice at all*, she thought. In addition to the usual purchases of food, she displayed replacement settings of inexpensive tableware for Sarafina's approval. In a household with so many children running about, knives and forks and especially spoons seemed to disappear, sometimes found under the house where small hands transformed small mounds of sand into English castles and Asian palaces, the theaters of choice for their carefree imaginations.

"Did they ask for me?" inquired Sarafina, looking over Kamille's shoulder and quite discretly tabulating the estimated cost of the morning's venture.

"No, Puan," said Kamille. "She's not that ill. But Anca did ask that I bring some tonic for her mother next week. It helps with her cough. More than just tea." On the corner of the table, unfolded respectfully, she placed the few dollars and assorted coins in change as she had done for years, her mistress never having to ask for it or remind her.

"She has enough to last till then?"

"Yes, Puan."

Sarafina made a note to herself that she herself would once again do the marketing next week. She would bring a small bottle of her remedy. A gift, to be placed conspicuously on the counter when Anca would begin to total the purchase of goods Sarafina would select from the modest stock on the shelves and from the barrels in the small Chinese shop. Kamille *had* paid too much, she told herself. Or perhaps pocketed a bit of the change. Distrust. Always, distrust.

"And what was that you were humming, Kamille?" A question with the pretense of innocence.

"Oh ... it was nothing, Puan. Just an old Malay lullaby." How ever she answered, whatever she answered, was of no importance, and this Kamille knew, having been a servant to Sarafina these many years now. It was the puan's reminder that she expected austerity of all who worked for her, especially the house servants.

And that austerity had been compromised by a stroll through the kampong, inhaling the aroma of good will, three months old, since Che' Wan's pilgrimage to them. The air still had the taste of honey to it, and it felt wonderful to let it linger on the tongue, to hum.

Kamille knew that Sarafina was intensely suspicious of anything that created pleasure. Except for her cigars. *But that was a pleasure born of flame, wasn't it,* thought Kamille. All her favorite rituals called for fire. Even the offering of candles with occasional prayer. It had nothing to do with light and darkness. It was the fire that intrigued her mistress. And fire unlocked the pleasures of her cigars. Kamille prudently kept this observation to herself, for her own good.

And what she also kept to herself was the true nature of the prevalent gossip in the kampong.

There was *only* talk of Che' Wan. Her power. Her beauty. Her generosity. Her love. And there was talk of the precocious granddaughter, and Che' Wan's discovery of the miraculous sign on her palm. How everyone bowed to the child that day. Kamille knew nothing of this until Sarafina stopped accompanying her on market days.

And there was talk of the encounter on the verandah, in which a proposition from Che' Wan had been refused by Sarafina Madrigal D'Cruz. The audacity. And *that* talk, Kamille knew full well, depended upon *her* for the telling and re-telling. She was the definitive authority of *that* installment of the gossip, having dutifully served tea on behalf of her mistress, tea that would not be taken by their honored guest.

It was approaching noon. "Kamille, it's time for the children's bath before *makan*. Go and find them, will you, Kamille?" A command, masquerading as a request. Kamille did not mind at all. Spinster though she was, she enjoyed the responsibility of bathing and dressing the children, brushing their uncooperative hair, feeding them rice from a common bowl as they sat in a circle upon the floor.

"Yes, Puan." She finished clearing the table of the few things that she had purchased, storing coffee and rice on the shelves in the pantry adjacent to the kitchen. All that remained on the table was a broad basket of fruit, most of it grown on the plantation, and she judiciously covered it with a canopy of cheese cloth to frustrate the fruit flies. She departed through the back door to find the children in any one of a dozen of their secret places within the walls of the estate.

Sarafina was alone once more in her house. She ambled over to the propane stove. The limp she had cunningly falsified for years to create the deception of weakness was becoming endemic to her walk against her will. A disguise no more.

Ever present on the stove top was the morning's cauldron of white rice, neutral in taste and color and temperature, rejuvenated for consumption at each meal by the flameless fire of curry and spices. Next to the rice was a pot of very thick tea, faithfully boiled by Kamille each morning before the men would rise. This, too, would last all day, diluted with hot water from one of several flasks that Sarafina's daughter Joyce would see were kept full during the course of the late morning and into the early evening.

Since her husband, Tony, had run off six months earlier, Joyce had come into the fold once again, bringing her two children with her. Sarafina had pragmatically dismissed a servant, generously permitting her daughter to fill the void, and assume a servant's duties within her household in exchange for her old room and a place at the table for herself and Marta and Nestor.

Sarafina found her favorite cup from its prestigious niche on the shelf and poured herself a blend of the strong tea and the hot water, and took her place at the table. It was always the same place, clearly inherited when her mother died shortly after her father himself had gone to the other side. From her chair she reached up to give a gentle tug on the cord to the overhead fan. Electricity had been brought to the house for two years now, but she never ceased to be amazed by the effortless work of the fan. It was still a novelty to her. She could remember as a child that young boys would stand unobtrusively in the corner during the heat of mid-day with a broad palm leaf, moving the air ever so slightly with the slow rhythm of up and down strokes while her family ate together.

The twirling fan, perhaps, might blow the mysterious presence from her kitchen that she could sense had infiltrated the house when Kamille had returned from marketing. Sarafina still did not know quite what to make of it. But she would find out...

Except for the whir of the blades, the house was soundless. Rarely would she permit the children to play inside, though during the monsoons which came upon them twice yearly it would not be unusual to find them under the house, which was elevated perhaps to the height of a man's shoulders from the ground.

That had been Sarafina's domain as a child. She mused briefly about a childhood unfairly abbreviated. She remembered how she would tie sarongs from post to post, making her own little fortress, and play forever with the children of the servants. Sarafina had been an only child. Her birth had been difficult, she was told, and it damaged her mother, who never completely forgave her. The bonds to the children with whom she spent so many blissful hours were slowly discouraged, and when she was old enough to know to enter the house without mud on her feet, her grooming as the heiress to the estate commenced. She was weaned from the freedom of childhood and from playfulness under the house a bit too early ...

The back porch was the working porch of the house. The place where sweet potatoes were peeled, where clothes could be washed and hung to dry on a rainy day, and where small, naked children could stand and grit their teeth while water was poured over them to wash away the lather after soaping up in the big round tub.

Kamille had found the children, all five of them including Catherine, and successfully herded them back to the house, the promise of makan distracting them from the pending bath, which they always seemed obligated to resist.

They wiggled and shook and squabbled and one by one were clean and dripping dry, as Sarafina stood in the doorway, leaning against the jamb, her mug of tea in hand. *Where was Joyce?* she thought to herself. *She should be helping. After all, Nestor and Marta are hers. She should be taking care of them herself. And help with her brother's children, for that matter.*

"Kamille?" she began, "Was Joyce with you in the village?" It occurred to her as she spoke that lately, and with greater frequency, Joyce was not to be found during midday.

"No, Puan," she said, making furtive attempts to dry off the last of the children.

"Very strange," said Sarafina, out loud, inviting Kamille to agree with her.

Kamille said nothing.

"Oweeee." complained Nestor. "So rough, lah."

He was right.

"Hold still," ordered Kamille, indifferent to his protest as she quickly worked the towel over his damp head. Too briskly.

"Very strange, indeed," repeated Sarafina, this time expecting a reply, but getting none. Sarafina put down her cup on the back rail and picked up a towel to help dry the children. Draped over the rail were assorted sarongs for the girls, and baggy trousers with a draw string for Beni and for Nestor, who was rubbing his head as Kamille finished with him, giving a little pout that would mature into a scowl as he got older. His sister covertly stuck out her tongue and quickly passed under Sarafina before he could retaliate.

Catherine wrapped her own sarong around her shapeless, little-girl body and tied it behind her neck, and willingly did the same for Fin, who had just turned four, before following Kamille into the kitchen where they all sat down upon the woven mat in the center of the floor.

Sarafina followed, and retook her place at the table, watching Kamille dish out rice into a large wooden bowl as the children waited with no more patience than baby birds in their nest, about to be fed.

Kamille seemed to be consumed with her duties. *A reasonable explanation,* thought Sarafina, of why she seemed to be oblivious to the subtle beginnings of an interrogation. *Ahh, well. Not important. I will know all things, in time.*

But not this thing, thought Kamille, who was far from oblivious. Not from these lips. Kamille could keep a secret. Especially one that, if exposed to air, would no longer smolder, but would ignite, would engulf them all in the flame of Sarafina's rightful fury. It was not a secret born of trust or confidence, but one mandated by an accidental discovery. And it was best that Sarafina never knew. For her own good.

Chapter Eleven

Joyce entered the house from the back door, slipping out of her sandals, which held clay from the damp earth of the fields and sand from the long driveway to the house. Here her entrance would be most unobtrusive. It was the servant's entrance.

She stepped inside the kitchen to find the children midway through their meal, and her mother midway through her tea.

"More tea, Momma?" she asked, taking the initiative.

Marta stood up, rice and drool spilling from her cheeks as she reached possessively for her mother, who gave her an obligatory hug and sat her down with the others.

Sarafina had yet to reply. She had cultivated a way of using silence very effectively. It had become instinctual to her nature to pause a very long time before responding to even the most innocuous of comments or questions. Others would often fill the void with words they might not otherwise have volunteered. So it was with Joyce.

"I was in the fields, Momma. I brought Papa and the boys their *makan*." Joyce took the cup from her mother and replenished it with a blend of strong tea from the stove with hot water, and she ignited the burner beneath the kettle to replenish the water in the flask. She spooned and stirred sugar before setting her offering before her mother.

"Thank you, Joyce," she said, after some time.

Joyce could sense that her absence had drawn attention. Attention usually led to scrutiny, which was an agonizing ordeal even when there was nothing to hide. But she had been hesitant to disturb her napping mother to tell her where she was going, not wanting to risk irritating Sarafina by waking her. She hadn't really been gone so long, she thought, and could not have known that her mother had awakened prematurely. She would now pay the price of her miscalculation.

"Why don't you fix me more tea, and then finish up for Kamille," said her mother, giving Joyce some direction.

"Yes, Momma," she said, dutifully. Her mother's question was, of course, not a question. She stood quickly and prepared tea for her mother.

Kamille relinquished her place on the floor and handed Joyce the wooden bowl of white rice and cooked vegetables. "I have cleaning, Puan," she said, and dismissed herself, leaving Joyce to fend for herself, if that is what was to follow.

Sarafina sipped her tea, heavily sugared by her daughter, just the way she liked it. "This is very good tea, Joyce." Sarafiina realized, of course, that Joyce had been in the fields when she saw that she had entered the house with the empty basket. Still, every explanation had the potential of becoming a confession. And now, what Sarafina was determined to ferret out was an explanation for the damp stains she could not help but notice on the back side of her daughter's sarong.

"Thank you, Momma," she said, anxious to get on with her duties of feeding the children, and perhaps lose herself in the maze of their demands upon her, spooning food into their upturned little beaks.

Sarafina studied her daughter for a while, in between sips of tea and inhalations of the soothing vapor from the cup. "This is very good tea," she said again. A compliment to draw her out.

But Joyce knew her mother very well, and this cued her that she was under some additional investigation. She became wary. And angry. *It's none of her damn business*.

She could never be in the presence of her mother without being angry, and could never quite explain the phenomenon to herself, let alone justify it. Her mother had done nothing to her. But still, the anger. It never ignited. Her mother saw to that. It only smoldered, turning her bones hard, prematurely, and dehydrating a face more wrinkled now, than her mother's. A face that had at one time the potential, the promise of beauty, but now had the permanent demeanor of disdain.

The fire deep from the interior of her volcanic spirit scorched her hair, ash gray, though she was not yet thirty, and burned everything that might have grown, charred each thought, smoked each spoken word.

For Joyce the cost of returning to the security of her mother's house would be to accept the brunt of responsibility for raising Eric's three children, whose mother had left them. With that burden evaporated any hope of ever escaping this house, of ever finding another husband again, of ever being anything but a less-than-trusted servant.

How she hated Catherine for this. Not quite safe enough for Joyce to hate her own mother, who enslaved her, but safe enough to hate the powerless one who so resembled that jungle woman. That savage. That Iban. The one who did those evil things so freely with her brothers. And maybe even with her father.

And yet, this incinerating hostility needed some disguise. It was too ungodly, and needed to be Christianized. The only acceptable explanation that Joyce could live with was that the object of her wrath must be evil. The angrier she became at her obligation to Catherine, the more evil Catherine had to become. It was the inescapable destiny of those coerced into believing in God, and who could not possibly accept that anger was inherent to their own character and a defensible component of the human condition. To Joyce, anger was an intrusion upon the perfect soul God had endowed them with, and cautioned them to protect. God would not approve of such a selfish flaw. It therefore did not exist. Joyce negotiated with God, denying that she was ever angry. Only self-righteous. And God approved of her shared contempt for those who were evil.

It was an easy thing for her to do, sacrificing Catherine to the child's grandmother. Because Catherine was evil.

"Momma," she said, "this one has been teasing Marta." She looked fire-cold at Catherine, who had no idea what she was talking about. Marta was a sickly child, and in spite of being well fed, even pampered, always had the look of being undernourished. Her legs were quite spindly and never seemed fully developed. She could easily evoke her mother's sympathies, but more importantly, Joyce had discovered that for some obscure reason, Marta was Sarafina's favorite grandchild.

Catherine, suddenly realizing that she was being falsely accused, wanted to speak in protest, but choked on the mouthful of rice her aunt forced down her throat.

"YOU, lah." fired Joyce. "Chew your food properly. Don't spill."

And suddenly, with a little bit of meanness directed towards Catherine, Joyce was a servant no more, but her mother's beloved daughter.

"Why, what has she done now?" Sarafina's first genuine question. She wanted to know.

"She's always teasing Marta about her legs."

"More rice." said Fin. It was her turn in the circle and she saw no reason why her aunt should hesitate.

"It's true, Grandma," said Nestor, having no idea he was accidentally supporting his mother's diversion with a lie of his own. Catherine seemed to be getting too much of the attention because that temple woman had come. Everyone in the kampong bowing to her and talking about her. He quickly improvised. "And she shoved Marta down. In the *dirt*."

Even without proper schooling in the matter, Nestor knew enough to emphasize the 'dirt' rather than the 'shoving'. He intuitively knew his elders would be more concerned that Catherine had caused his sister to get dirty rather than hurt or humiliated.

Joyce was startled with this revelation. Maybe it was true. Surely her son would not lie. She continued the momentum. "And Catherine climbs the trees too much. It is not proper for a young lady."

This, as calculated, was enough to trigger Sarafina's recollection of the mother, of the jungle woman, who was forever in the trees, even in the orchard before the house, like a gibbon or wild monkey, indifferent to Sarafina's commands that she return to the house and behave herself, as if the tree tops were beyond her domain. Openly defiant of her.

And it was that easy for Joyce to deflect her mother's inquisition. Joyce had no love for Catherine. She had herself, and her two children to watch out for. And that contempt for Catherine not only gave her God's blessings and sanctioned her hostility, but it also gave her access to Sarafina's good graces, just as Nestor was accidentally discovering how to garnish his own mother's approval. Sharing contempt, and anger, and disdain became as bonding in the family as sharing love might have been. It was a bond not unlike that between Sarafina and Sister Masselin, who felt a special solidarity reassuring each other that the world was corrupt and evil.

"More rice," said Fin, blissfully.

Joyce looked down at her niece's gaping mouth, and filled it with a ball of rice, irritated by the child's playfulness. In turn she then fed Beni and Nestor, then Marta, and Catherine once again. Out of habit, that which she spooned to her own children, even from the same bowl, always had the bit of chicken, or pork, or fish. Eric's children would get only rice and vegetables, and perhaps a bit of egg, but any meat was by accident. For a long time, now, Joyce had stopped being discreet with her favoritism. No one suggested it was unjust.

So, this is my brood, thought the matriarch of the family. Sarafina sipped the last of her tea and drew in a heavy breath. The cacophony of her grandchildren, unlike the electric fan, was no longer an intriguing novelty to her. It was just an annoyance to be tolerated. Somewhere in this generation on the floor in her kitchen was the one who would take care of her in her old age. She seemed fairly certain that she would outlive her boys, and probably Joyce.

She hoisted herself from the table, this becoming more of an effort of late, and shuffled through the kitchen and parlor, making a brief excursion to the humidor before ascending her throne on the front verandah. There she rocked and smoked, wondering which of those whining children would be conscripted for her care, as she aged, and which were expendable.

It required very little thought.

For the child's own good, she thought, *I will follow Masselin's advice.* She became more sure of herself, as the cigar neared its end. Yes. And why not in the morning? No oracle to consult. No confirmation required of her husband or solicited from her indifferent son. The answer to the most difficult questions always appeared to her quite clearly from within the blur of smoke that surrounded her rocker.

And so, having informed no one but Kamille, Eric's two daughters, Fin and Catherine, were neatly scrubbed, properly dressed, and with bags appropriately packed were ushered through the gates by their grandmother in the predawn darkness the following morning to begin their exile from childhood.

A hint of moonlight illuminated the well-worn path through the kampong, the houses and the palms, colorless silhouettes against a silver-tinted indigo sky. Lamplight yet to emanate from any window, a morning hearth yet to be stoked. They followed the serpentine path without so much as disturbing a dog, Sarafina leading the way, holding the hand of her granddaughter to keep her from straggling. Behind the two of them was Kamille, carrying Fin who was not fully awake, and a few steps behind them the gardener, pressed into service this early morning to carry the few small bags that contained all the evidence the two girls had even lived at the plantation.

They could hear the river whispering gently ahead, and reeds along the bank rustling together to breeze and to current, a low morning chant. As they approached the bridge, the outline of the vast jungle on the other side of the river seemed impenetrable, its path that would widen and lead to the road hidden by a graying darkness.

Halfway across the bridge they could hear the first words of the *muzzein.* "*Allaaaaaaah, O Akbahr ... Allaaaaaaah, O Akbahr.*" God is great ... God is great."

Catherine paused with her grandmother for a last look at the village, which was now being summoned into wakefulness and prayer. She had no idea where her grandmother intended to take her, or why, and was unaware that childhood could be lost as easily, as completely, as irretrievably, as by crossing the river.

"Where are we going, Grandma?" Catherine had not been away from the kampong in two or three years. Not since her mother ... she forgot the details. It was almost half her life ago.

"Hush," said her grandmother, though not harshly. "You will know soon enough." The bank on the other side of the river began to take on form, began to be more than a flawless wall of darkness. The sky continued to gray, and the entrance to the trail, the only trail, became visible. "Watch for snakes," cautioned Sarafina. Prudent advice, especially where the trail was so narrow.

There was enough light to support their unhurried though deliberate pace. Sarafina was becoming heavier, slightly, as she aged, and the weight overworked her lungs in the damp air of dawn and aggravated her limp. Still, it was she who set the pace, indifferent to Kamille who had the burden of a sleeping four-year-old on her shoulder, or to Amir, given charge of the baggage.

After some time, they had come to the clearing where Che' Wan made the transition from her Mercedes to the garruda, but the clearing was no more. Three months had seen to that. The jungle had swollen over all traces of the event, new growth coming not only from the soft dirt, but also in a tangle of vines from the canopy above, as well. Only the proximity to the river, void of a living filter of trees, permitted them enough light to amble forward.

But soon the trail became gravel and widened, and the sky above them began to have a few traces of morning color. Upon a recently fallen trunk they sat to rest, though only for a few moments while Sarafina rubbed her knees. Fin was awake, now, and rubbing her eyes, having no recollection of being lifted from her mat where she had been sleeping between her brother and sister.

They continued to walk. Kamille took the handbags, now that Fin was awake, and Amir lifted the sleepy girl, who had yet to speak or inquire about their journey and hoisted her upon his shoulders. After another half mile a quadrant of the jungle had been transformed into a pineapple plantation, not unlike the expansive fields originally cultivated by Sarafina's father, half a century ago. To accommodate the harvest, a road bisected the fields, ending at the river's edge. Here, clearly morning now, the travelers turned inland. The utility road would eventually intersect a main highway, where a twice-daily bus could be flagged down sometime before mid-morning.

It was still early morning when they reached the crossroads. The notion of a bus 'stop' had little relevance here. Stopping the bus was a matter of hailing it anywhere along the road, but this was as good a place to wait as any. They had come early enough, should the bus arrive at the shallow end of its sporadic and unreliable schedule. But it was fairly predictable that it would pass their way sometime well before noon, and by mid-afternoon they would find themselves on the outskirts of the capital city.

Sarafina dismissed Amir. Fin, being awake now, could walk together with her sister, and Kamille could manage the two small bags they would need to start their new lives. Certainly, they did not need Amir for protection along the road. His puan was a far more intimidating presence than he was, anyway.

He bid them good day, pausing for a privately sad moment to gaze upon the two children. He had not been informed of their destination or purpose of the trip, but seeing that their bags were packed, and that Beni was excluded, he rightfully imagined what was ahead for them. He would miss them, especially the tomboy who had so much spunk.

Sunshine, morning rainbows, and an ever-so-slight sprinkle of rain marked his departure, as he shuffled gently back down the lonely red clay road between two pineapple fields towards the river. He saw no point in looking back. After all, he had work to do.

Inevitably, the children became restless, finding it an almost impossible task to sit with their grandmother, who spread a small blanket on the ground and was propped against a fallen log at the corner of the road. The baggage that they carried served as a buffer against the coarse trunk, and Sarafina could lean back comfortably to watch the day progress. From her day bag, which she herself carried, she produced a flask of tea. She helped herself, being as tolerant of the children as she could, cautioning them not to squirm into her and make her spill.

Kamille offered some tea to the children, who took it from boredom as much as thirst, and she offered them rice cakes from the kitchen, which kept them occupied for a while. They huddled together and nibbled at the food, pretending to be two little mice.

There was a bit of traffic on the road now. Mostly foot traffic. Men coming to work the fields, and an occasional cart. One or two automobiles also passed, both in the direction of the city, and several lorries with clay on their tires and mud spattered and caked on the side panels.

Kamille did her best to entertain the children. "Kamille, can't you keep them quiet?"

Kamille ushered them down the road a bit, out of earshot of their grandmother. A stranger, a coolie, offered them a pineapple at the edge of the field, slicing it politely for them with his parang. "I know who she is," he said, interrupting Kamille who started to explain to him her mistress's importance. Sarafina looked once in their direction but only briefly. The coolie was of no importance to her.

"These children, they are hers?"

"No, her grandchildren."

"Oh. I see." He looked discerningly at the children. "But ... they look Chinese?"

"Their mother was Iban."

"Oh, yes. That could be. I have seen an Iban woman. She looked Chinese. She was crazy."

"What?"

"The Iban woman I saw. Maybe two or three years ago. She was wild. She crossed this very road, blood in her eyes and running like an animal. But I saw her face. She looked Chinese."

"You must not speak so loud. You disturb my puan."

"Sorry, lah."

He sliced another pineapple for them and went back to his work in the fields.

Sarafina fluttered an occasional breeze with the fan from her bag and waited dispassionately for the bus. The road was straight in both directions as far as the eye could see, rising slightly upon each horizon. The sunshine was just becoming uncomfortable when at last, slipping down the center of the road haphazardly in the distance came the bus from the interior on its way to Kuala Lumpur. Sarafina winced for a brief, uncharacteristic moment, as she envisioned what lay ahead for Catherine. She did not dwell upon it. After all, it was for the child's own good.

Chapter Twelve

The bus, as expected, was overcrowded and brought all the usual discomforts this condition implied. Bodies of strangers sweating in close proximity, and stagnant air fermenting their odors, co-mingling with the toxic perfume of diesel oil, and the exhaust fumes that only in theory were expelled behind the bus. The sweet scent of the pineapple fields was simply too refined to enter the vulgar, rambling chamber on wheels that made passageway through them.

All this was aggravated by the jolting motion on the pockmarked road. At the moment it finally became intolerable, the red clay and loose gravel miraculously became black asphalt, and with a little extra speed a warm breeze was forced through the open windows of the bus.

Stops were frequent, but brief. Passengers would insist on getting off where there appeared to be nothing at all but wilderness or unpopulated pineapple fields. Sometimes whole families would appear out of nowhere, inexplicably hailing the bus, dressed in their finest, with no evidence, not so much as a footpath, to indicate from where they had come.

The only stop of any duration was quite naturally for the mid-morning call to prayer, initiated by the driver himself.

Although the discomfort distorted time, making it seem infinite, it was less than a few hours before they approached the more tangible evidence of a city. There was now traffic, more frequent crossroads, stalls alongside the road to accommodate travelers, and nameless kampongs displacing what had been either jungle or cultivated fields. They even crossed over railroad tracks.

"Is that where we're going, Grandma?" Catherine's incredulous eyes opened wide to a citadel in the distance, with spires and towers and minarets, more than she could even count, the most spectacular shimmering gold in the midday sunshine. A high wall, so much higher than the wall to the house back home, seemed to surround the entire hill. It was spilling over with vines in flower, and on the other side, a jungle, untouched, undisturbed, except for the enormous palace at the pinnacle miles away on its commanding rise.

Catherine, with the special kind of impatience known only to a seven-year-old, asked her unhearing grandmother once again. "Is that where you're taking us?"

"Hush," said her grandmother, who had taken the window seat. "No. It isn't."

"Very few people are permitted there," spoke Kamille, leaning forward from the seat behind Sarafina and her granddaughter. "That," she further explained, "is the palace of our king."

"Really?" said Catherine. "Grandma. That's where Che' Wan lives." She squirmed in her seat, stretching to the window for a better look.

"Yes, and you will never go there," said her grandmother, adamantly, gruffly seizing the girl by the nape of the neck and restoring her properly to her seat.

"But, but ..." stuttered Catherine, "Che' Wan said ..."

"Che' Wan is a witch, and is evil, and uses black magic," came the remark from the witch, who was evil, and used black magic. It was her most seething condemnation.

"But ...'"

"Hush."

"Yes, but ...'"

"Catherine," Kamille put her hand on Catherine's shoulder, having repositioned Fin who had fallen asleep on her lap. "Catherine," she said softly, "hush." She did her best to still the enthusiasm that she could see was clearly provoking Sarafina's ire.

"But ..."

No, no, no, girl," encouraged Kamille, sympathetic to the sweet, indomitable wonder she herself had once felt for the world. Kamille did her best to maintain harmony, or at the very least prolong its illusion until they reached their true destination, miles, it seemed, from the road or from the wall.

Sarafina D'Cruz looked sternly ahead, resolute about her granddaughter's future.

Catherine stared at the wall that encapsulated the palace and its private preserve. It seemed endless and would periodically snake down and border the road. At one point the wall curved away from the road and increasing traffic, forming a crescent-shaped alcove that designated one of the lesser-used entrances. Twin towers, almost as high as the trees of Borneo that her mother had told her about stood as sentries on either side of the gated road that led between them. The road itself, from what she could see, disappeared on the other side of the hill where it made a steep climb to a second wall not even visible from the main highway.

The driver slowed, as he passed, intrigued as was everyone on the bus by what life must be like on the other side of those formidable walls.

But soon it was all behind them. The city was not more than a few miles ahead, and shanties on the side of the road were replaced by respectable rows of houses, two stories high, with shops and vendors below, living quarters above.

Undeveloped stretches along the highway were fewer now, but the hills that sloped behind the houses were still swollen with jungle, which looked as if it could burst at any time and wash over civilization's toehold on the way to Kuala Lumpur.

And the structures were no longer exclusively made in wood, or roofed in corrugated zinc. Brick and mortar and pale stucco were the construction materials of choice, and red tiled terra cotta roofing gave civilization a more permanent appearance, the partial legacy of British rule.

Affixed below almost every window on the second floor were a half a dozen steel holsters, sleeves into which could be slipped bamboo poles that protruded over the street to hang the damp laundry in sporadic morning sunshine. It made the approach to town quite festive, the sarongs and blouses that festooned each building resembling flags and banners, heralding gay festivities and adventures within the city proper.

The bus moved very slowly, now, and the passengers discovered that it did, in fact, have a horn. It seemed to trumpet its own importance several times down each block to bicycles and pedestrians that had not quite learned to co-exist with the recent incursion of the automotive age.

Some would scatter at its approach, others would linger indifferently before it, proceeding at the reasonable pace of a tri-sha. Now that there was cross traffic, each intersection offered to stop traffic all together, as an increasing number of drivers brought their personal philosophy of road etiquette to the confusing ritual of right-of-way.

Fin was awake now, and Kamille let her sit on her lap at the window, taking in all the sights that were brand new to her. Catherine had seen this before, but that had been when she was her sister's age. Her grandmother turned in her seat to look out the window herself, and she effectively blocked Catherine from seeing anything at all. Her impulse to thwart other people's pleasure was not only conscious, but instinctual, exploiting every opportunity. Catherine was getting only a frustrating view of this strange world through the dusty windshield so distant from the back of the bus. Kamille invited her to sit with her, and with Fin, Sarafina be damned.

The row of shop houses was interrupted by another parcel of green, stretching along the road for about half a kilometer. And then, right along the road, a wall as high as the window of the bus, straight and even, massive and purposeful. Broken bottles, amber and green and diamond-clear had been embedded in mortar troweled upon the top of the wide, gray wall like frosting on a cake.

From the vantage point of the bus Catherine could see a complex of buildings from within, all very symmetrical and painted with a dull gray that at one time may have had a hint of blue that had become disinterested and faded away.

Sarafina rose to her feet, and called to the Malay driving the bus, "*Sihnee.*" Here. He came to a stop, and Sarafina marched to the front of the bus and made her exit, leaving the formalities of a thank you to Kamille, who ushered the children before her and struggled down the narrow aisle with their baggage.

The bus rambled ahead and disappeared after cresting one final slope before entering the city. Catherine could see the outlines of the buildings, some of them a full five stories high. But it was Sarafina's intention that they get no closer to the city than they were at that moment. She took her granddaughter's hand.

A gravel road led up the hill where the wall made an abrupt right angle from the main highway. Trees and very dense undergrowth, jungle, stood ready on the other side of the path to retake the trail at the first signs of neglect, and in fact surrounded the entire compound except where it bordered the highway.

As the little band entered the gauntlet, the corridor formed by masonry on one side and by trees on the other, a colony of monkeys scrutinized their approach from the canopy above. They were baring teeth and snarling and had become so daring as to drop from the trees. They made an attempt to snatch at Sarafina's day-bag, which still had the potential of a cache of food. Sarafina whacked a would-be robber with her scrolled parasol, and with his retreat the others followed into the trees. They regrouped and swore at the passers-by below them.

Catherine was perplexed. They were so unlike the monkeys who co-existed on the perimeter of the kampong at Sentul. *What had made them so mean?*

They were almost halfway up the hill, a hundred yards, at least, when the dispassionate wall cornered once again. Sarafina paused to catch her breath, oblivious to the hardship the trudge up the hill made for Kamille who was shouldering one bag and struggling with another in her arms, her stride broken awkwardly by the additional task of herding a four-year-old behind the grandmother.

The stop was brief, and the walk continued another fifty or seventy-five yards, until at last they came to a simple wooden door hinged within an even larger wooden gate that could open to let infrequent vehicles in or out. A tether by the side of the entrance dangled from a brass bell that pivoted from an ulin crossbar that spanned the gate.

Sarafina pulled abruptly on the bell twice. It rang sharply, devoid of music. It was purely utilitarian. In a moment Catherine could hear a bolt sliding from within. The wait had not been long; their arrival announced formally by the howl of the monkeys.

"What *is* this place?" asked Catherine, in a whisper, to Fin or to Kamille, or anyone who would answer.

The massive door, thick but narrow, pulled open to the inside, concealing whomever it was who was letting them in. Sarafina stepped inside, with Fin directly behind her, followed by Catherine, and of course, Kamille. The door shuddered behind them, drawing the girls' attention, and the bolt was slid back with a sharp rasping sound by a woman who dressed just like Sister Masselin.

When the girls turned forward again, their grandmother had stepped aside, and there, right before them, was an Englishman, almost naked, bleeding from a wound in his chest, and rail-road spikes through each of his hands and another through his feet, all this holding him to a post embedded in the dirt among the roses.

"Aaeeiii!" screamed Fin, as did Catherine, who ran to push aside the gatekeeper and undo the bolt.

"Catherine. Catherine. It's all right." Kamille put her hand and weight to the gate to keep them from leaving.

"Let me go."

"Catherine. Calm down. It's all right."

"CATHERINE." Bellowed her grandmother. "STOP ... AT ONCE."

Fin had run along the perimeter of the wall and found a patch of bushes in which to hide, with Kamille chasing after her when it became clear that Sarafina would deal with Catherine herself. *This* they had not at all anticipated.

"Girl ... it's Jesus .... *it's Jesus!*" Sarafina grabbed Catherine by the shoulders and lifted her off the ground, slamming her hard against the wooden door. "LOOK." She dropped Catherine to the ground and then thrust the girl forward to see. "It's WOOD. You stupid girl."

Catherine was gasping, breathing hard, and refused to look. Her grandmother, behind her now, clasped either side of her head, and forced her to look. "It's WOOD."

Slowly, it made sense. It was wood. It was a statue. Painted. Made to look like a man. A statue. "Fiiiin." said Catherine, still trembling. "He's not real ... he's a statue."

But Fin was still in the bushes, where Kamille could not retrieve her, huddled over and crying and waiting for her sister to come and protect her, as she always had.

"It's made of wood. It's a statue, Fin. A statue." Remarkably, Catherine had regained her composure, and her instinct now was to come to the aid of her hysterical sister. Then it occurred to her, Fin would have no idea what a statue was. Catherine crawled into the bushes.

The commotion had by this time brought the Mother Superior, and her secretary, Sister Masselin. The elders exchanged a few words, and from windows of a second story, a colony of curious orphans abandoned their studies and peeked to investigate. And when their teacher left the classroom to see what assistance she might lend to the others, the whispers became talk, the talk became chatter.

The children scampered from window to window, and back again for a better view of the intruders. They began to point and jeer at the girls in the bushes, as one of their classmates figured out what had happened, and explained it all to them. They began their cruel laughter, until the cacophony annoyed Mother Superior, who turned her head sharply in their direction, which was enough to silence the howl of the monkeys. They instantly retreated from the windows to avoid her stare, scampering back to their places and were silent once more.

In a few minutes, Catherine led her sobbing Fin from the thorny bushes, her sanctuary. "You see. It's only wood. Like the garruda. In the mosque." Catherine went up to touch the man on the cross. Even the bound and bleeding feet that had terrorized her, too, just moments before. She rapped on it with her knuckles for her sister, for herself. "It's wood."

The brunt of the scare being over, Fin waddled over to Catherine with her arms overhead, and Catherine picked up her baby sister and let her cry some more. She turned and faced her grandmother, suddenly aware she had done something wrong.

"You *stupid* girl," said her grandmother, with disgust but not much feeling, relieved that her burden was just about over.

Vaguely, Catherine recalled a picture of the man in the garden from her grandmother's bible, but that had been long ago, and she was beaten for going through Sarafina's things. Still, she thought, she should have remembered.

"Is this the one?" asked Mother Superior, waiting sternly to see if it would be Masselin or Sarafina to first provide an answer.

"Yes," asserted Masselin, sparing her old friend further embarrassment, "this is the one."

Catherine set her sister down and bowed her head, noticing that everyone had a necklace just like her grandmother's and Sister Masselin's, and the pendant was in the same shape as the lumber that supported the frightening carving of the dying man.

Mother Superior turned to go back inside, not bothering to invite them in, knowing they would follow, all of them.

Catherine stood, for just a moment, Fin by her side, beneath the agonized symbol of her grandmother's faith and her moral compass.

So this was Jesus.

"How do you do.

"My name is Catherine Madrigal D'Cruz, daughter of Edward Eric, and this is my sister, Fin."

Jesus said nothing. He had problems of his own.

Chapter Thirteen

Antoinette had been among those who had witnessed Catherine's debut three days earlier. It was she who had figured out the shouting and the screaming had something to do with the scarecrow in the rose garden that greeted all newcomers. It was she who explained it to the other children, and it was she who decided it was comical. And it was she who determined the appropriate response was ridicule.

Now, from her command post in the cafeteria, she sent Luka to find out what she could about the girl, and report back to her.

"You, take this." Luka offered Catherine a slice bread, which was no mean sacrifice.

"For real?"

"Yeah. Sure. Take it. What's your name?"

"Cat. Catherine."

Catherine divided the windfall with Fin, who had clung to her fearfully ever since her first encounter with Christ.

"So, the old woman was your grandma?"

"Yes," said Catherine, pleased that someone had taken an interest in her.

"And the other one, with the bags. Her frien'?"

"No. Kamille. Our servant."

"You got a *servant*?"

"Yes. Of course. And I have a papa and a mama, too. Only, she doesn't live with us on the plantation."

Luka understood this to mean that Catherine's family worked on a plantation. Had Catherine suggested that her family *owned* the plantation, Luka would have concluded that Catherine was just another orphan with an invented family, like so many of the others.

Luka was just shaking her head in amazement. "Nobody here has anybody. We're all orphans."

"I never met an orphan. I never even knew anybody who died."

"You shouldn't be here," said Luka, forgetting that her purpose was to glean information, and not to make friends with the girl. "Not if you've got family on the outside. There must be some mistake, or you're lying ... You really got a servant?"

"I'm not lying. Honest. Fin, tell her."

Fin was too young to follow what they were saying and said nothing. Luka believed her anyway, impossible though it was. There was something very straightforward about Catherine that she liked, though she knew she wasn't supposed to.

"The girls over there." Luka nodded in the direction of an exclusive table. "Outsiders. They come just for the school. They got somebody. Somebody brings them every morning. Somebody takes them home every night." And then she paused, announcing with some distinction, "But we got nobody." Except, she thought privately, for Antoinette. We have Antoinette, who was glancing over occasionally to let her presence be felt. She reflected a moment before asking again. "You *sure* that was your grandmother?"

Catherine nodded, determined to reassure the first girl to talk to her. She had no idea that the reason she and Fin had sat alone was that it had been the decree of the girl, about her own age, who sat on the other side of the room and awaited the return of her lieutenant. But someone was at last sitting with her, and Catherine hoped she had made a friend in Luka. She seemed nice enough.

"Luka. That's your name?"

"Yes. How you know that?"

"I heard that other girl talking to you. She called you that." She pointed her spoon to the girl at the center of the table near the doorway.

"That's Antoinette."

"Ang Tuah Net?" Catherine repeated the name, making it sound a more recognizable Chinese.

"No, no. It's ANN TWA NET. Antoinette. It's English, or French, or something. They gave most of us new names. They let me keep my name 'cause it sounds like 'Saint Luke'. He was a holy man."

"Luka? How come nobody talks to us?"

Luka took a sip from her bowl of broth. She shrugged her shoulders as if it were a mystery to her as well. To lie wordlessly, with a gesture and falsified look of bewilderment, was less sinful than to speak words that were untrue. It was a diplomatic way to deceive Catherine and still remain within the perimeters of honesty.

Fin dipped the last of her bread into her bowl just as Sister Marcella was approaching. The lunch hour was almost over, and it was time for her nap. Fin was not quite old enough to join the others in school, and spent her days in the nursery with the younger children. But she could take lunch with her sister, and supper as well.

The evenings had been difficult for Fin. She had never slept without her sister before, and it made parting now more difficult and uncertain.

Sister Marcella patiently peeled Fin from Catherine's side, giving her a moment to hug her sister, and carried her through the open doors to one of the many courtyards and down to the nursery. Sister Marcella shared the duty of caring for the very young with Sister Gertrude. More accurately, Sister Marcella obeyed the commands of Sister Gertrude, respectful of her seniority. Sister Gertrude had been there since the end of the War, having come all the way from London, and Sister Marcella's vows to Christ were more recent. But she went about her duties almost cheerfully, and Catherine could see that Fin seemed to like her. Fin waved goodbye to Catherine over her shoulder.

Catherine had been meaning to ask someone, and better to ask Luka than an adult. "There are no boys here?"

"Of course not. This is a convent. What do you think? And all the grownups are nuns. Except for the two gardeners, and they're very, very old. And the cook, too. He's Chinese."

"You not gonna make it here, girl. You not tough enough. What are *you* doing here, anyway?"

The truth of the matter was, Catherine hardly knew the answer. It was explained to her abruptly the morning after her grandmother had finished a cognac with Mother Superior, and departed with Kamille and Amir. All Catherine knew, all Catherine was told, was that it was for her own good, the answer given so often by those who did not care enough to give her either the truth or the details. Catherine had heard the phrase often enough in her short lifetime to understand it was always followed by something unpleasant.

Catherine was trying to formulate an answer, for Luka and for herself, but was spared the struggle by the entrance of Sister St. John. She had come in from a door that had been closed, carrying a tray with eight or ten empty wooden bowls. She sat the tray down, as Catherine had seen her do the day before, and closed the door behind her. Luka could sense her curiosity.

"That's not for us. You *never* wanna go in there."

"Why? What's in there?"

"Tell you later." Luka could see that Antoinette was leaving for the courtyard before classes were to resume, and when she rose, her entire table stood and followed. Luka departed as well, making no gesture, giving no sign, that it might be all right for Catherine to join them.

Catherine was alone again at her very long table, as she had been before Fin had joined her for lunch. She had never seen so many children. There must have been fifty or sixty of them, still at their chairs, eating or talking, some starting to wander outside to play. A few of them, she thought, gossiping about her. Some were mixed blood, like herself. There were some Chinese, like Luka and Antoinette. Most of them appeared to be *Bumi Putra*, Malays, and a few were dark enough that they must be Indian.

As Catherine looked about her, wearing the new blue and white uniform issued to her on the very first day, she thought herself to be an observer, and not really there. Within months that thought would become a wish, then a hope, and with the kind of irony that only Christianity could provide, when she had mastered the ritual of prayer, she would pray that she would be only an observer, and not really there.

Those who would teach her the ritual had a table to themselves superfluous with food. Their vows of poverty and self-denial apparently did not extend to the supper table, where they ate abundantly and were seemingly oblivious to the knowledge that the children Christ had entrusted to them were barely getting enough. And they were indifferent, or oblivious, to the knowledge that when they left their table each day to return to their duties, a spy by the door would give the all-clear sign before the kitchen help came to clear the table. An elite group of children, Antoinette's gang, would swarm upon the carcasses of unfinished chicken, uneaten fresh vegetables, and half-eaten sweet rice cooked in coconut milk, and even an occasional mooncake.

Catherine had seen this now, for two days running, and the nuns were preparing to get up and leave. Antoinette's spy appeared in the doorway, casually leaning against the jamb.

Catherine herself had been given only broth and bread and unsweetened tea, and made up her mind that she, too, would get something more nourishing for herself and for her sister, if it were there to be had. She, too, could wait for the nuns to leave.

Stealing food was not new to her. She knew Auntie Joyce always gave more to Marta and Nestor, depriving her and her siblings even when there was plenty. Though she was not old enough to understand it in words, her intuition was acute in one so young, and she realized that doling out extra food to her own children at the expense of Catherine and her siblings had nothing to do with her Auntie's motherly instincts for Marta and Nestor. It was an expression of meanness towards her brother's children who inspired so much resentment. There was so much venom in the woman that it needed to be milked at every opportunity to keep it from killing her.

Catherine protested only once, and it happened to be in the presence of her grandmother. Very little seemed to be said about it, except of course for Sarafina's obligatory remark that Catherine was ungrateful for the charity the family showed towards her, being abandoned by a mother who had been so irresponsible. But the next day, when Auntie Joyce found Catherine alone, she retaliated by giving her a beating to restore the equilibrium her protests had imbalanced.

And so Catherine had become quite adept at stealing food from her own family on behalf of herself, and Fin and Beni. She would never take freshly steamed rice, because the surface in the cauldron would be flat and unbroken. She would wait until either Joyce or Kamille would stir it in the pot, and then she would spoon out a small portion onto a banana leaf, careful to mix the rice again, covering in any depression left by the ladle.

She would never take a leg or a wing from chicken in the pot. The wings were her grandmother's favorite piece, and its disappearance would be noticed. But chicken that was cubed and left the day in the wok with other vegetables could be pilfered along with a few beans and spinach, and no one would notice.

It also made her aware that Joyce had certain days when she would routinely be absent for a full hour, bringing food to the men in the field a bit earlier than usual, while Sarafina took her morning nap.

Catherine was never caught. Neither was Joyce.

Children and nuns flowed one by one through the cafeteria doors to the outside courtyards. One table, now vacant, had been occupied exclusively by girls who came each morning for schooling, and were picked up at the gate late each afternoon.

The outsiders.

Their families had money and could afford to support the convent through donations. They were compensated by having their daughters learn English and western ways. It was rumored that some were even royalty, wanting their children westernized in preparation for the new world order that seemed inevitable since the end of the war and the consolidation of the Malay people into one nation. The

Sisters made no attempt to convert the children of the devoutly Islamic families. The patronage of their parents was their most essential subsidy.

Their children always brought more food in their sanitary little lunch kits than they could eat, and their half-eaten sandwiches prepared by their servants each day were unceremoniously scraped into the waste bins at the end of the lunch hour. But this was not fair game. This, too, was under the jurisdiction of Antoinette's gang. This, Catherine could not have known, but was soon to find out.

She waited patiently for the last of the Sisters to finish their tea, or at least put down a half empty cup. Even the tea was a spoil to the marauders, for every last one of the Sisters had a sweet tooth, and the tea was heavily sugared. Some even with milk and honey. The orphans, prudently, were never given sugar. Bad for their teeth. Milk might give them diarrhea.

Sister St. John was the last to leave. A slight breeze or disturbance had made the door to the cellar come ajar. It caught her attention as she stood up from the table, and she strutted over and shouldered the heavy wooden door into place, this time dropping the hinged latch to secure it. She made a quick survey of the room, and when she saw Catherine sitting plaintively alone, she made a note to herself. Catherine was supposed to be outside, with the other children, but since she was still adjusting to her new life, Sister St. John granted a rare concession and decided not to reprimand the girl.

She strutted down the hallway, very hard shoes making a very hard sound on a very hard floor. A march.

When Antoinette appeared in the doorway, summoned by the one to whom she had given the special privilege of being look-out, she was stunned to see sitting at the head of the nun's table, in a spot vacated by Mother Superior herself, Catherine Madrigal D'Cruz, the newcomer, sipping tea still warm and cleaning the sweet meat of chicken from a bone. And looking like she belonged there.

Clearly, a lesson was in order.

"Who told you to take our food? ..." Catherine was unimpressed. " ... Your mother?" Luka stood in the doorway behind Antoinette, and Catherine could see her flinch and recover, her mission exposed. Luka had told her everything ... but why?

"It's none of your business," said Catherine.

The talent that had helped Antoinette rise to her position through the ranks of the disenfranchised was her innate tendency to put everyone on the defensive as her first tactic of domination, but Catherine was impervious to this kind of assault.

She had learned to deflect the meanness of her Auntie Joyce and tolerate the cruelty of her grandmother. But here was someone about her own size, who did not have the advantage of brute force, like an adult.

Antoinette entered the room, and a half a dozen of her gang spilled in from behind her, anxious for food, and eager to get a closer look at the newcomer that was so foolishly defying their leader.

"Your mother's a whore." said Antoinette, coldly. Clearly an invitation to fight.

"No, she's Iban." Catherine had no more idea of what a whore was than Fin knew what a statue was, but she remembered her grandmother call Che' Wan the same thing. Her pretended indifference to the remark inflamed Antoinette even further. Her schoolmates were dumbfounded.

Catherine sipped tea from Mother Superior's abandoned cup, and licked chicken from her fingers. *My mother is Iban*, she thought to herself. *Warriors.* Her recollections of her mother were vague, it having been so long ago. But she remembered her mother telling her the legends of her people, and Catherine herself was the granddaughter of Jon the Poet, a very brave man and a very fierce warrior. "His blood is your blood, Catherine, and you are invincible," she heard her mother's voice.

Antoinette knew what an Iban was but refused to let herself be distracted or her intent diffused. Words of intimidation seemed to be without impact on the newcomer, an outsider at that. Someone guilty of the inexcusable offense of having living relatives, and yet quarantined among those who had no one.

All of them knew what was to follow, what Catherine's defiance had brought upon herself. One of the girls went to guard the door, looking for the approach of either a nun or the kitchen help.

Catherine continued to pick through the leftovers from Mother Superior's plate. But she herself recognized that a fight was now inevitable. A fight usually meant a slap or two, like Beni and Nestor, striking impulsively to assert themselves, but never with any thought out malice or willful attempt to do harm.

This was going to be different. This, too, Catherine could sense.

A fight differed from a beating. It was obligatory to tolerate the beating from an elder. After all, what could she do? They were so much more powerful. But she remembered the one, late afternoon, when Sarafina decided that what Catherine's own mother needed was a sound beating, and she sent Eric to the fields. Catherine had hidden herself under her grandfather's bed with her brother and sister, and they were all absolutely terrified. Sarafina cornered Miri in the bedroom where the children hid stiffly beneath them.

"You think you can get away with that in *my* house." That was all the explanation that Catherine could hear or understand. Their grandmother had expected no resistance. After all, it was her own daughter-in-law. And Sarafina was her elder. Was she not obligated to submit? Then the terrible bamboo cane came down upon her mother.

But it came down only once.

Miri seized the cane from the matron of the family, and slashed her vengefully across the shoulder with it, and then tossed the stick angrily behind her, first breaking it upon her knee.

Sarafina was both shocked and outraged and came at Miri with her powerful hands to choke the life out of her. The two of them fell upon the bed that almost broke with their brutality, and Catherine and her siblings could hear but could not see and trembled but kept their silence.

They could hear their mother scream, but it was not a scream of pain. It was the empowered, defiant scream of a warrior.

In a moment, falling to the floor beside them, the interlocking bodies of their mother and grandmother, gouging and punching and crippling, wrestling, oblivious to the children beneath the bed.

Miri prevailed and sat upon Sarafina's chest and gave her the beating of her life, a fistful at a time, upon a face that had never shown her anything but contempt and anger. And when Sarafina was no longer conscious, Miri stood and kicked her once in the ribs before running out of the house in which she had never really been welcome, over the trimmed grass and through the orchard, and then vaulted the stone wall, effortlessly, like a magnificent tiger of the jungle, never to return.

It was several hours before at last Sarafina opened the eyes of her pained face. As she lay upon her side, her first vision was of the offspring of the heathen who had done this to her, quivering in their own urine beneath the bed, pinioned in place by fear. It was a vision that neither Sarafina nor Catherine would ever forget, the kind that invades the realm of sleep at will, and becomes more hideous with time, like the face of Sarafina Madrigal D'Cruz.

Catherine's secret, the one that made her fear her grandmother more than anything else, should she find out, was how proud she was of her mother for defending herself so bravely against her grandmother's injustices, how she could feel herself in her mother's body as she watched each fist-fall upon the corrupt face of that foaming woman. And how good it felt. Especially, how good it felt ...

And so, Antoinette naively thought that the arrogant little urchin was about to be her next victim, as all who circled the table had been before her. She had never had a serious challenge to her authority.

Until now.

And Catherine had never had the absolute luxury, the privilege, of being provoked or attacked by anyone where it wasn't mandatory for her to just simply grit her teeth and take it.

Until now.

Catherine kept on eating, very much aware that each bite further antagonized the ugly little waif who stood at the opposite end of the table grunting orders while her disciples surrounded Catherine's chair and blocked any avenue of escape.

"You. Outsider."

Catherine did not even stop eating.

"Care for some chicken?" said Catherine, discovering sarcasm for the first time in her life. She held the bone, stripped clean, to the girl at the far end of the table, who was taken off-guard by such self-assured defiance.

"That food is for us ... you never get food from this table without first getting permission from me."

"Pass the salt, please."

And at this, the short-fused Antoinette, who had been leaning forward on the table, shoved it hard against the girl in the chair, and came straight over the table for her. A burst of anger in the form of a scream intended to paralyze Catherine was anticipated and therefore ineffectual. She was met with a hard wooden bowl of rice to the face, giving Catherine a moment to push herself back in her chair, which fell over as she stood to greet her attacker.

She took advantage of Antoinette's momentum and grabbed a handful of hair and pulled her to the bruising tile floor. Catherine had recovered quickly from the jolt to the ribs by the force of the table, and she simply held the girl's hair low to the ground and dragged her backwards to keep her from getting a footing. Stunned orphans backed out of their way, too amazed to say a word.

The lookout by the door was drawn to the spectacle but fearfully held her post to watch for the inevitable arrival of a nun or other adult. The excitement proved to be too much, irresistible. She was ultimately consumed by the unexpected sight of her leader being humiliated and abandoned the door for a better look.

Antoinette reached up, clawing blindly, digging her nails into Catherine's wrists and forearms, drawing the first blood. Catherine let go, but before Antoinette could stand, Catherine sat on her chest and beat Antoinette's face, her energies not yet peaking.

No one had noticed the approach of Sister St. John.

The back of her hand caught Catherine on the side of the head, knocking her off her perch and started her wailing. She rolled on the floor, like Antoinette, holding her ear as if it would make the pain go away.

The other girls gave what comfort they could to their fallen Antoinette, and Sister St. John loomed over Catherine, the obvious troublemaker, and clenched her fist before declaring, "In this place of God there will be *no* violence!"

An elder. How unfair. She curled up on the floor to prepare for the inevitable. She had no reason to believe that this adult, costumed though she was in the uniform issued by God himself would be any different than any other enraged adult. As hands and fists came raining down upon her, she could see Antoinette sitting on the floor smiling cruelly to amplify the pain of each strike.

Catherine began to cry. Of course, everyone thought it was pain and fear, and even Sister St, John was quickly satisfied that Catherine had had enough, and stalked out of the room after chasing the other girls outside and ordering Antoinette to the infirmary. But Catherine was not in that kind of pain. Catherine was in mourning. What had died was any hope, faint though it might have been, that the fires of Hell would be any less incinerating here, on the grounds of God's palace, than they had been at the plantation where Auntie Joyce gathered kindling, her Uncle Joe chopped firewood, and where her grandmother stoked the fires herself.

And what had died was any hope that she might be accepted by the other children, be liked by them. Be less lonely ...

It was a miserable place. Catherine was much in need of her best friend, but Tippy had wisely stayed in Sentul.

Until now.

Chapter Fourteen

It had taken two days for the rumors of the legendary fight with Antoinette to distort the truth beyond Catherine's recognition. Catherine was the aggressor. Catherine threw steaming rice in Antoinette's face. Antoinette was just recovering from the foul way Catherine got the advantage and was about to thrash Catherine soundly, but Sister St. John broke it up. The black and blue mark beneath Catherine's ear was the one punch Antoinette was able to land before the Sister intervened. Even the witnesses began to believe the amended version of the story they invented and circulated.

There was no one to take her side, or even willing to listen to her side of what happened. Certainly no one to give her any comfort. She could overhear small clusters of girls talking about her between classes, and they disbanded as Catherine approached, or spoke defensively of their beloved Antoinette, or scolded Catherine disdainfully as the outsider whose parents lived yet did not want her.

It was unfair, and beyond a young girl's comprehension, that Antoinette, who started the whole thing, should get all the sympathies of the victim.

Never mind. I'll show her. I'll show them all. With no one to avenge her, she would avenge herself.

She sat up in her bed, a lower bunk in a dormitory. So many children, and yet, so separate. It began with the sleeping arrangements. Alienation from one another in a subtle, less than remarkable way. Beds evenly spaced, all in a row. *This must be how westerners sleep,* she thought, the nuns who were not British doing their best to be British, deferring to a superior culture and a superior God. How she missed sleeping with her brother and sister, and even Nestor and Marta. Interlocking limbs on a cool floor on a soft mat. Sleep always held the possibility for enchantment, for dreams that had no structure.

How strange all of this was. Sleep here was a ritual of devotion. Kneeling beside the bed, forty or fifty girls communicating simultaneously with God, pulling down the light blanket, removing their bed slippers, and, on the command of a Sister, sliding into the envelope of a bed. All of them encouraged to sleep upon their backs, in the center of the bed, the blanket tucked under their armpits, and their hands folded on *top* of the blankets. The nuns would see to that, for baffling reasons known only to themselves.

It was Sister St. John who had the duty this evening, to instruct the girls to pray for God's forgiveness and protection. God's son looked down upon them from a wall with half-dead eyes as they prayed, and agonized as they slept. *How much protection could God give her,* she thought, *if he let that happen to his son? My grandpa wouldn't let that happen.*

She prayed to him anyway. Tonight, especially, she wanted his protection, as unreliable as it might be. Tonight, she would give it a test.

She let an hour pass, in mock sleep, before opening her eyes in the dimly lit dormitory. She sat up upon her little steel bed and inched her feet into bed slippers. But then, she thought, perhaps I can be more silent without them.

The monsoons were upon them, testing the sanctity of the terracotta tiles overhead, finding them without fault. Catherine went to one of the several windows that lined two opposing walls, a very tall affair with arched shutters, typical of the bungalow houses of which the British were so fond. Sister St. John had seen no harm, apparently, in leaving the windows open to let the breeze refresh the air in the room.

But the breeze had become wind, and it carried with it the salt-less tears of heaven and spilled them on the cold tile floor around the three windows to windward. Across the courtyard Catherine could see that the nuns had also retired for the evening, no lights from the row of small windows in their private quarters. Sister St. John would not be returning, and Catherine took it upon herself to close the shutters against the rain and the wind whose slight chill might shiver her sleeping schoolmates. Her instinct was to spare them from the cold, but in closing the shutters against the rain and the wind she realized their unbroken sleep was important to her plan, and she wanted no one shivering themselves awake.

She was dressed in bedtime clothes, the uniform of sleep also issued to her upon her arrival. Even in sleep, in neat rows of beds, conformity was valued above all else. Her pale-yellow gown was like everyone else's. *But this is a good thing,* she thought. *If I'm seen, I'll look like anyone else.*

She glanced about the room of children upon their beds absorbed in sleep, and Christ upon his cross absorbed in his suffering, and, certain that she would not be missed by either Jesus or his flock, made her way down the first of many hallways. Some were dimly lit, others in complete shadow and darkness.

She was not yet comfortably familiar with the labyrinth of hallways and doors and stairwells. She knew not what was contained or concealed behind many of the doors. Some were expressly forbidden, some seemed less significant, never opened though they fronted the more commonly used hallways of the second floor.

She needed to loop over the passageway that linked the dormitories to the offices and private chambers of the Sisters, find the hallway that led to the stairwell, creep downstairs and follow the colonnade to yet another cluster of buildings on the far side of the courtyard. There she would find her ultimate destination, the kitchen. Food.

The plan was brilliant. She would find her way undetected to the kitchen, and once there, eat a very full, indulgent meal. And then, when she was quite full, leaving subtle evidence that someone had been there, she would creep back to the dormitory and her bed, but not before first sprinkling a few grains of rice on the pillow where Antoinette laid her head, and scattering half a handful by the side of the bed where she slept.

It was an elaborate trail. The straightforward alternative would have required her to exit the building where the doors opened almost directly to the small cottage shared by the two old gardeners. They would be asleep, undoubtedly, but they had a German Shepherd who curled judiciously upon their porch every evening. It had both bark and bite, having been poisoned over time with the meanness of the place, perceiving everyone as a potential intruder. In her first few days there, Catherine had made unsuccessful attempts to befriend it, innocently thinking that it might offer and accept affection.

She hesitated before attempting the long corridor that both joined and separated the two buildings. It was narrow, with a row of full length, shutterless windows on either side. A bridge, really. The overhang of the roof was sufficient enough that even with a monsoon-powered wind the rain would never quite have the velocity to break upon the sills, and spatter upon the floor. But if those for whom sleep was a prison of nightmares should escape into wakefulness, they could see anyone crossing the long corridor.

When she made up her mind that no one was watching, she quickly crossed the vulnerable span, and then became obfuscated in shadow on the other side, flattening herself against the wall as she waited to see if she had been discovered.

There was a quick blur of movement in front of her, and she caught her breath. *I miss Fin.* A quick alibi she spontaneously formulated to explain herself if she were caught. *I got lost trying to find where she sleeps.*

But she had only startled the cat, *Sa'ang Hitam*, Sir Black. Except for a tuft of white on its breast, it was as black as the habit of a nun. It was Sister Masselin's pet. Its reflexes had been dulled by the good life, and Catherine was almost upon him before he detected her. It caught mice only for sport and was made plump by scraps from the kitchen.

The cat rounded a corner, and Catherine decided to follow. Taking the correct turn was strictly a matter of speculation, or of chance, and perhaps the animal's instinct was escape, having been startled, and it could lead Catherine through the complex maze of doors and hallways.

Furthermore, the heavy sound of the rain diluted her concentration. This was harder than she had thought.

The cat led her deeper into the sanctum of the nuns before she lost sight of it all together. But in the minimal light of a candle burning on a small altar honoring their savior, Catherine could make out a stairwell at the end of a long corridor, ending the most treacherous part of her mission.

She tiptoed down the wooden stairs, the obligatory creaking made indistinct by the complicity of the drumming rain, and she found herself in the cafeteria. From here she knew the way, and not even the heavy sound of rain on the terracotta could distract her.

She followed a long hallway branching off from the cafeteria and opened to a covered walkway that crossed and divided another courtyard and led to the kitchen. A single light bulb dangled and swayed under the eaves, the only light for the entire courtyard, distinguishing the kitchen door from others. To the left, to the right, no one. She scampered across the walkway and slipped inside the door, and at once glanced through the open window to see if on the final leg of her endeavor she had been discovered.

"*Oi*," she gasped out loud and quickly covered her mouth with both hands as if the sound had not yet escaped and she could hold it in. Sa'ang Hitam had preceded her, coming in through the open window and rubbed himself against her calf as Catherine spied past the window and through the curtain of rain that rippled from the edge of the low roofline just outside the kitchen.

She was not overly surprised to find Sa'ng Hitam had preceded her. He had twice succeeded, now, in startling her. Catherine shrugged his attention away.

She turned to survey the room for which she had exposed herself to so much risk. Filtering in through the windows from outside was the light left burning to discourage the pilfering that Catherine was now intent on accomplishing. She could see it was exactly as she imagined. There was a cauldron of rice on the stovetop, several large preparation tables, a deep sink for washing food. Glowing dimly before her was the polished door, one of so many forbidden doors in this place, the polished door that sealed a walk-in cold-box.

It must be where the food is kept, she thought, though she had never seen a room within a room, like this. She pulled the latch and opened the door towards her and relied upon the existing light to survey the interior.

She was not disappointed. Here was a baffling abundance of food. Liars. They said it was so scarce. They said there was very little. They said be grateful. Without pausing to really take inventory, Catherine discovered on a table a tray with at least half a dozen cooked chickens basted with the sweet scent of ginger and browned in soy sauce that had never made it to the dining hall.

All for the nuns. And for the children whose parents paid to have them come daily to learn to be proper Europeans. And for the cat.

Catherine could understand the nun's greed, hoarding the best food for themselves. But she was angered and disgusted to see the way they indulged the cat, even feeding it from the table at supper time, completely oblivious, or maybe indifferent, to the fact that every orphan saw every scrap so casually tossed to their mascot. She'd never seen an animal as bloated as the cat. Fin could probably survive on what they fed that animal for their own amusement. The cat now shamelessly expected something from Catherine, having shown her the way to the kitchen.

Catherine sat on the floor with a pot of chicken in her lap, and hissed as Sa'ang Hitam made his first, and last attempt to intimidate her into feeding him. He backed himself into the shadows, where he himself hissed at the child for not recognizing his importance, his status as the pet of Sister Masselin. Catherine spat a feline growl under the table where he thought himself hidden, and at this he turned and ran, abdicating his throne on the kitchen floor without a fight.

By the dim light of the single bulb, Catherine devoured almost an entire chicken. She startled herself as she realized how much food she could hold. A thief should be more subtle. Would Antoinette not know this? It was too late to refine her plan, and she was secretly grateful that she hadn't thought about it until after she had indulged herself as she did. It was the first time she had been full since entering the convent almost a week ago.

She walked the pot back into the cold-box, the denuded carcass that would scream attention to itself in the morning when the cook arrived. There was so much food, hoarded on the shelves and even stacked on the floor. Potatoes and yams, crates of fruit and vegetables, and that icon of Asian well-being, rice, in bulging burlap sacks stacked like sandbags holding back a monsoon flood of starvation. Did anyone else know? Did these orphans, so thin and so gaunt, have any idea how much food atrophied here? This was not a cold-box. This was a vault.

It was dangerous to know about this. She could tell no one, not even Fin. Seeing such opulence, which she had ignored when she first entered to take the chicken, made her regret the careless way in which she had consumed so much. It would have been better, she thought, to have stolen in the more inconspicuous manner that had served her so well in the kitchen of her grandmother. She wished that she had thought of some other way to strike revenge upon Antoinette, for now, too late, she realized that she had spoiled her chances of returning to steal successfully anytime soon.

The hypnotic rain, which possibly was all that held everyone now in the trance of sleep, had suddenly stopped, as is the way of monsoons. Catherine was focused, once again, upon her true intent and her plan. She closed the cold-box door behind her, having fought the temptation to smuggle something for her sister.

From the cauldron on the dormant stove, she helped herself to a handful of white rice, fed upon it, and dusted her hands to leave a conspicuous trace of thievery on the floor, hoping that mice would not consume the evidence by morning. She doubted that Sa'ang Hitam, dulled by the good life, would take interest in anything but napping, and the mice could scamper in the kitchen unchallenged. She put the lid back on the cauldron, leaving it just slightly off center, and as she left the kitchen, clutching a kerchief in which she had wrapped no more than a spoonful of rice, she left the door slightly ajar, speculating that it would immediately arouse the suspicion of the cook and lead to further investigations.

Her mission was nearly completed. She had now only to return undetected to the dormitory and sprinkle the rice, as planned, at the side of Antoinette's bed before crawling back into her bunk. No new lights were visible as she began to make her way back, and she complimented herself on a job well done, and for having been clever enough to leave her slippers. She was soundless as she moved, and there was no longer the drum roll of rain to disguise her step. The rain that lost its grip upon the slick terracotta tiles plummeted to a soft death upon luxurious grass adjacent to the walkway shielded from assault by the huge eaves.

Catherine hurried herself away from the single light that strangled on its cord that hung like a noose from the ulin truss just outside the kitchen door. Swift enough to have been an apparition had she been seen by half-awake eyes, she was now in the sanctuary of benevolent shadows, hidden once again, and making her way back to her point of origin at the dormitory where she could only hope her absence had remained undetected.

She found herself in one of the many hallways that starved for light. It sucked what it could from the dim glow in the cafeteria ahead, where, upon a table against a wall next to a colorless color picture of Jesus in prayer, a lamp with a single bulb that cleverly simulated the shape of a candle, was left lit by a nun who cleverly simulated the shape of humility. A night-light, leaving the features and color of the room indistinct, but leaving the room dim rather than dark, outlining the features of tables and chairs and making passage by night a possibility.

Catherine entered the room that had been the scene of the victory so unfairly twisted into a defeat. She calculated that she had been less than half an hour on her enterprise. There was still much night ahead of her.

The sealed, forbidden door through which she had seen Sister St. John make her entrance routinely at lunch times begged plaintively as Catherine passed. A halo of light from the other side escaped through its imperfect fit in the jamb, an irresistible beacon for an irrepressible young girl. How could she refuse?

She looked gratuitously around her, confirming that she was alone. *Why not*, she thought. There was something about the white light that condoned the violation of one more commandment, for while Luka had only warned her not to go down there, Sister St. John had expressly forbidden her to do so when she had noticed Catherine's curiosity.

But the light.

It occurred to Catherine that it was the first authentic light she had seen since being in the convent. It was soft and inviting. Not harsh, not false. Not an appliance intended to assist the nuns keeping inventory of meandering children or wandering souls. Not intended to discourage thievery or deprive the girls of private thoughts that permissive darkness encouraged. Not an offering to Jesus in an alcove, or the currency of prayer like so many candles abandoned together at an altar in the chapel. Although Catherine did not think these things in words, she felt them in spirit just as knowingly.

She had to see for herself. If this were the palace of God, and God watched over them as they slept, could it be that the light burned from his private chambers? All the pictures she had seen in her short stay there showed God and his son with light all around them.

She had seen only the Sisters go through that door, especially Sister St. John. Since she always seemed to have instructions for them—God wants you to be good. God wants you to study. God wants you to obey—could it be that beyond the door was where he held audience with her? It made sense. Besides, every time Sister St. John came through the door, she had a tray with many empty bowls. God would have a huge appetite and would be allowed to eat all he wanted.

With burgeoning expectations that displaced all fear, she opened the door. Indeed, there was a stairway, but it led neither to heaven nor to God. Yet its discovery was no less impressive. The convent had a cellar.

Catherine closed the door behind her as best she could and stood upon the landing at the peak of a long row of stone steps eaten by darkness on the other side of a single bulb that hung unceremoniously above her. Apparently, it was left burning because each time that Sister St. John passed beneath it her hands were holding a tray and she never bothered to come back to pull the cord.

If this was not where God slept, then who ate the food? Being silent, being unseen, were two of Catherine's best skills. She could be these things until an adult's wrath or lust had subsided and been forgotten, or when compelled to steal food either from the pantry or occasionally from the Chinese store in Sentul. Her skill gave her confidence to proceed, though she was fearful once again upon discovering that God was not the source of the light that had enticed her to open the forbidden door. She was determined to find out who was so important that they had food brought to them and did not have to eat in the cafeteria with the rest of the children and the Sisters.

She made her descent, having no idea that the cool steps were the petrified cinders of Hell and the increasingly damp walls were its disguised flames, and its blackness a blinding fire.

She stood a long time at the bottom of the steps, the belly of the convent, until her eyes had adjusted to the absence of light, which seeped through the floor having spilled from the stairwell. It was cavernous. It was huge. She could see no limits, which was as much a function of its vastness as it was the darkness. Stone and mortar pillars began to appear in orderly rows in all directions. The floor was cement, but she could detect a channel, covered with heavy ulin planks, that gurgled with the run-off from the heavy rain that had so recently subsided.

Instinct guided her to stand by a column, merging her silhouette to the stone. Gradually she could make out, faintly, the outline of several windows against a far wall. The darkness outside somehow held more residual light making it distinguishable from the different darkness in the cellar. The windows were small, and high above the floor, just beneath the ceiling.

She proceeded, pillar by pillar, in the direction of the tiny windows, and could make out a corridor parallel to what had to be the outside wall. She could see the outline of several doors to the hallway, but no doors against the outside wall, which she concluded must be buried up to the windows.

But this was not the revelation that riveted her to the pillar. There was movement from an obscure pillar. She was not alone.

After a moment that could not be measured by time, or by depth, Catherine spoke in her most anonymous voice, obscuring her location as best she could with a whisper, a question. "Tippy? Is that you?"

Her voice fell, like a cloud falling from the sky, soft, even upon the hard floor that she was certain that she now shared with someone else. But there was no reply. "Tippy? It's all right. It's just me."

Still there was no response, and no movement from behind the pillar. This was unlike Tippy. This could not be Tippy. And if this was not her best friend from Sentul, then who could it be?

Catherine regretted having given away her position. But it became obvious to her that she had been watched for some time before she had noticed someone else in the catacombs. She stepped from behind the pillar, moving cautiously to the center of the space, and closer still to the pillar that she was certain concealed whomever it was who had been watching her. Her eyes dilated further in the darkness, and she took a step closer towards the pillar. "Who's there?" she braved, leaving herself completely vulnerable, but trusting in her own speed and agility to outrun whomever it might be back up the stairway which had the latch that was always secured from the other side.

There was no answer, and she inched forward, placing her hand before her, unable to guage the true distance to the pillar in the frustrating darkness. "Who is there?" she voiced with some insistence, now.

But no one was there, at least, no longer there, behind the pillar.

"Maggie," a docile voice imploded behind her, but it might as well have been a Chinese firecracker. Catherine spun around, completely taken by surprise and backed herself to the pillar, and saw a faceless silhouette limping softly towards her, a darkness against a greater darkness.

Catherine pressed herself into the coarse stones of the pillar, and the apparition approached almost within arm's length, features no more distinguishable than they had been from three times that distance, the form further obscured by an apparent blanket or cloak, that swayed with each step, accentuating the limp.

"Maggie," mumbled the voice, once again, a feminine voice, a child's voice. The apparition turned and shuffled away, further into the catacombs, until she disappeared altogether, only to reappear in the explosion of light from a bulb, her hand having invisibly found a cord that illuminated part of the cellar, condemning the other parts to harsh shadows, innumerable pillars standing like mummified sentries. The girl standing beneath the light turned slowly towards Catherine. From a face that was not formed the way other faces are formed came sound that was not formed the way others form sound. The words were rounded at the edges, indistinct, almost muffled, as if robbed of their clarity somewhere along the passageway from her chest and through her throat and into the open air. Crippled words, limping together and holding forward a beggar's bowl.

"Maggie," she gurgled once more.

Catherine did not know how to respond, certainly did not know what to say. As her fears receded, she took a small step forward, feeling a small pain between her shoulder blades where she had thrust herself blindly against the jagged stones of the pillar behind her. She had never seen anyone quite like the girl, if indeed it was a girl, standing passively before her. More sounds, spoken slowly and deliberately, were offered up to Catherine, but she could not make them out. A few of the syllables sounded like English, but the only word that was audible was the repetition of the girl's name, as if it were the most rehearsed word in her repertoire. Maggie's speech, Maggie's words, were the shadows of real words, and perhaps comprehensible only to herself. Yet she spoke as if she assumed Catherine understood, and smiled when she had apparently finished what she had intended to say.

Maggie reached with her free hand slowly from under the bed sheet that she clutched towards Catherine, who instinctively cornered herself into the pillar once again. In spite of the soft nature of the words and the unobtrusive limp, Catherine was afraid, and the fear expanded like breath within her breast as the girl got closer.

"Maggie?" The voice of an invisible adult from somewhere behind Catherine down the long corridor brought the girl to a halt. Catherine once again stiffened, trusting that she was concealed by the pillar and had not yet been detected. "Maggie? Is that you? Come back to bed, child."

A light from behind now locked Catherine to the pillar, and she could hear the slap of slippers between heel and floor as the adult came closer. "That's it, Maggie. Turn out the light," encouraged the adult. "Come back to bed."

"Maggie," said the girl, as she passed Catherine, smiling still, and obeying the voice of her night guardian. Catherine could hear the nun, surely a nun, patiently scolding Maggie for having strayed again, but certainly not angry or meaning her any harm. The light behind her suddenly was extinguished, and Catherine heard the firm closing of a door at the end of a hallway that had, apparently, several if not many doors. One of them must certainly be another passage out of here, she thought, the latch on the door from the cafeteria not accessible from the inside at the top of the landing.

Ten minutes, at least, had passed. Catherine had slowly let herself down to the floor, where she sat against the pillar and waited for her eyes to adjust to the darkness again after the invasion of light had left her blinded. She made her way back to the bottom of the angular stairwell, which now offered light from the top of the landing. Wasting no more time, and recalling her original mission, she hurried up the steps and into the cafeteria, closing and bolting the door behind her, certain she had been seen only by Maggie.

Why so many bowls, she thought. Sister St. John always had a tray full of bowls when she came up from the cellar. Making her way back to the dormitory, she astutely concluded that Maggie must not be the only one down there. There must be others, like her.

Catherine entered the dormitory, and, peeking through the shuttered windows that she herself had closed an hour, or almost two hours earlier, could see no new lights across the courtyard in the nun's wing. Everything was as she had left it. Jesus was still on the wall; children were still in their beds. Catherine padded over to the final row of beds in the far corner of the room where Antoinette slept, and without the slightest remorse unrolled the kerchief from the pocket in her night gown, and exactly as she had visualized, sprinkled rice in a halo around her sleeping head, on her blanket, and on the floor. She even pressed Antoinette's slippers into the rice on the floor, for the sake of being thorough, before arranging them neatly at the side of her bed.

Feeling quite content, quite accomplished, Catherine returned to her own bed, a lower bunk, and, certain there was no evidence to implicate herself, climbed smugly under the blanket for a very restful sleep. She had stolen food, disobeyed half a dozen directives from adults, and carried out a very intricate plot of revenge. Rarely again would she feel so proud of herself. The nuns would see to that.

Chapter Fifteen

There was no bell, muffled by the distance to a bell tower, to gently or lyrically announce morning and coax the children from sleep into wakefulness, nor were there subtle sounds of the wilderness, the monkeys, the birds, or the rustling of trees, nor lightening of color of the night sky, to usher the children from the private sanctuary of their sleep into the public, stark world of the convent. Morning was not determined by dawn, but by the more reliable clock in the quarters of the nuns. Morning was then forced upon them by the invasive ritual that began with a peaking crescendo of footfalls upon the hard tiles of a distant hallway.

Wakefulness was something commanded, an elder's first opportunity to demonstrate authority. A nun's first opportunity to inflict a little power, the ability to create suffering without personal consequence. A duty to perform. Usually this was accomplished by Sister St. John, who would slap her hands together, making the air sound out in pain, so harshly and so abrupt, snapping the gamelan tranquility for those girls fortunate enough to be sleeping without nightmares. Hard light would then fall upon them from above, pulled from a cliff by a nun tugging firmly on the leash of an electric lamp. Sleep, that had gathered like untamed animals to drink harmoniously from the same pool after building up confidence in the darkness, would scatter as light shot at their flesh, and the young girls winced, closing their eyes more tightly. And then the voice of the nun would trespass into the fragile tranquility that surrounded each private bed, and each word would fall and shatter like a porcelain teacup upon the tile floors.

The children never really got used to this. This was the way adults were supposed to rise each day, with the striking of flesh to flesh, with sleep something broken, and made useless and forgotten. A new day. Sleep and wakefulness were not a continuum, but two very distinct experiences, and each had its time, and time was something to be managed, something that could be controlled by slicing it into pieces, with each piece assigned to some activity. Time to eat, time to study. Time for class. Time to brush your teeth. Time for bed. Time to sleep. Time to wake. And for those who were English or pretended to be, even teatime. And as they matured, the children would see the sense in all of this. Some of them already had made the discovery.

Childhood was nothing more than a strained apprenticeship to adulthood, and the nuns considered themselves the reluctant but best qualified tutors.

On this particular morning, Sister St. John had not come alone. God and the cook had come with her, and Sisters Elsa and Cirese. The soundless air was not broken with the conventional crush of her slapping palms, for her right hand was bleeding sweat around a choking bamboo cane, and was thus preoccupied. The air erupted instead with that horrible word that she vomited upon them: "GIRLS!"

They were, without exception, instantly awake. Some of them sprang up in their bunks, some of them audibly gasping instinctively in panic at this brutal attempt to commandeer their final remnants of sleep. Then the light went on, and nighttime and all its possibilities simply were no more. The cook stood rather sheepishly behind the Sister. He had at first been indignant when he rushed to find her, telling her what someone had done that previous night in the kitchen. But even he was a little frightened by the tone in Sister St. John's voice, though the fury he had unwittingly released was not blowing in his direction.

"Girls." Most of them were sitting up now and looking in the awful direction of the voice. "One of you is a thief." Upon hearing this, almost every girl trembled in fear and in guilt, for few among them had not stolen something recently or one time at least, and most of them stole habitually. A pencil here, a spool of thread from the sewing room. Something to bargain with for more food from the other orphans. And now one of them was caught. It must be something big.

"Who did it?" No one knew yet precisely which thievery she was talking about, except of course for Catherine. They looked at each other for a clue. Something so important to bring Sister St. John like this could not have happened without everyone knowing. It would have been something to secretly boast about. Stealing not only served the purpose of providing a little currency in their black market, it gave them a sense that they were not completely consumed by the nuns. A way to defy them and assert themselves without consequence if they could avoid getting caught. But no one knew. No one had heard anything about it.

Luka got up from her bed and started to trot to the door, which Sister Cirese theatrically closed to her. "I have to go pee-pee."

"You will wait," said the Sister. She needed no coaching from Sister St. John, who was clearly in command.

"But ..."

"You *will* wait. Now, get back to your bunk."

Luka went back to her bunk and sat down, squeezing her palms together, prayer-like, inside her legs holding herself back. She looked plaintively towards Antoinette, who was rubbing sleep from her eyes, and paid no attention to Luka, not wanting to do anything to draw the attention of the nuns, who had begun a predatorial stalking between the aisles to ferret their prey from the bush. Who would tremble, and bolt?

Sister St. John then announced the specific nature of the crime, and in so doing narrowed her list of suspects. It would require a particular boldness to do something like this. "Someone in the night trespassed into the kitchen and stole food. Do you know how precious little food there is in the world?" She did not really expect to find evidence, or to provoke a confession. Upon hearing the audacity of the crime, the girls themselves began eliminating suspects. They did not know Catherine very well—some barely knew her name. But she had shown cowardice in her fight with Antoinette and cried when Sister St. John barely hit her. It was doubtful she had that kind of courage. All of them by instinct knew that it could only be Antoinette. They glanced, as discreetly as they could, to find a sign from her. It had to be her.

Sister St. John walked down the aisle where the new girl had been given a bunk and looked suspiciously at her. She looked suspiciously at everyone, regardless of the occasion or circumstance. It was both a strategy of intimidation and an endemic part of her character to do so, but as she looked upon Catherine, her suspicion was genuine. She, too, could hardly remember the girl's name, but she remembered giving her a brief thrashing, of course, and that the girl had not yet learned to sustain punishment without crying. She stared upon Catherine's face, *a handsome face,* she thought. Catherine radiated just the right amount of fear to be innocent. The guilty one would be stone-faced. Like Antoinette. She passed by Catherine, but not without making a note to be wary of this one in the future.

Sister St. John knew that Antoinette was not so easily intimidated. Certainly not by this. Nor did she expect a spontaneous confession. But the more she thought about it ... yes, she must be the one. She slapped the cane upon the steel bunk of an unsuspecting, unsuspected orphan, to regain any attention that might have drifted away while she had been distracted in thought. "Girls... that food was intended for you." Of course, no one believed her for a moment, although she was prepared to believe herself. "Until the thief is caught, you will not eat. There will be *no* food for you."

This, they believed. She resumed her slow and deliberate march between the rows of beds, staring at each girl only long enough to feel their fear, or invoke it. She came to the row in which Antoinette was sitting up, Antoinette who was very, very still. Motionless the way one is motionless when it is whispered, *a snake is coiled upon your blanket.*

Antoinette had discovered but without reacting, the telltale spattering of rice on the floor beneath her bunk. She did not, at first, know what to make of it. Analisa, the girl who slept in the bunk overhead, was far too timid to make such a raid, and yet, if she did, she would also be careless enough to trail in some evidence. Antoinette was accustomed to girls performing some act of bravery to impress her, to win her approval, which they certainly valued above the approval of the nuns.

Luka, in the bunk across from her, was straining and rocking, and her eyes opened wide as by accident she saw the rice on the floor. Antoinette looked angrily at her, for not better concealing that she had seen, and Luka instantly knew she had erred, closed her eyes, and turned her head away. The nuns had not seen any act of inadvertent betrayal by Luka and assumed the contortion in her face was her agony at not being able to relieve herself.

From halfway across the room Catherine could see the suppressed agitation on Antoinette's face, as the nuns made their way down her aisle. She squirmed just enough on her own bed to willfully draw Antoinette's attention, and, in that one instant, revealed by Catherine's ever so slight smile, Antoinette knew she had been set up. She would deal with that later. Sister St. John was approaching, Sisters Cirese and Elsa behind her, the cook having departed at the first covert opportunity.

"You will starve, girls, because of the actions of one." This she said as she looked directly at Antoinette, bypassing the other girls whose bunks preceded hers, so that there could be no doubt in anyone's mind that Sister St. John knew that it was Antoinette who had done this thing, Antoinette whose influence she had tried for so long to break.

Her eyes were fixed upon the girl, to the exclusion of all else.

To the exclusion of a few grains of white rice on a red-brown tiled floor.

Antoinette avoided a second look at the evidence that now was directly beneath Sister St. John, her prosecutor. She propped herself up on her pillow and could feel the distinct compression of soft rice beneath her palms, even as Sister St. John lowered her head to get face to face to the little pug-nosed urchin. Often, they would test each other's will by staring into each other's eyes, waiting to see who first would blink, or look away. None of the other girls would even raise their heads when speaking to Sister St. John.

Antoinette waited patiently for her face to be slapped, which is what usually happened if she failed to blink first or give way. Luka was fidgeting behind the nun, the springs on her bed drawing fire. St. John turned around and stood erect. "All right, all right, *go!*" she said, and Luka tumbled out of her bed and went running to the door and down the hall to the toilet.

Sister St. John looked around the room made harsh and jagged by the electric light that burned overhead and repeated her threat. "Remember, girls. No one eats until the villain is found out and punished." These were, of course, her instructions to the girls to force them to turn upon Antoinette. She knew that it would not be long, for while Antoinette had a core of very loyal followers, there were others who had been as terrorized by Antoinette as they had by the nuns and might privately turn her in after a missed breakfast. She turned to make her departure, but not before first slapping the bamboo cane on yet another steel bunk to punctuate her intent.

I'm almost going to get out of this, thought Antoinette.

"Sister St. John." She was almost to the door. "Sister." Sister Elsa, who had stood dutifully behind Sister St. John, had made the discovery.

Chapter Sixteen

One by one, defectors fell from Antoinette like overripe fruit from a tree, and, one by one, Catherine gathered them up before they rotted and spoiled. Over the course of the next year, the number of her followers grew. No longer did she sit alone at a table during lunch. She sat at *her* table, where others would save her place.

She remembered nothing, almost nothing, of the stories her mother had told her about Jon the Poet, the competent chief of the Ibans. Her natural tendency to lead must have been an inherited quality, his legacy to the grandchild he would never see, and not something merely imitated, for she could not recall the complete accounts of any of his heroics.

It was not enough to be brave, though this she certainly was. Fistfights with Antoinette were at first frequent though brief, with neither girl emerging as a clear victor. The fighting established Catherine as a warrior, and one not intimidated by the prospect of sudden or certain violence.

It was not enough to be cunning, though this was a vital skill. Cunning meant an intelligent, purposeful deceit, elevating deception to a virtue. Catherine had seen many of the children, lacking the fundamental ability to lie straight-faced, bent down in submission to ever-inquisitive nuns, never quite able to stand erect again.

Antoinette was certainly not lacking in these skills and was respected by all. But what distinguished Catherine from her mean-spirited adversary was Catherine's willingness to apply her talents for the good of others. She would lie for those inept at doing so. She would fight, quite spontaneously, for those usurped of the ability to fight for themselves, pouring back into their spirits a sense of worth drained dry on a daily basis by the nuns. *You are of no value* was the message of the nuns. *You are worth fighting for* was the message of Catherine.

She would take an occasional beating for some orphan less adept at stealing food, confessing to other's crimes, and no one from Antoinette's gang would dare to steal food from anyone loyal to Catherine.

Gradually Antoinette was compelled, begrudgingly, to accept Catherine's presence in what had been exclusively her domain. Territories were established. Boundaries were drawn. There were even improvised attempts at diplomacy.

Wednesdays, Antoinette's gang would not pilfer garbage cans for food. Thursdays, Catherine instructed her followers to abstain. On other days, the usual turmoil and territories would apply, carefully monitored to ensure compliance and respect.

But while Antoinette had a *gang*, a band, or an army—something very western and orthodox—Catherine, with the blood of her mother and of Jon the Poet surging primitively in her body, had something altogether different.

Catherine had a *tribe*.

Every child conscripted to Antoinette had been personally beaten up by her. It never became a formal ritual, a rite of sisterhood, it just seemed a natural expression of domination. Fear was terribly cohesive. The first reward of obedience to Antoinette was to be spared her anger. The absence of her fury in that perverse society was pathetically mistaken for affection. Real approval only came after convincingly emulating her. That which offended Antoinette was offensive. That which entertained Antoinette was entertaining. That which pleased Antoinette was pleasing. In increments children who had nothing surrendered themselves to Antoinette, if only to be her shadow.

Catherine offered a real alternative. She never fought someone because she didn't like them. It was never an expression of arrogance, or an attempt to humiliate someone. When Catherine fought, and she fought well, it was either to bring a halt to someone else's aggression, or to fight for food.

The one exception, the only exception, was Antoinette. The dislike was genuine, and mutual, and when they fought, it was with real passion. The source of Antoinette's dislike of Catherine was knowable, understandable. The root of Catherine's dislike, constant anger, was more subtle.

No one had seen Antoinette for three days, following the discovery of evidence of her thievery by the side of her bed a year earlier. When she was reunited with her classmates at last on the evening of the third day, she looked but once at Catherine, as if to say, "This, you have done to me."

Her face was badly bruised, and one eye partially swollen shut. For several days afterward she was hesitant to speak, for when she parted her blistered lips to form words, it revealed two teeth broken. She had survived her punishment bravely, but to be disfigured now caused her great humiliation.

Remarkably she had not implicated Catherine. There would be no point. She would not be at all believed and would have received additional strokes of the cane for lying. She knew all this without having to be told. Thoughts only of revenge sustained her through the ordeal.

And upon seeing Antoinette's broken face, Catherine felt ashamed. She had wanted Antoinette to be whipped, to be punished for her cruelty towards her, and for permitting her gang to spread those other lies about her to everyone. But she was not prepared to see a young girl, her own age, beaten so mercilessly by the nuns. This type of brutality she thought only her grandmother capable of, or her Aunty Joyce. This had not been her intention at all. To look at Antoinette now and be responsible for having inflicted those wounds upon her, made Catherine feel terribly guilty, and in that confusing circle of blame felt an outrageous anger at Antoinette for making her feel that way.

The war continued, as, one by one, the days became casualties of childhood.

"Catherine? Have you heard?" whispered Fatima, urgent to tell a less-than-urgent matter. "Two new girls. Taken in today."

Of course, Catherine had heard.

"Tell me," she said, looking discreetly around the dining hall, to see if others were listening, helping Fatima believe in the importance of her secret.

"They're buggers. Indians."

"Really?"

"They have purple skin. I saw it myself." Fatima was quite proud to be the first, or so she thought, to relay the information to Catherine. In fact, several others had already rushed to tell her the news.

"Purple skin? How can that be?" Without even any conscious effort on her part, Catherine intuited that Fatima's self-esteem would be elevated if she thought that she had actually been the first to deliver the news. She let her continue.

"My god. We only got two other buggers heah and they both with Antoinette."

"We'll take a look at them," said Catherine. "Does Antoinette know yet?" This was a genuine question. The others who had brought the rumor didn't know.

"Yeah. She does. I was talking to Luka when the bell rang. I don' mean the class bell. The other one, by the gate. Sister Masselin came to the gate, and they come in. Right then and there the Hindi start to beg the sister to take the girls. Masselin say they Indian and she don' wan', but the woman say it O.K., and she take the Sister by the sleeve, like this—" Fatima was very demonstrative— "and say 'you *gotta* take 'um.'" I don' yet know they names. But I know they poppa was Indian. An ol' woman bring dem heah, and she had the sign of the Hindi on her head. Like this." Fatima licked her finger and wiped dust from the table, smearing it in a spot on her forehead. For a moment what Catherine saw was the mark on the forehead of Che' Wan, hidden by an emerald.

"Really?" said Catherine. "How ol' you think they are?" Catherine already knew.

"I don' know for shuah. Maybe three or four, the one. The other a little older. Maybe six or seven."

"Outsiders?"

"No. Like us. I mean ..." Fatima corrected herself, "like the *rest* of us. Orphans."

"The momma and poppa?"

"Dead. I don' know how. But the woman who bring them. She bring some money and she no care if they gonna be Catholic, and believe in Jesus. They got nobody else. The Mother Superior, she come down from her room. She see it all, lah. And then they argue a little more, and the Hindi woman pull up this pouch from her neck where it hang, and she give it to the Sister. Mother Superior scol' her, but they keep the pouch, and the woman go away. Luka right there with me, all the time."

Catherine could see Luka talking intensely to Antoinette at the far table, undoubtedly talking about the same thing, asking the same questions if she didn't already know the answers.

"Catherine." One of the younger girls ran to her table, obviously upset, and oblivious to the conversation between Fatima and Catherine. Interruptions were things that children did to adults. Among themselves it was never perceived as such. It was only a spontaneous change in the direction of a conversation. No one took offense. At least, not within Catherine's tribe.

"What is it?" she asked, not at all annoyed, and sensitive to the girl's distress.

"Look," she said, holding out her hands in which was crumbled her ration of toast for the morning. "Sarah did it."

"Sarah did it? Did what?"

"Smash my toas', lah."

"And what did *you* do?"

"I didin do nothing." The girl was emphatic, though not entirely believed.

"Send her over here," said Catherine. "Tell her it's my orders."

"Yes, Catherine," said the girl, certain the justice for which she had petitioned would be delivered. In a few moments, rather defensively, Sarah showed up at Catherine's table, and sat down across from her.

"Tell me what happened," said Catherine. Fatima understood that this settling of a dispute would take priority over her audience with Catherine, and she accepted this shift of attention with dignity.

"Nothing," said Sarah.

"Why you crush her bread?" said Catherine. Catherine could speak the Queen's English very well, and yet, when she spoke to many of the girls who had been given vocabulary and grammar commensurate to the food that sustained them, just enough to get by, she spoke as they would speak, and they were not ashamed.

Sarah did not answer, looking down at her hands folded on the table.

"You know what?" said Catherine. "I don' care why you did it. You *never* do harm to food. It's bad luck."

Sarah remained impassive. She had no choice. It was a matter of face. But Catherine could detect that she was recalcitrant.

"Go to your table. Did you eat your bread yet?"

"No."

"Bring it to me."

In a moment, Sarah returned, and held the bread to Catherine as an offering for leniency.

Catherine looked at the girl who had come expecting justice, and the one who had returned expecting punishment.

"You," she said. "Give me your bread." This she said not to Sarah, but to her accuser. "Yes, the crumbs." She deposited a pile of dry crumbs on Catherine's plate. As Sarah waited for the inevitable, Catherine instead offered the girl, who had stopped whining and crying, her own, unspoiled slice, the only sustenance until suppertime. "Here. Take it." Catherine had spoken. There may have been reluctance, but there was no choice. She took the slice and headed back to her table, leaving Sarah standing before her, holding her bread, which Catherine had refused.

"And you. You will stand there." As Sarah stood before her, Catherine ate the crumbs deposited on her plate, and drank the watery soup meant to accompany their slice of bread. She knew that the crushing of the bread was an attempt to humiliate. "We don't do such things to ourselves. It's enough the Sisters do it to us.

We stick together or we never live to get out of this place." Catherine ate the crumbs, without shame, and this was not lost on Sarah. "Go to your seat. Be grateful you got bread."

Jon the Poet could have done no better.

Chapter Seventeen

In the shade of one of the few trees permitted to grow within the walls of the convent of the Most Holy Order of the Infant Jesus, Catherine peeled the skin of a rambutan that had miraculously survived long enough on the branches to reach maturity. It had actually fallen in a small cluster of ripened fruit, overlooked by the pruning knife of the gardeners, who harvested on behalf of the nuns, and bypassed by the marauding monkeys on one of their raids from the higher treetops on the other side of the wall.

It was a relaxed moment between classes and chores, and she floated on her island of shade upon an ocean of tropical afternoon sunlight. Even Jesus, who was not an Englishman at all, seemed content to brown in the sunlight in his place among the roses, the scene of the crucifixion where he had first greeted Fin and Catherine upon their arrival to his palace. Catherine could see him from where she sat, while she was propped up against the tree, peeling another rambutan, stowing the remaining three or four from the fallen cluster in her school bag, to be eaten later, or traded, or to be given to Fin when they passed through the halls.

Fin had not fared so well. The only mother she had really known was a scant three years older than herself. Catherine had always taken care of her, good care of her, filling in the many voids left by her Aunty Joyce. The nuns discouraged the two sisters from playing together, believing it a worthwhile goal to make the two of them more independent, or, more accurately, dependent upon the nuns themselves.

When Fin was hungry, she was told to wait until lunch. When she needed the toilet, she was told to wait until their break time, and when Fin awakened in the night, alone in her bed, unable to dream anything but nightmares, she was told to sleep, and be silent, and wait until morning. Fin was constantly waiting, but she knew not for whom, or for what. Slowly the cravings for her big sister dissipated. Perhaps the Sisters had been right.

Catherine had the shade and the big tree all to herself. Trees always gave her a sense of well-being. Every time she would climb the mosaic of branches, hundreds, thousands of feet into the sky, she would invariably find her mother. Together they would share a guava from the rattan kit on her mother's back, and they would watch the rest of the world below them. Her mother, pointing out tigers before Catherine could even see disturbance in the grass so far below. Her mother, hearing things soundless, like the movement of great snakes, and feeling the motion from the wings of butterflies in the still air. Her mother, teaching her how to see, and to feel, and to think. How to be a hunter, an Iban, and how to be a woman, braiding her hair combed free of knots and tangles, all from altitudes above the earthbound people skilled only in the ways of hurting. There was always safety in the trees. There was always adventure, and there was always her mother. Catherine survived on small moments like this. Catherine had waited, for a moment like this. She was completely alone but not at all isolated.

Catherine laid upon her back, her hands beneath her head, staring into the filigree of branches above her, seeing herself, and her mother, seeing the entire forest of Borneo, up so high the clouds could be eaten like shave-ice, up so high not even the garruda would nest for fear of falling.

She closed her eyes, and as the shepherd sun encouraged the shade to graze elsewhere, Catherine could feel the wonderful, warm light filling her breast, and stroking her shoulders, her face and her brow, like the touch of her mother, or the momentary touch, never forgotten, of Che' Wan.

The last cloud of the day slipped between Catherine and the sunlight. She opened her eyes.

It was not a cloud. Antoinette, too, had waited for a moment like this.

Catherine sat up abruptly, taken off guard. How could she have been so careless? "What do *you* want." she said, trying to retake the initiative.

"Nothing I don't already have."

Focused so intently upon Antoinette's eyes, Catherine had not noticed that the girl was holding Catherine's schoolbag, which Antoinette lifted slowly into view. "Need this?"

Catherine had not been coiled to spring, like cobra or tiger. Nevertheless, she lurched forward from her back as an animal would, making a failed pass to snatch the bag from the arms of Antoinette, who spun before Catherine had left the ground, and began at a gallop down the mildly sloping lawns as Catherine rose to her feet and sprinted in pursuit.

Catherine had not been thinking. *Where was Antoinette's gang?*

But Antoinette had been thinking. Antoinette had been planning. And she knew where her gang was.

The girls were equally matched, both as runners and warriors, though Antoinette had the advantage of size and power. She was also at an advantage because she knew exactly the course she would run, and several times she turned a corner that could not have been anticipated, and Catherine lost the gains of her own momentum.

But Catherine was tenacious, confident in her own stamina, and certain that she would run down once and for all the girl who had been so consistently nasty to her. And she would retrieve her bag. Even in the fury of pursuit, these things she thought and visualized. Antoinette did not have a chance.

Antoinette took another turn, running now in the passageway between one of the outbuildings and the main dormitory. It was an uphill path, a bad choice for Antoinette, for Catherine knew from midnight forays that the course dead-ended with the next turn, and that Antoinette had trapped herself. There was a fire exit to service the dormitories, but the door was always kept locked to prevent the girls from doing mischief out of sight from the nuns, and to keep the flames of Hell that burned from within from being visible in Kuala Lumpur should anyone care to look. Always locked—this Catherine knew—having often tested the door herself.

She was almost gleeful that Antoinette could have been so foolish, running the path that she did. The chase had invigorated Catherine, and she was ready to take on the girl, once again, her energies peaking.

For a moment Antoinette disappeared behind the last blind corner, and Catherine could find no cause to slow down. Inertia was on her side, her momentum making her bigger with each quick stride. She herself turned the corner, and as visualized, there was Antoinette, with her back against the wall, and nowhere to run, to escape.

But Antoinette was smiling.

Catherine stopped in her tracks, jolted instantly as she realized what that smile implied, and she herself turned, and it was in fact, too late. It was not too late for Antoinette, but for Catherine. A dozen or so of Antoinette's most obedient followers had quickly blocked the exit, from where they had been waiting as ordered.

"You're trapped, you little bitch."

Catherine spun round again, this time facing Antoinette with renewed venom for having been duped, and self-angered for having been so reckless as to fall into the trap. In her typical style, she was determined to inflict as much damage upon Antoinette as she could before she could be taken down, and without hesitation or a glance to the rear, she sprang, now like the cobra, now like the tiger, taking Antoinette completely by surprise, who thought the sight of so many of her enemies would have immobilized Catherine and reduced her to fear and to begging. Antoinette was hit by a flurry of bites and scratches amid a peppering of fist-falls, and she herself was paralyzed by Catherine's war cry. Her soldiers, though they had been given explicit instructions, were still very slow to react, stunned as they were by the bravery and insanity of the little she-demon, unprepared for such fury. But it took just one of them to recover, and lead an assault from behind, to break the spell that seemed to hold them all in check, and they were upon her.

Strangely, those discarded orphans, addicted to Antoinette, had already lost to Catherine. The purpose of this entire episode, weeks in planning, was to humiliate the girl. Causing her pain was only a tactic, almost incidental. Her valor undid any intended disgrace. This moment of supreme triumph had already been ruined by the unexpected audacity of their victim, who even now, with a swarm of orphans overwhelming her, continued to strike and even to wound Antoinette. Where was the fear and the trembling this violence was intended to inspire?

They pulled her off their fallen leader, and held her to the ground, at least one girl to sit upon each arm and limb, and still Catherine convulsed as if it were not over, and that she might break free to inflict one more blow. It was Antoinette, and not Catherine, who felt afraid.

This was not going at all as she had planned. Antoinette's face and skin stung in a dozen places and trickled red from the claws of the pinned tiger, and her cheek and jaws were already beginning to throb from those unstoppable, bony little fists. Nevertheless, she had a plan, she had purpose in luring Catherine so far from the window of Mother Superior, or from the view of any prefect, or from the playground where Catherine's tribe had not yet noticed her absence or could hear her wail or war-cry.

"Turn the bitch over," said Antoinette. She had visualized telling Catherine exactly what she was going to do to her, the many times that she rehearsed this moment in her mind. It would have been a great pleasure to torment her in that way. But the quick little beating she had endured, rescued only by her gang, usurped any satisfaction her long awaited moment of revenge may have held out for her, and she wanted to get this over with.

Catherine's bravery angered her, witnessed as it had been by her own gang. Catherine was tough. Antoinette was only mean. Catherine was defiant. Antoinette was only cruel. And now the sound of these differences was amplified in the echo of the abandoned courtyard. *Could these sounds be heard*, thought Antoinette, *by my gang? Yes, best to get this over with quickly*, she judged. *Muffle the sounds of Catherine's courage.*

The girls did as they were told, and they turned Catherine on her stomach, and flattened her to the ground as they stretched her arms and legs. She could not shift from side to side or rear up to spring free. Antoinette had gone to the corner of the courtyard, where a stout bamboo laundry pole had been propped in place the day before. "Get off," said Antoinette dryly to the girl who sat upon Catherine's shoulders. "Put this in her mouth," she ordered Luka, handing her a sock. Catherine's head was twisted towards the daylight by one of the girls, her hair pulled tautly back, immobilizing her. She could not see Antoinette, who was behind her, or the bamboo. There was only Luka, before her, on her knees, prepared to do as she had been ordered.

Virtues are so few in number, and rarely do the virtuous have more than one or two. Goodness, like rice, was available to everyone, but in very small rations. But real virtues, like a spot of chicken or pork, were in even shorter supply, something rare and coveted, an occasional event, like mercy. Luka had but one virtue, and that was loyalty. And though it was misplaced in Antoinette, still, it was all she had. Everyone starved there, in that place, for food, for love, for touch, for virtues, for a sense of worth, for hope. Luka *had* a virtue, and though Catherine had hoped ever since her first days among them that Luka might become her friend, she would respect her for the one virtue her impoverished, abused and undernourished spirit managed to sustain. Catherine had many virtues, and Luka had but the one, and this evoked from Catherine a bit of compassion for this conspirator knelt before her. Had any other girl tried to force the sock into her mouth, there would be bloody, even broken fingers for it. But this was Luka. Luka who suffered private things that only Catherine had seen and understood.

Catherine looked upon her plaintively and gave little resistance. She bit down hard upon the sock, expecting a beating momentarily. But this was not what Antoinette had in mind. Her plot for revenge had incubated for more than a full year and was more refined.

"You like to be high, Catherine. I seen you in the trees. I watched you in the trees. You like to be high up there, don't you?" Catherine could hear the voice, calm, in control, the anger almost undetectable, coming from behind her. "I watched you many times when you are alone. Who is that you talk to? I never see anyone. Oh. Can't answer. Sorry, I forgot. The sock. Got rice in it. I combed the rice from my hair."

None of the girls knew what Antoinette was talking about, and it sounded a little crazy, starting to scare them a little bit. All that the girls knew was that their leader was going to do something bad to Catherine. They had no idea it was revenge from the incident a year ago. Having endured her beating with two broken teeth to show for it, Antoinette decided that the thievery for which she was falsely accused might actually enhance her reputation. Such a bold thing to do.

She had said nothing about the matter, then, or any time since, and let the girls conclude that it really had been she who had run the gauntlet of the nun's quarters and down to the kitchen that night long ago. But she had expectations of revenge to cushion each strike of the cane upon her, and now those expectations would be met. Only Catherine would know what it meant, the rice.

"Do you like to go out on the far branches?" She took the bamboo and rested it upon Catherine's shoulder.

"Should I beat you with this?" she inquired politely.

She tapped the rod a few times upon Catherine's shoulders, letting it fall and bounce of its own weight.

By craning her neck Catherine could look up to the sky that spilled sunset into the courtyard, falling a full three stories. From the three sides and protruding from holsters beneath each of the upper floor windows were the bamboo poles, like the one on her shoulder, that held the day's laundry, drying, in what had remained of the sunlight. Delicate linens, airy pillowcases and bed sheets, here and there a pastel yellow night gown.

Catherine had already shut out the sound of Antoinette's mortal, vengeful voice. In that hollow of sky in the ring of the buildings, it was not laundry at all, but white clouds and angels, floating and drifting, and come to her rescue.

A door from the ground floor opened from within. This, too, according to plan, opened with a purloined key. Antoinette, too, was a skilled and discreet thief.

"All clear," said the girl, who had opened the door, startled to see Antoinette bleeding.

"Good."

A nun, a gardener, or any of the waifs pledged to Catherine might wander by accident or to investigate the air discolored by pain and anger, and Antoinette knew her pleasure could be halted at any moment. She wasted no more time taunting her victim, exquisite though the sensation was. She slipped the bamboo pole through the gap between Catherine's pressed blue shorts and her buttocks, and under her blouse along her spine, exiting again at the collar behind her neck. She motioned the girls to hoist the pole and shoulder it among them, and Catherine resembled a deer skewered and bound for the fire pit, there to be turned upon a spit.

They marshaled her into the building, careful to lock the door behind them, and proceeded directly for the stair well. Catherine began to struggle, and Antoinette ordered her hands tied to the pole as well, letting only her legs dangle. A belt cinched around her head held the sock in her mouth and she could not spit it out to cry for help. They awkwardly rounded the stairwell to the second floor, and then the third. Except for themselves, the building was empty.

Snared as she was, Catherine could think only of getting free. She had no idea what Antoinette had planned for her. A girl double-checked on the third floor that there were no nuns, and no sympathizers of Catherine's to interfere, and they smuggled their prisoner into a room overlooking the courtyard from which they had come.

Angels and clouds and laundry, affixed to the sky on bamboo shafts were shaken free and drifted to the courtyard below, as space was made on a holster for the human laundry to dry and twist in the air.

"You, lah. Take the front of the pole. That's it." Antoinette barked urgent orders as she opened the window. "You. Hold here like *this*, lah. Don' let drop." They maneuvered the pole to the window. Antoinette herself held Catherine by the hair, and stood on the windowsill, her other hand clasped firmly to the wooden molding of the window frame. Other girls shuffled and struggled, and the pole made its way outside the window. Catherine was now motionless. She could see the fallen angels broken on the brick three floors below, half obscured by a cloud that could no longer defy gravity and had come crashing down upon them. Her angels, her clouds, had failed to rescue her, and the height screamed fear that Antoinette could only whisper.

The girls struggled to slide the pole into the holster. It had never been intended for anything except the weight of drying laundry. Hardly the sixty pounds of the girl now straining the bamboo pole.

Their work was done.

"Someone comes." The warning of the sentry, always posted by Antoinette. The girls scattered, vacating the room, and rushing truer than rain down the back stairs. Antoinette lingered a moment, even at the risk of discovery. This was a moment that she could not allow to pass so quickly. Her moment of conquest, dubious and assisted though it was. She held Catherine's hair from above while cantilevered over the precipice of the windowsill. Slowly she released her grip on the tangle of hair, watching the pole flex as it took the full weight of the girl. Never again would she see Catherine so vulnerable.

Antoinette's own instincts for self-preservation tugged at her sleeve and spellbound though she was by the sight of Catherine's helplessness, she fled down the hallway herself as she heard footsteps coming up the other stairwell.

There was no urgency detected in the step, which seemed deliberate and slow, but it echoed in the hall with the weight of an adult. Catherine never knew who it was, and the steps got closer, closer still, then more distant, without stopping. The bell in the distance summoned the children to supper.

Catherine was alone. The sky above slowly turned colorless, and then the dark, melodic blue that sings its color to the night. Seduced by the song, the moon let fall its feathering of clouds, and in unashamed fullness, slipped with opal smoothness upon the passionate indigo, pausing as it discovered Catherine pinioned to the canyon-courtyard precipice, giving what comfort it could, with its healing, yellow glow, summoning stars to watch over her.

Catherine could feel the bamboo straining. Any attempt to move could snap it at its base, but even the panic of fear could not prod her into motion. To move would be to die. *I will be motionless. I am a tiger. I am stalking through the grass. I do not move. I am very powerful, and I make the weak tremble. I will hold this pose, though the wind may blow, until my quarry makes a move, but I myself will be motionless, until that time.*

And Catherine was missed at dinner.

And when the tiger slept, the garruda awakened. *My wings are so vast, the world beneath me so helpless, so far below me. I can soar in this breeze forever. I can stay aloft forever. What is that below me, a mousedeer? Prey? Tonight, tonight it shall be spared. I choose to feast instead on the pleasures of flight, this bloodless flight that has no end, with these wings of mine upon a breeze that has no limits. Wait. Not a mousedeer. Not a mousedeer at all. A human, but who? Who is that?*

Somehow, perhaps during that relaxed amnesty when struggle and death reach an accord or temporary arrangement, the ropes that bound her hands before her had come loose, and she was held now only by the bamboo passing under her trousers and jersey. She spread her unencumbered arms in the fantasy of flight.

Pale beneath her, a shadow, and then a form, three floors below. A girl, making no sound, come to look up at the eclipse, the crucifixion, a silhouette in a perfect ring of

147

moonlight. *But who is this beneath me, so very far below?* Too much darkness, too much distance, to know for sure. Someone come for absolution.

Catherine's body went limp with sleep, hidden in the laundry that protruded on bamboo from windows on either side of her like two thieves.

She could hear men gasp beneath her, as the sun came up, their animated Chinese voices waking her. They fumbled for keys to unlock the door in the courtyard, and one of them rushed inside as the other one remained below, as if losing sight of her would somehow make the bamboo break.

Someone had alerted them.

Chapter Eighteen

The young orphan, Luka, was well into the journey from one day to the next, floating down current in the darkness on her little, separate raft like all the other little girls on their beds in the dormitory, but she was not asleep.

She never slept very well. Kuala Lumpur, either by night or by day, steamed its waters into the air like a kettle of steeping English tea, except during the monsoons, which offered some relief and cool nights. But the monsoons were gone, and the girl struggled in the thick air, both for breath and for comfort.

Sleep did not offer many rewards, anyway. Some girls told of dreaming beautiful things when they slept. Their dreams were formed by the shape of their deprivations. Beneath a layer of thin sleep, the whitewashed walls of the dormitory became tapestries like the palace of the king. Stale bread was transformed into mooncakes. Nowhere in their dreams could the black and white habit of the nuns be found, all dress was flowered batik, and all their elders were servants. The snarling watchdog of the gardeners became a tamed panther. Elephants and peacocks strolled the courtyards, platters of fresh fruit begged attention upon every table, and the scent of mutton, or chicken, embodied, emboldened with the aroma of lemon grass and ginger and invigorating spices flavored the air to arouse hunger that never went unsatisfied. The harsh bell that beat them from one class or activity to another became soft and subtle as gamelan.

These things, the girls would dream, and then, in wakefulness, in the playground and between classes, they would share these dreams with the others, like stolen food.

But Luka never brought that kind of purloined vision to the table, or under the tree where they would gather, away from the nuns. Her dreams, when she dreamt, never developed the animal momentum to leap the high convent walls and escape into jungle or city or palace. Never fanciful, like Catherine's dreams. Instead, she dreamt of Sister St. John, or of Masselin, or Gertrude, or Beatrice. Often, she dreamed of Sister Beatrice. Often, Sister Beatrice would come to her in dreams, and lead her into private chambers where she had never been. Her dreams, sometimes vague, sometimes vivid, were of this, and of the cane, or of hunger punished with more hunger, or of endless hours in her chair while a sister scratched sharp chalk across the board and intimidated her with facts that she could never remember about countries and continents she would never see. The events of the day, like the repetitive strokes of a cane, delivered themselves upon her when she slept, until at last there was no difference at all between wakefulness and sleep. Her dreams. They offered no escape, and some mornings she would awaken with a rancid, inexplicable scent in her nostrils.

But those who dreamed of worlds other than their own would generously share with her when they would gather at the cafeteria or in the playground. Catherine, in the darkness halfway across the room, was probably dreaming those wonderful dreams, even now. Catherine always had the best dreams. Catherine always told the best stories. Like Jon the Poet, the grandfather Catherine had never seen, but who sometimes brought her stories in the night. How envious was Luka of the outsider. Luka laid upon her little cot, perspiring under the sheet that she was not permitted to remove.

She had gone several days now, without sleep, except for dozing off in class, like so many of the other girls, awakened by a quick and occasional rap across the knuckles with a little wooden ruler. Sleep was for the fearless, a war fought in the darkness, and she was a nocturnal casualty of the perpetual saber of fear. It was not safe. But she knew that eventually, if not this night, then the next, the weight of so many hours upon her shoulders would take her down, like the weight of a tiger can take down even a water buffalo, and she could only hope that the sleep would be swift and dreamless.

How wonderful to be like Catherine, fearless not only in the face of Antoinette and the Sisters, but even in sleep. Fearless enough to dream. Overcoming an occasional skirmish with a rogue nightmare, and free to dream again of better things. Fantastic, colorful, liberating visions.

Exhaustion began to overtake her. She cowered under the sheets, curling herself up into a tight little citadel. The dream, the bad dream, was coming again. She could hear it, barefoot though it was, creeping down the hallway from the direction of the nun's quarters, as it had on many nights before, all silhouette and shadow, smoke and mist, singling her out, stalking the aisles, stopping at her bed. A serpent, a *naga*, a dragon, lifting her from her cot into cavernous arms and carrying her through a dark tunnel to its lair, where it would eat her. If she could but stay awake a little longer, surely, she would be spared. This apparition would only come in dreams, and dreams would only come in sleep, and sleep would only come in darkness. "Oh, Jesus on the wall. Make the sun come up."

He, too, was asleep.

She could hear, she could feel, the coming of her nightmare, the breathing of her beast. Sometimes, if she were very, very still, the rasping rhythm of that breath would pass her by, like a whining arrow that missed its target, and the beast would choose another to devour, carrying the child away quietly. Miraculously, when dawn at last blew away the smoke and the darkness, the chosen sacrifice would somehow be back in its cot, asleep. No evidence of struggle. *Of course not*, thought the girl, *because these are only my dreams*. She asked no questions and told no one what happened in her dreams. Her dreams, deformed, like the girls rumored to be in the cellar, frightening and shameful.

She did her best, her very best, to stay awake. But she was too frail, she was too exhausted. She could feel hot breath upon her forehead. Sleep surrounded her like the lifeless cloak of a nun and carried her down the hallway. She was condemned to dream the dream one more night ...

Morning, which was never inevitable, had arrived outside the convent walls and gained admittance through the heavy wooden doors. She was awakened with all her night companions in the customary way, abruptly and brutally, but was disoriented for only a moment. She expelled but a single breath, purging herself of the horrors of her night, when a brand new fear, fresh and invigorated, leapt into her bosom with the first breath that she inhaled like a fly upon an open wound. She had wet her bed.

The overhead light oscillated on the wire like a snared animal, sprung from its path, the light cord pulled by Sister St. John. She slapped her hands together, breaking night into day in her usual fashion, chopping up silence with her meat cleaver hands.

The girl looked up at Jesus, in whose wisdom she half-believed in spite of his poor choice of wives. *Don't let her walk this way. Don't let her walk this way.*

The girls began their ordinary stretching, the yawning, the sitting up and looking about, the rubbing of sleep from their eyes. The insistent voice of Sister St. John herding them into collective wakefulness, letting no one fall behind into the comfort of bed and pillow, letting no one drift back for an unauthorized helping of sleep. It was, after all, morning, or would be very soon.

"Come along, girls. Up, up, up." She worked her way to the vast shuttered windows, her cloak spreading like the wings of a bat as she opened the shutters to a sky not yet gray. A light, here and there, like low grazing stars, glowed from across the courtyard against dark buildings. Proof of dawn's return—the morning sounds of waking animals—had yet to be emitted through the immense jungle on the other side of the perimeter walls.

Soon there would be morning prayers, and it was Sister St. John's duty to see that the children were alert, washed, and dressed before the ringing of the chapel bell. Hair to be brushed. Children to be bathed.

Beds to be made.

She opened the last of the shutters. Two nuns had joined her, and a third was preparing the washroom. Some of the children, particularly the older ones, had already made their way down the hall, where any remnants of sleep that may have clung to them would be washed off in the splash of water doused upon them from a scoop at the cistern. The washroom was similar to the toilets, which adjoined it. Square lime green tiles covered the floor that sloped slightly to a central drain and tiles wrapped around the walls as high as the shoulders of the tallest of the girls. Half a dozen sinks of white porcelain were evenly spaced against the far wall, and opposite to that were low wooden benches beneath a rack of stubbly pegs that held a personal towel for each of the girls. Against the remaining wall was the immovable cistern, as wide as outstretched arms and hip-high, built into place with concrete, and lined with the same tiles. It was kept full at all times by a single spigot protruding from the wall, awkwardly out of reach but to the tallest of girls or to the nun, who stood in attendance as the first of the girls came staggering in, and hung their night gowns on their designated peg with their towel, and lined up to be rinsed with a ladleful of the standing water after lathering up their hair at the sinks.

On their way from the dormitory two or three girls passed Luka, who was sitting up. Her eyes were glazed open in fear. The girls could see the sheet upon her bed had been wet, and they quickened themselves from the room lest their shock draw the nun's attention. Bedweting was a serious matter. It was forbidden. It was punishable. It was punished.

Catherine passed the bed as well, one of the first to leave the room. Once or twice, when visions of her Uncle Joe or her grandmother had torn through the ether barricade separating dream from nightmare, she too, in her terror, had wet the bed, clinging to the mattress even in sleep rather than risk waking up. In those moments of hallucination and confused perception, only fear was courageous.

One of those times she had been found out. It seemed to be something the nuns looked for. All during breakfast, she was made to stand in the cafeteria with the wet sheet draped over her head in the corner, while the girls filed past, or sat to eat. It had, of course, been humiliating. Surprisingly, Catherine quickly got over it, and it did not slow her ascent to leadership. Most of the girls had wet their beds, even the older ones, transfixed to their cots as Catherine had been, and most were subjected to some form of humiliation when the nuns were feeling more creative than simply to rely upon the stroke of a cane. The commonality of punishment diffused any long-term impact of the intended degradation.

Still, Luka would no doubt be singled out that morning, and as a repeat offender who had recently been warned to control herself at night, her punishment would most likely be severe. Such willful disobedience.

Catherine left the room to join the others down the hall, a sense of relief that it was not she who had faltered that night. She stood in line with the others for a turn at the sink after relieving herself, and low rumors were already circulating about the girl so reluctant to get out of bed. By the time Catherine had brushed her teeth and lathered her hair, it seemed as if everyone in the room, except for the nun splashing them down with water, knew what had happened.

And in a moment, the nun, Sister Beatrice, would also know.

Back down the hallway Luka continued to cower beneath the sheet, attempting invisibility, her only possible escape if this was not more of the bad dream. No. Not a dream. This is not part of the bad dream, thought Luka. And the bed *is* wet. My bed is truly wet.

Surprising herself, she sat up, letting the sheet fall in a bundle on her lap, in so doing its dry fringes fell upon the evidence of her mistake, as Sister St. John made a first pass through the aisles. The few remaining children, in sleep's half daze, sat up themselves and pivoted in their places, their feet blindly finding the little slippers arranged neatly by their beds the night before. The Sister, like wind burglarizing the branches of a tree, blowing the children from their tenuous clutch on their cots a leaf at a time. Until there was but one.

"Come on, now. To the bath," the Sister said, without detectable malice. The girl swiveled in her bed, as if to comply, concealing the evidential sheet in her little-girl hands, testimony of her night accident still unrevealed, unspoken, but incrimination pending. And then, remarkably, her will to evade detection simply vanished. It all seemed so pointless, so futile. She would be found out. The girls were always found out. And her nightgown was clinging to her skin in acrid dampness.

"I can't, Sister."

"Well, of course you can. Hurry along, now, and join the others."

"No, Sister, I can't," her words the preamble to her complete resignation.

"*What* did you say?" The Sister was dumbfounded by such non-plus refusal to obey her authority.

"I've wet my bed." Her surrender of pretense accomplished, bypassing fear, feeling a momentary relief that her confession had come so easily.

"What?" The Sister, too, shocked that the child spoke of the matter so casually, as if there would be no consequences. She had been warned several times, and the escalation of her punishments should have left the girl trembling. And yet, she seemed so indifferent to what would follow, what had to follow. Sister St. John's faith, if not in God, was in the power of fear. Fear. How else to give order to the lives of so many anonymous children? The girl was not courageous, not at all. She was simply without fear, having accidentally discovered that fear becomes impotent if the victim it intends to manipulate gives up some paltry resistance. The girl offered none.

Down the hall, above the splashing of water, the voice of Sister St. John could be heard as it vomited disgust at the girl. Sister Beatrice paused, hearing the commotion, thrusting her free hand out upon the motley assembly of naked children in a stern gesture to silence them. Beads of swelling water clung desperately to dripping hair, unwilling to break the silence commanded by the nun with their pending fall to the tile floor.

The girl, with unexpected decorum, had stood up. Nothing in her demeanor suggested apology as she walked to the corner of the room, returning without hesitation to place in the hands of the nun the obliging bamboo that stood sentry every night as they lay in their beds. She waited passively for Sister St. John to beat this most recent sin from her body, if not her soul.

Sister St. John felt vaguely challenged, the power of the moment usurped by the girl's unexpected cooperation. She held the very tempting switch in her palm, striking it once or twice against her own palm in the unconscious manner of a horse flicking its tail even when there are no flies.

The girl was unflinching at the rhythmic prelude to inevitable violence. All terror seemed to have evaporated, visibly annoying Sister St. John, whose concentration was broken when she suddenly perceived the splashing of water down the hall had come to a halt. Perhaps the terror was there, hidden among the bathing children.

"Put this back where you found it."

"M'me?"

"Put this back in the corner."

The girl did as she was told. She had no idea what turbulence would fall upon her if a simple, knowable caning were not the punishment of choice. The calm of her resignation, like a pool of still water, began to ripple once again as Sister dropped a first pebble.

"So. You think it's all right to wet the bed, and your gown?" A question not casting for an answer. Sister St. John was leading the poor child down the hall holding the flesh of her ear between two, compressing dagger fingernails, formulating other absurd questions that also expected no answer as they walked. "Are you an infant? Do you need nappies, still? Should we have you sleep in the nursery? Or perhaps in the *basement*, with the other girls who can't control themselves?"

She ran out of questions by the time she had marched her to the washroom, all but one, perhaps improvised. "Do you like being wet?" The girl squeezed her eyes tightly, but it seemed to make no difference to the sharp pain from Sister St. John's hold upon her ear. She blinked and could see the troubled faces of all the children in a row, some half-dressed, some naked, but all suffering with her.

"Girls. We've got a bedwetter here." Of course, they all knew that. Was this nun actually trying to arouse disdain in them? Did she actually think they would share her sense of disgust? Amazingly, that is precisely what Sister St. John thought. And she would avenge the children for this crime.

"You ... get in the tub." She thrust the girl in the direction of the cistern, releasing her ear at the last moment. Fear had found the child once more, who held her ear with both hands, and turned helplessly to face all the equally helpless children. "Get in the tub."

The girl was paralyzed, but Sister St. John saw only that the hesitation was further defiance. She slapped the girl on the face and shoved her once more into the direction of the water, until she did as she had been told, though not quickly enough to satisfy the nun. Slipping, she tumbled into the cistern, water overflowing the green tiles and escaping towards the drain. She sputtered, coughed, having swallowed water upon entry, and she held the sides of the tub under her arms to regain her breath, her pale yellow nightgown floating up behind her like the petals of a water lily.

"You want to be wet? Now you're wet, aren't you?" The words throbbed within her, echoing in the bath chamber off the green tiles before they fell to the floor and escaped through the drain with the cascade of water. The children no longer had faces for her, all was blur. She could not see them. There was only Sister St. John, who kept mumbling words she could no longer understand, two nuns who stood at the door, and Sister Beatrice at the side of the pool. Sister Beatrice, the face of the dragon in her dream, just a dream.

This was all far too passive to satisfy Sister St. John's appetite. Intuitively Sister Beatrice averted the helpless gaze of the child and stepped aside as her colleague trudged forward to the edge of the cistern and took the girl by the nape of the neck, twisting her face left and then right, forcing her to look at all the children whom she could not see, dousing her with humiliation. The nightgown had lost its buoyancy as it absorbed water and sunk like a shroud around the girl chest deep in water.

"I think you should pray, my dear." It took a moment for her to realize that the nun expected her to pray, to fold her hands, no doubt to pray to Jesus that she be forgiven for wetting the bed.

"Jesus, forgive me, for I have sinned ..."

"Wait. Wait. Wait. When we pray, are we not to be on our knees?"

And then the horror came, as the girl, as all the girls in that prison of a room realized what had been said, what had been intended, perhaps all along. The girl folded her hands prayerfully, and took a deep breath, and submerged herself to pray as instructed by the teacher of prayer. She sputtered to the surface, her full chest of air swelling her with buoyancy, and she found she was unable to keep from floating.

"Here," offered the nun. "I'll *help* you." She took another breath, and as she folded her hands, Sister St. John helped her to pray properly, on her knees. Sister St. John, named for the Baptist, the one who held Jesus underwater in a ritual the children did not really understand.

As she held the child underwater, she looked upon the faces of the girls who surrounded the pool, and she saw at last, with great relief and satisfaction, what had been missing up to that moment. Her authority had returned. Every one of them. Every one of them was afraid. She was euphoric.

She felt the struggle of the child beneath the water and was annoyed that her moment of pleasure was interrupted. Small hands broke the surface of the water and clawed at the air for escape. But a moment more. *I will hold her a moment more.* A gush of air broke the surface as well and several of the girls, Catherine included, instinctively motioned forward to help her, only to be held in check with the admonishing snarl of Sister St. John.

The struggle seemed to stop, and Sister St. John pulled the girl up by the hair and draped her over the edge of the tub. Her face was blue, and for a moment breathless, until a cough fought its way through her lungs, and swallowed water burst its way from her body.

Defying the unspoken command to stay where she was, Catherine lurched forward and helped the girl remain upright as she continued to expel water and displace it with air. She held the girl tightly, who surrendered all her strength when at last someone was there to help her. Other girls, emboldened by Catherine, came to her aid and they lifted the girl over the rail.

Sister St. John at first said nothing. She looked at Sister Beatrice, who awkwardly, tactlessly, looked away, and in that gesture, it occurred to Sister St. John that perhaps she had gone too far. The girl was cradled in the laps of others on the floor, and Sister St. John, careful to show no emotion and certainly nothing that suggested regret or error, hovered over her just long enough to ensure herself that the child was breathing.

And the child *was* breathing, even alert. "So. You want to wet your bed? You go and sleep in that wet nightgown today. All day." And she bounced an order off the tiled walls to no one in particular: "Put her in her bed ... and no food today." She left the room to recover her face, leaving the other nuns to carry out the morning duties. As if to persuade herself that this was all part of her plan, and not obsession gone awry, she turned as she left and said to the girls, "Let this be a lesson to all of you."

Indeed, it was.

The girl did not come down that day, the whole morning. She was the talk at lunch time, the lunch she was forbidden to attend.

But Sister St. John was in attendance.

Girls refused to look at her, at her face. It was not in fear of her, fearsome though she was. They watched her sit, even pray, dine with Sisters. But they could not look upon her face, because of what they felt. Not what they felt about her, but what they felt *for* her. And what they felt for her was shame, pity. This … is not what we were meant to be. Not this. Not cruel. Not so terribly cruel.

Mutiny, of course, was out of the question. But there was a collective feeling that what she had done to the girl she had *over* done. No one deserved that. A beating, a stroke at a time, perhaps. After all, she had wet the bed. A caning was an adult's prerogative, but not something as terrifying as what they had seen, the baptism in the room that glared with incandescent light and green tiles.

Someone should sneak her some food. Not fair that she miss lunch, too, denied that. An armistice existed that morning between Antoinette and her gang, and Catherine's tribe. This was too big. It was decided that the master thief smuggle in a bit of makan. Who better than Catherine?

She tiptoed up the back steps while children finished lunch and entered the courtyard, where the talk was not of play, or of dreams, or even of food, but of the girl still banished to the bed in the dormitory. They would distract the nuns if need be. A staged fight or the like. That always brought the nuns. Anything to let Catherine accomplish her mission.

Soft, midday light comfortably filled the room though the shutters were half closed. As with every covert enterprise, Catherine entered the room slowly and deliberately, watchful for nuns, and suddenly aware that she really had not prepared an excuse or had an explanation in mind if she were to be intercepted.

The girl was still burrowed under the pastel yellow sheet, so thin an armor to deflect the indiscriminate arrows snapped from the bows of God's chosen archers. Catherine approached, speaking in whispers, knowing how even the sound of a voice could break a porcelain spirit. "Hey. It's me. Cat."

There was no response. The girl refused to move. Catherine continued to coax her. "I brought you some food, and some tea. We stole mooncakes from the table of Mother Superior for you."

Catherine sat on the little cot across from her. The ordeal must have been exhausting, for she still slept. Catherine reached gently, almost maternally, for the hub of a shoulder curled tightly against a cheek, and prodded her once, twice, to draw her gently from her sleep. Not harshly, not brutally, like the nuns, but gently from her sleep.

But she was not asleep.

Luka was dead.

Chapter Nineteen

The Mother Superior, who had of course, never been a mother, sat upon the corner of the stage on the lone chair that had been provided for her. She felt compelled to call this special assembly, even at the expense of disrupting the daily routine that gave order to the lives not only of the children (eighty-three, at last count, the number having been deleted by one due to that unfortunate accident) but to the Sisters as well.

There was nothing at all foreboding about the room. In fact, it was quite pleasant. It had a very high ceiling, and was the only room equipped with ceiling fans to move air made stale by the presence of so many people. Two sets of double doors opened to the courtyard, but in addition to that there was a stage entrance that opened directly to the outside, plus a few doors that led to minor offices and storage rooms, and from there to the inner labyrinth of the Sisters' private quarters.

It had been the intention of the British who designed the complex that this be a recital hall, and the comfort was only compromised by the hard wooden benches, pews really, directed to the stage, now occupied by a motionless Mother Superior.

By her side was a lectern, and behind her was a piano, black and white like the habit of a nun, and rarely in tune.

Sister Gertrude and Masselin herded in the last of the girls, who knew well enough to stop being girlish once they entered the room and could see the static violence that awaited them on the stage. The Reverend Mother said nothing. She had not yet cause to speak, and she knew it would be enough for the girls to see her with her hands folded in her lap, holding a flat, yellow ruler. Her scepter.

Doors closed behind them, mocking thunder, and the woman on the stage had yet to even blink. Her eyes were black. All the kinder colors were already taken, and black was all that was left. Her skin was a chalky white. Layers of dust had fallen and stratified over her skin in her continuum of sleep, and she examined the wrinkled archaeology of her face daily. God, her lover and husband, had long ago become bored with her, preferring the younger Sisters in his harem. Her marriage was a failure, leaving her terribly disillusioned. It was only the unfair secession of her youth that caused His eye to wander. Upon her shoulders fell, like a guillotine, the daily burden of keeping up appearances of fidelity.

An assembly called by Mother Superior was rarely a pleasant event, but Catherine was relieved to have been called indoors. Posted on the door at eye-level to the girls was a list of all who had failed the math test, and Catherine's name was inked upon it, inviting ridicule from the taunting children, whose numbers and whose cruelty was overwhelming for her. A few of her closer friends said nothing, but none were brave enough to give her any comfort or support.

Even Fin avoided her sister and was not strong enough to defend her against the endless teasing of her peers. Those (and there were many) who had a genuine dislike of Catherine had free rein to trample her vulnerable, little-girl's spirit, without reprisal from the Sisters. They wasted no time in humiliating her in the exact manner calculated by the nuns. "A *zero* on your math? You're so stupid."

She had answered not a single question correctly on the exam earlier in the day. In fact, pencil had scarcely touched paper. She could think only of Luka, whose vacant seat sobbed all during class.

Through the palms and feet of the paper— they pinned her test to her blouse— a bleeding red crayon announced the score.

Even those for whom she had stolen food showed no mercy. It was so rare that the nuns would hint at affection for any of them. Here was an opportunity to gain their approval, simply by betraying Catherine and joining in her condemnation, which the nuns instigated and encouraged. To share the commonality of indignation and contempt. Like Nestor betraying Catherine to win the approval of his mother, Joyce. Like Joyce betraying Catherine to win the approval of her own mother, Sarafina. "You are so stupid," chided the faithful.

There seemed to be such delight on the faces of all the children who ripped at her spirit. She would have much preferred a caning, and then realized that would probably come later in the day, anyway. Her resistance weakened. *I must be stupid,* she began thinking to herself.

Now, in the presence of Mother Superior, no one dared speak.

Catherine hid herself as best she could in the rear of the auditorium, trying to make herself smaller and smaller, her arms folded over the humiliating test that invited so much pain. *If only I could be so small that no one could see me.* Everyone around her became taller and taller, but at least they were no longer looking at her, or saying those things about her.

Mother Superior drew in a deep breath, the first, it seemed, since she had been up on the stage. She sucked in light and spirit, and exhaled darkness over the apprehensive audience of young girls, who submitted to her their full attention. Blurred in the smoke of her own exhaled breath, their fear looked something like respect to her, respect for her authority.

She began to speak, words excavated from within the cavern of her chest like granite stones and falling on the stage and upon the girls who shuddered as every syllable hit the floor. "I am told by the Sisters that some of you have not been doing your work." She paused long enough to give each child the opportunity to envision that she was speaking directly to them. "In particular, some of you have not been doing your studies." Again she paused, as her wrath began to have focus. Some of the girls began to feel relief. If this was her purpose, they had passed their exams and were not this morning's target.

"I am going to call the names of those girls who did the worst jobs on their tests. You will join me on stage when you hear your name called."

But by now Catherine could hear nothing. She was in the vast pineapple fields, in tall, soft green grass, lying on her back with Tippy, watching clouds swirl by. "Agnes." The first girl was called. "Antointette." Mother Superior hesitated long enough between each name so each girl who stood would have an agonizing moment to reach the stage, and be the full focus of everyone's attention. Each girl was tearful, and, like Catherine, had their tests pinned to their blouses with the score written upon it with a red crayon.

"Sylvia." The roll continued. Eleanor. Mary.

"And, of course, Catherine." It was no coincidence that she called Catherine last. She wanted to prolong the tension of Catherine waiting for her name to be called, wondering if she would be next.

"Catherine." She repeated herself, half pleased that Catherine was proving herself difficult.

But Catherine was elsewhere. She was high upon her grandfather's shoulders, with monkey rain spilling all around her.

"Catherine D'Cruz."

Sister Masselin came to the aisle behind her and reached up and yanked her from her grandfather's shoulders, and Catherine fell crashing to the hard wooden floor of the assembly hall.

"Catherine D'Cruz ... get up here ... *at once.*"

Catherine picked herself up off the floor, and all the girls had turned in their seats to see her stand. She was still confused about where she was, and who all these faces were staring at her. Mother Superior, who had been coiled upon her wooden seat stood and took a step forward, and Catherine knew exactly where she was, the place to which she had returned.

She was again tearful, and she approached the stage, under the merciless eyes of the Mother Superior.

They saw Catherine cry, broken. Astonishing.

Mother Superior, whose arid face was so dry that her lips would crack had she not continuously moistened them with her tongue, hissed as Catherine passed to take her place at the end of the line and stood at attention with the other girls, facing the audience.

"These girls," began Mother Superior, "*these* girls have been especially bad."

Bad, the girls had learned over the course of the time, meant disobedient. *Bad* meant playful. *Bad* meant girlish. *But* mostly what they learned was that bad meant Catherine, the rebellious one.

And now Catherine was going to get what she deserved.

"You are so *stupid*. All of you." She looked down the row of repentant children. "Girls," she said, addressing the audience once more, "you do not want to be like *these* girls." She procrastinated, to give everyone time to agree, as she pointed to the failures on the stage with a ruler that measured only the depth of violence when brandished by Mother Superior.

"*These* girls," she continued, "have neglected their studies."

Everyone was waiting for her to finish speaking, and just get on with it.

"Agnes." The girl shuddered as her name was called. "A *zero* on your math."

Agnes could not look up, could not look at the faces of all the girls staring at her. She was crying and all she could think about was that she had better not wet herself in front of everyone.

"Hold out your hands."

Agnes fearfully complied.

"No, no. Knuckles up."

No sooner had Agnes turned her hands than the swift yellow ruler came rapping down across her knuckles, and the trickle of tears gave way to a flood of tears, as the pain traveled up her hands all the way to her chest.

"Sit down."

Agnes vacated the stage, almost stumbling to her seat, her eyes blurred with tears, and she was unable to look up at any of those who had seen and been part of her humiliation.

"Antoinette," said the Mother Superior, moving down the line to her next victim. "You, too. A *zero*."

Antoinette did not wait to be told. She had been through this ritual before, and knew it was better to get it over quickly. She extended her hands and gritted her teeth. Her reputation was at stake. She would do this more bravely than any of them. Her face would betray no pain. Her eyes would produce no tear. Nor would she even blink. Swiftly and hard snapped the brittle little ruler, leaving her knuckles raw with the first crack, bleeding with the second. She took her punishment, and returned to her seat, satisfied with her courage, and wondering immediately how Catherine would fare.

But Sylvia was not so brave.

"Sylvia."

And as her name was called, she began sobbing uncontrollably, almost hysterically. "No, no. Please don't. I'll try harder."

Mother Superior was delighted. She grabbed the young girl's hand and whacked her twice on each hand, making her knuckles bleed, and horrifying the breathless audience, which had never quite learned to become numb at these assemblies.

Mother Superior's momentum and wrath grew stronger as she moved down the line, feeding off the pain she created, growing stronger from it.

"Eleanor."

Eleanor was catatonic. She, too, knew the ritual, and knew it was inescapable. She knew it when she took her test. She knew it when it was returned, with a zero scrawled upon it. She knew it when the test was pinned to her blouse and was cast out to fend for herself among her depraved peers. Eleanor simply submitted, closed her eyes, and silently took a rap upon each hand and returned to her seat, not really feeling pain until moments later, when her smoldering little fingers turned to flame before her very eyes.

Mary was quite different.

Mary had been freshly orphaned. There was nothing spectacular about the death of her mother whose husband had long ago abandoned her. Just a consequence of poverty. Mary was only seven, and until she had been turned over to the Sisters thought that cruelty in the world was something from which adults protected you. She had never imagined they were its source. It was her first assembly.

"Mary," began Mother Superior, "Who told you to get a *zero* on your math test?"

Mary had never taken a math test before. She wanted to explain, thinking she might be shown some mercy, but she was too petrified to speak or even move.

"Who told you? Who?"

Mary was frozen. She was only vaguely aware that Mother Superior had pulled her hands from her side, but when she saw the ruler about to strike, she quickly awakened and pulled back her hands, and made an impulsive rush and leaped from the stage and ran.

Sister Masselin caught her in the aisle, and the girl was small enough that, despite her attempts to kick and scratch, the Sister had little trouble carrying her back on the stage, where Mother Superior was drooling with anger.

While Sister Masselin held her wrists, Mother Superior slapped repeatedly until the knuckles were bruised and bleeding. Sister Masselin, herself excited by the frenzy, carried the young girl to her seat, and dumped her like a gunnysack of rice.

And that left Catherine on the stage, alone.

The Mother Superior had saved her best pleasure for last. Mother Superior, in her long, black cloak, stood herself behind Catherine, whom at last, after months of effort, she had broken. It was evident by her tears. It was evident because she could not bring herself to look into any of the spellbound eyes upon her. "This one is the real culprit. *Isn't it so*, girls?" They all trembled as one. "This little thief. This saboteur." She drew her words from her mouth as if from a scabbard. "This girl," she said. "This girl," she said again. "You do not want to be anything like her. This *stupid* girl."

She paused, postponing climax, prolonging her pleasure.

"Perhaps if you had spent more time studying and less time stealing ... Oh yes. I know all about it ... you might not have gotten a zero on your numbers test." She slithered in front of Catherine now and lowered her face for a more intimidating glare. Her dead breath blew across Catherine's face.

"Catherine D'Cruz ..." she said, and then she turned slyly to the captive children. "Or should I say, Catherine *Tikus* ... Catherine the rat?"

She redirected her gaze back upon Catherine, who was sobbing with this added humiliation. It was a nickname the girls had given her very early on in her residence there, the Malay word for *rat* pronounced very much like her last name.

"Oh, yes," said the Reverend Mother. "I know that's what they call you."

Mother Superior stood fully erect before Catherine now, perhaps three feet before her, her black wimple spread around her face like the hood of a cobra, ready to strike. "Catherine Tikus ... put out your hands ..." Her command, her commandment, thundered.

Catherine was almost motionless.

But she had stopped crying.

She lifted what had been a shameful gaze from the floor, following the black folds of the woman coiled before her, upward, until she locked into those serpentine eyes. "Catherine Tikus ... put out your hands."

But Catherine heard a different voice. *Someday, I will teach you how to do it. You have to know when to strike.*

"... NOW, Catherine," said her grandfather.

For a fraction of a moment, Mother Superior became paralyzed by the crippling intent of Catherine's eyes, and in that moment, the time to strike had come.

Catherine leaped up, clear off the floor, as high as her grandfather, and grabbed the cobra by the head, grabbed the insidious wimple and lurched it from the head of Mother Superior, crushed it to death in her hands, beat it to death on the chair, trampled it to death on the floor, and a completely immobilized Mother Superior watched on in horror, her face, colorless for centuries, turning blood red, as she reached in disbelief to find her shaved, vulgar head, uncovered and wrinkled, and humiliating in front of the entire assembly of girls and of Sisters.

She was hideous.

She looked out at the jury of faces, suddenly so naked, suddenly so vulnerable, suddenly so ... powerless. The girls new it instantly. *My God, what had Catherine done?*

Someone started to laugh. Everyone started to laugh. Mother Superior was still in shock, holding her hands over her naked head, all composure lost, and she ran off the stage and unbolted the double doors, running in disgrace to her private chambers, smoke trailing behind her.

All this in the time it took to breathe a single breath.

The children watched Mother Superior stumbling through the upper terrace, and then turned to see Catherine breathing deeply, and triumphantly upon the stage.

Sister Masselin slammed the doors, the concussion having the stark finality of a gavel that smashes any hope from the air in a courtroom of the condemned, and the girls were instantly silent. They turned slowly in their seats, until all eyes were upon Sister Masselin. She had managed to shut the door before all the evil had made its retreat.

She sharpened her dagger stare at the girl upon the stage, intending fear, but Catherine was beyond the threshold of fear, and felt only the exhilaration of outrage.

Catherine easily deflected the blade of contempt hurled by the Sister who barred the door. She ripped the telltale math test from her jersey and crumpled it in her hands into nothing.

"I am *not* stupid," she said, with invigorated defiance.

"Get her," ordered Sister Masselin, with invigorated disdain.

Sister Gertrude and Sister Beatrice overcame their shock and rushed the stage. Catherine seized and threw the single chair, catching Sister Gertrude effectively on the jaw and knocking her off her feet into the aisle where her fall tripped Sister Masselin who had come running from the rear of the auditorium.

Sister Beatrice pressed on, tripping but catching herself as she scaled the steps to the stage, but as she charged, Catherine sent the lectern, too heavy to lift, crashing in her path, and she, too, tripped, leaving Catherine free to run past her and try the first of several stage doors, before finding one ajar, the other three nuns in attendance distracted, though only for a moment, with the fallen Sisters and with the children who were now explosive in their seats and in the aisles and adding to the spontaneous combustion of the moment.

Sister Masselin was barely audible as she called for order, and there was none to be had. Several of the girls, frightened by the escalating terrors, ran for the door, now unattended, and burst their way clear, and spilled into the courtyard.

With the doors open, others followed, some rushing through the aisles, some climbing over the pews. Someone, an anonymous ally, cried "Fire!" and with this added panic Catherine was able to get through a door that entered into a long hallway before the nuns could catch up with her. But it was *not* an anonymous ally. It was a reliable enemy, Antoinette, with a spontaneous impulse to charity she could not explain to herself.

Other of the Sisters, who had not been in attendance, could hear the commotion and stepped into the hallway to investigate, turning to stone to see Catherine running towards them.

She made no efforts to dodge them, and she became more powerful with each step. She plowed through Sister Marcella, who she left rolling on the floor with the wind knocked out of her.

She did not look behind her to see the tidal wave of black with white crests building behind them, and as she passed each crucifix and icon of their faith, either on a pedestal, or in a niche in the wall, she sent it crashing to the floor.

It was purely an eruption of anger, not a spontaneous strategy of escape, but it slowed down the force waiting to overwhelm her, as each of the nuns, comically, stopped to bless themselves as they passed each fallen Christ or prostrate Virgin Mary.

The door at the end of the corridor was open and led to the lower terrace and gardens. Catherine was through it and slammed it shut behind her, but the fury of the impact sprung it open again as Catherine charged ahead, still no plan in mind, and only the raw instinct of flight to propel her.

The nuns were now in force as Catherine realized that avenues of escapes were becoming fewer. She could hear the nuns clattering behind her, and found the door to the kitchen, which had a rear exit, was open.

She lost little momentum and ran inside, startling the cook, who had no idea what was happening. As she passed a table her right hand instinctively grabbed a butcher knife, and she was out the back door before the cook could recover from his astonishment.

Nuns in crude-oil black flooded the kitchen, the wet floor taking another casualty, but three or four of them passed through the back door, unaware that Catherine now had a knife. They pursued her under the colonnade, and Catherine took a confused turn that led her into an exit-less alcove, occupied by the tortured replica of the man they loved so much, miniaturized like the trophies of Jon the Poet, but grotesquely nailed to wooden boards. Sister Masselin's favorite cat was awakened from a curled sleep on the bench, fat with food from the kitchen that never made it to the orphans.

Catherine turned to retreat, but it was too late. The nuns had rounded the corner, and their numbers were swelling.

But they stopped short, as they saw Catherine brandishing a knife, made more grisly by the fact that it still had blood upon it from a chicken slaughtered in the kitchen. Sister Masselin caught up with the rest of the Sisters.

"Catherine. You evil girl. Put it down."

Catherine was poised, and ready to strike. "Go chew your balls," she said. "You *whores*." The word still held no meaning, but Catherine knew it held power. She whispered the word to amplify the vulgar shape of its sound.

The cat, of course, so abruptly awakened from its nap, and having nowhere to run, did as Catherine did, made herself taller, and hissed. Catherine could see it, Sister Masselin's pet, from the corner of her eye.

As the nuns inched their way in upon her, Catherine snatched the cat by the nape of its neck, and, before the disbelieving nuns, slit its throat.

They scattered as she threw the dying animal in their direction, and Catherine flew through the void they made, renewing the chase that could have but one conclusion.

Catherine ran through the archway into the garden shrine dedicated to the Virgin Mary, whose statue stood placidly in the center of the lawn. From here there was no exit, but the wall in the back was only as high as the wall to her grandmother's estate, which Catherine had learned to scale when she was only half her present size.

If she could make it to the wall, she might actually do it, she might escape. Over the wall she could run down into the street that led to the city, or over the hill and quickly be lost in jungle where they could never find her. Like her mother had done.

Disastrously the two gardeners and their shepherd dog stood directly in her way. She hesitated beneath the statue, and turned to make a retreat, but the nuns, in force, had recovered, and now blocked her only exit.

They shouted something to the gardeners. The circle around her became smaller and smaller, but it moved cautiously, she still had the knife.

Her back was against the pedestal, cornered truly like a rat. In the instant that she realized there was to be no escape, Catherine Tikus decided to take one more victim. With a burst of energy far in excess of a ten-year-old girl's capacity, she toppled the poured concrete statue of the Virgin Mary.

It did not shatter, but fell humiliated head first, puncturing the thin layer of green grass, parting the skin of the earth for a glimpse into the Hell just barely below the manicured surface.

Catherine was satisfied with her triumph, and waited, knife in hand, for the first one brave enough to take her on.

It was the dog.

He leaped at her upon command. She turned to catch it in mid-air, and as it fell upon her, its weight fell upon the blade.

It took Catherine to the ground with him, and the gardeners wrestled the knife away from her, before she could retrieve it from the depths of the dog's convulsing body.

But it was not the gardeners who beat her into oblivion.

It was the Sisters of the Most Holy Order of the Infant Jesus.

Chapter Twenty

The portrait of Catherine's pain was painted in red upon the cold, gray stone floor in the cellar of the convent, where she had been deposited to repent and recover, in that order. She was lying face down where she had been dropped, and upon a tenuous awakening made a valorous effort to draw her body into an instinctive fetal position.

This she could not do.

Her disobedient body had been beaten so badly that any movement brought new punishment. Her eyes were swollen shut, and the throbbing in her head was agonized by even the gentle pulse of her blood. If she could only stop her heart from beating, she thought, she could stop the pain.

She had no way of knowing how long she had been there, but her eyes were, in addition to being swollen, caked shut with her own blood. It was too soon to make an effort to open them.

Though her anger had delivered her from humiliation, it provided her no comfort now. She needed strength of a different kind. Some way to bear this pain.

By sheer willpower she forced herself to think of more pleasant times. Ripe durian fruit. Mangoes. Climbing trees. Che' Wan. What was it she had said? She couldn't remember. No matter. It was enough to see her face, and imagine her voice. Imagine her touch. Her motherly touch. *Momma? Where are you? Are you in Singapore? Momma, look what they did to me.* A memory, jarred loose, her father, beating her mother in Singapore. *Why, Papa? I can't remember. Why? Georgie. Yes, that was it. Georgie. Momma?* "Your father sold him to clear off a gambling debt." *Che' Wan? Where are you? Che' Wan, help me. All the wonderful food. Oh yes, I like to dance. Tippy, come, please. Tippy would not like it here. Tippy would not like it here. Tippy? Is that you? GET AWAY, LEAVE ME ALONE, UNCLE."* Joseph. Where have you been? You should be in the fields." *Fin, look out. Grandma got a knife. Tippy, is that you? I am not stupid. Was Georgie my big brother, Momma? I'm so high. I'm so high, Grandpa ...* "Tippy, is that you?"

"Who is Tippy?"

Catherine at first did not recognize the voice.

"Who is Tippy?" It was Sister Marcella, sent down to assess the damage. Three days had passed, most of it without movement and only the frailest signs of life. The delirium was probably a hopeful sign. The death of an orphan was one thing; no one on the outside really cared. No questions to answer, not even a need to falsify any documents.

But this could be different. This could be difficult. This would at the very least involve an investigation, and besides, it exceeded even the mandate given by Sarafina Madrigal D'Cruz. This would not do at all.

Sister Marcella had brought water, both to drink and to begin, three days after the fact, to clean wounds that for the most part had already scabbed over. She took a clean rag, dipped it in the drinking water, and placed it to Catherine's lips, the first water in three days. She sucked gently and swallowed, her throat at first hurting for the effort it made, but resilient as the water trickled through her lips.

Catherine still had not moved. Sister Marcella came from behind her, and delicately turned her over, still uncertain if they had broken any of her bones in the frenzy of kicking and scratching and punching on that hideous day of Catherine's wickedness.

The only light came from the hallway, the door to the cell left open as Sister Marcella entered. She cradled Catherine's head in her lap, and she could see the girl wincing in pain with the movement, and Sister Marcella wept. The compassion was certainly a betrayal of Mother Superior, and it was an emotion with which Sister Marcella was not entirely comfortable. It was also likely, she reasoned, that it was out of place, inappropriate for a ten-year-old so evil. Maybe even possessed. Still, she wasn't sure what she felt, confused with her feelings.

Dry, brown blood covered the girl's skin. Sister Marcella dampened the cloth and cleaned off the tortured face in her lap as best she could, rendering it only slightly less hideous. The girl's eyes were black and blue, and her lips distended and blistered. But the scratches upon her face were only superficial, and even at this early stage of her healing it was clear the face would not be disfigured, and the broken teeth were the last expendable teeth of her childhood.

Catherine slept once more, while evidence of violence was cleaned off the floor, and her clothes were cut from her body and taken out and burned. Sister Marcella had hoped that someone else would have been given the duty to see to Catherine's rehabilitation, but she was nevertheless determined to do her duty well. She had a cot brought from the infirmary on which she laid her patient, and a rocking chair and small table for her own comfort. She drank tea intended for Catherine and listened intently to the rambling words escaping from Catherine's delirium, easier to understand as the swelling in her lips receded.

It had been very dark, those many months ago, when Marcella's tryst with Sister Gertrude had been interrupted by a young girl in search of a short cut to the kitchen. It had been Sister Gertrude who noticed and scolded the girl, Gertrude whose husky voice was easily recognizable. But in that confusing blur of blankets, had Catherine recognized her, as well? Sister Marcella had no way of knowing, and nothing about Catherine's demeanor the following morning hinted that she knew.

But of the many startling revelations that escaped during Catherine's fevered healing, there was nothing about the night that Sister Marcella could only hope made no lasting impact on its accidental witness.

Be that as it may, the time passed no less slowly for Sister Marcella than it did for the girl whose recovery was placed in her care, as she wondered how much Catherine had seen and remembered.

On the fifth day the fever cooled, the fire extinguished not so much by the occasional damp cloth upon her forehead, but because there was nothing left to burn.

Her pain now had a certain symmetry to it. Its sharp edges had been smoothed and dulled, like pebbles in a stream, so that no particular part of her wounded body screamed more loudly than any other. From her lips came the first word that indicated that Catherine's meandering sense of awareness had come to nest in the present, "Water."

Sister Marcella put down her morning paper, which had shaded Catherine from the stark light of a single bulb hung outside the little storage room designated for her recovery, distinguishable from a cave only by its hard angles and water pipes overhead but having all the other qualities of gloom.

Catherine could hear the sound of water poured from an urn into a tin cup, splashing like a waterfall, the sound throbbing in her head. It was clear she could not yet sit up, and Sister Marcella lifted her gently, if not carefully, from behind, and held the cup to her lips. Catherine was able not only to swallow, but to hold the cup by herself. And then, tentatively at first, opened eyes whose last conscious vision had been the crushing descent of the heel of a shoe.

The feel of the womanly body behind her, so warm and so soft, was the only human touch she could recall that was not an expression of violence. Except for

Grandpa. Except for Che' Wan. Except for her mother, so very, very long ago. Touch meant slapping. Touch meant a caning. Touch meant wrestling with orphans and biting and scratching. Touch meant a brush angrily drawn through tangled hair by a resentful Auntie Joyce. Touch meant the clumsy groping of Uncle Joe, whose face was so hard and so mean and smelling so strongly of cigarettes.

The stark light produced a pain of its own, now directly upon her face. She closed her eyes against it with only minimal discomfort, the swelling having gone down, and she was content to absorb the unfamiliar sensation of being nested in a woman's lap in the dark.

For Sister Marcella, too, it was strange bonding. Could this be the same child who had so cruelly slashed the cat, so viciously killed the German Shepherd? Could she be the demon that Mother Superior declared she truly was? How could one so frail have done those evil things, and have been so powerful to topple the statute from its pedestal, if not possessed?

And this was the same child, Sister Marcella reminded herself, who was the lone witness to evidence of her own evil, the one who could possibly incriminate her? She had found herself, earlier, at least, hoping for Catherine's death, though not bold enough to pray for it to happen. To pray for her death would require her to explain to God why she wanted the girl dead, and this she could not do.

Now, this human touch contradicted everything. She found herself wanting Catherine to live and had become genuinely determined to care for her. Later, she allowed herself to speculate, she might even show her Christ's love.

"Are you ready for some tea?" she asked.

It was easier to speak than to nod her head. "Yes, please."

Sister Marcella let the girl down gently, and in the absence of any pillows, maneuvered a spare blanket against the wall to give Catherine something to lean against if she was able to sit up. It proved to be still a bit early for that, and Sister Marcella once again cradled the girl in her lap, giving her nourishment like a mother bird. Later, there would be a bit of bread to dip in the tea, and after that a very weak rice porridge, boiled in a bit of chicken broth.

For her exertion, Catherine fell into sleep once again, but this time falling like a feather, gently and without resistance.

Mother Superior was anxious for Catherine to be in good health, once more, so that she herself could administer a proper caning. As the days had gone by, Sister Marcella began to question the wisdom of such an intent. She began to have other plans for Catherine, who slept between feedings, who in sleep went searching for the vitality of spirit that had abandoned her body. Could it be possible, Sister Marcella began to wonder, that the caning had nothing to do with either discipline or a mandate from God to punish the wicked? Could it be possible that the caning Mother Superior was so urgent to administer was something as basic as revenge?

These thoughts disturbed Sister Marcella, freshly twenty years old, and not yet as devout as she was told that she would become.

Catherine was awakened by the sweet, sweet voice of her best friend in the world, whispering her name into her ear. "Cat? Cat, it's me."

"Tippy, is that you?"

"Ssshhh, ssshhh. She'll hear you ... of course it's me."

Sister Marcella heard nothing.

"What have they done to you."

Catherine, who remained in the amnesty of sleep, told Tippy of the horrible beating of the week before. "But you should have seen Mother Superior. It was worth it."

"Catherine," said Tippy, telling her what she obviously had not yet discovered, "they've cut your hair."

At this Catherine woke up abruptly, all amnesty rescinded, startling Sister Marcella, and she groped for her hair, feeling nothing but ... despair. There was nothing there. Her head was bare, shorn by the nuns. Momentarily, empowered by the shock of revelation, she was able to sit up, as Sister Marcella maneuvered for a closer look at the girl with whom she had been so constant for the past few days.

Catherine couldn't believe it and looked about the room before realizing how absurd it was to think she would find a mirror to confirm the traitorous news of her fingers. Her hair was gone. Tippy vanished.

Sister Marcella easily interpreted her dismay. "Lice," she lied. Sister Masselin herself had extracted further revenge upon the girl shortly after she had been beaten into unconsciousness, brutally wielding shears and then a razor, her angered hands quivering with desire to do greater harm.

Catherine was resolved not to cry. Not here, not in front of the nuns ever again. Che' Wan whispered encouragement faintly in her ear, "... Be strong."

Catherine looked at Sister Marcella, in black and white. One of *them*. "I am not stupid," she said slowly, deliberately, dispassionately.

Sister Marcella trembled. She quickly needed a response to assure herself that she was not afraid, for she had expected Catherine's first words to reflect contrition. "Of course, you're not." It was clear this one still had a defiant streak in her, and if Catherine's statement was meant to be a challenge, Sister Marcella was not up to it. All of the nuns had been horrified by Catherine on that violent afternoon, and Sister Marcella was not about to instigate new fury by contradicting her.

Catherine studied Sister Marcella cautiously. Catherine had raided the barbarian territories of pain and despair, and returned alive, wounded but intact. For this her laurel was a new sense of confidence. She had been brave. She was now determined to compliment this freshly sprouted virtue with cunning. She could sense that Sister Marcella was afraid of her, and that fear made her less formidable. Catherine tested her new power. "I'm hungry," she said.

Sister Marcella dismissed herself to go to the kitchen, strangely aware that Catherine had changed, but not in ways at all anticipated. She didn't quite know what to make of it, but on her way to the kitchen realized that 'I'm hungry' was not the plaintive begging of one who had been broken.

It had been an order.

Catherine was alone now in her cell. The door had been left open. Apparently, it was obvious to Sister Marcella that Catherine did not have the strength yet to walk, at least not without the help of her demons. Sister Marcella felt no need to bar the door, though would later be admonished by Sister Masselin and Mother Superior for such a neglectful oversight.

Certainly, confinement had as much to do with punishment as with healing. *No matter,* thought Catherine. *I will become strong again.* She surveyed her small room, her accustomed eyes no longer pierced by the sharp edges of light of the single bulb that hung from its braided wire outside her door.

She knew this room.

When she had been insolent, it was here she had been taken and left isolated. When her fingernails were not quite clean enough, it was here she was to contemplate the virtues of cleanliness. And when "7 times 4" was 32, it was here she was sent to master her multiplication tables. Always in the dark. Always by herself. Always alone.

But not quite.

Completely unbeknown to the nuns, Catherine had managed to smuggle in her friend Tippy. Tippy was always there for her. Tippy was the one friend that Catherine could rely upon, who never teased, who never humiliated, who never hurt her.

And one day, after a customary caning when Catherine had been thrust into the familiar cell for infractions she could not even recall, Tippy had a surprise for her.

Michael.

And Karen.

And Angelica.

And there were others. Tippy brought her many playmates, and she swore to Catherine that they would *never*, never, let her be alone in that dark cell again. They would play for hours together, eating durian and mangoes, and climbing trees. Being tigers in the tall grass. Stealing pineapples from the cart. Eating roasted peanuts while watching the wayang puppets in the kampong. Having teatime together as rain pelted the zinc roofs outside their pretty little houses, like proper English ladies and gentlemen.

Soon after Sister Marcella left for the kitchen, Tippy merrily reappeared at the door, come for a visit with her best friend.

"Hi, Cat."

"Tippy. Where have you been? I've been waiting for you."

"Yes. I know, I know," said Tippy, a bit ashamed that she had kept Catherine waiting so long. "I've brought Michael with me," she added, thinking the news would cheer her up.

Michael appeared at the door, politely waiting to be invited in. Michael could be very shy and formal, at times. He was the tallest of her friends, and his form eclipsed the light bulb behind him, with light glowing from behind his head like a halo, like her grandfather against the sun.

"Look, Catherine," he said. "I've brought you a kite." And then, rather boastfully, he added, "I made it myself."

"Do come in. Do come in. Don't just stand there gawking."

Catherine poured her guests some tea. "Would you care for some cookies?" she asked. "They're fresh from the oven." She offered them on a serving dish from her finest China.

"Oh, thank you."

Catherine could see that they were each duly impressed with her cooking and her hospitality, and she, the hostess, began to blush.

"Catherine, that was really nasty what they did to you this time. And your hair," said Michael.

"Hush, Michael," interupted Tippy, knowing that Michael's innocent concern would nonetheless hurt the girl's feelings. "It will grow back in no time."

"Have you seen Fin?" inquired Catherine of her sibling.

Michael and Tippy looked at each other knowingly. "Yes," said Michael, reluctantly. "It's not good."

"Why, what is it?" asked Catherine, a sense of urgency in her voice.

"Well," struggled Michael, "it's like this. Fin is getting teased for being your sister. Some of the girls think it was really brave, what you did, but most of them are going along with what the Sisters tell them, that you're crazy."

"Tippy, what do you think? Am I crazy? Grandma says so, too."

Tippy looked admirably, lovingly, at her friend. "Catherine, you're the bravest girl I ever met."

Just then they could hear shuffling outside the door. Maggie, the deformed girl, had strayed from the big cellar room where she had spent and would continue to spend most of her life with the other similarly encumbered or even damaged children. She had a sense that someone else was in the catacombs, and her sense of curiosity was less ruined by accident of birth than her other limited abilities, and she gravitated towards Catherine's cell, where now she stood, in the doorway.

"Who are you?" asked Michael. But Maggie heard only Catherine's voice and saw no one but an almost skeletal girl recuperating under a thin sheet in which her undernourished body appeared to be little more than a wrinkle.

Maggie smiled.

She liked Catherine. She could not understand why Catherine got afraid when they slept together some nights, or why she wept so, sometimes throughout the entire night till morning.

"That's Maggie," whispered Tippy. "She lives here, in the basement."

"Poor thing," said Michael. Her round, cherubic face looked somehow different from other children he had seen, almost as if it were not fully formed, but it didn't seem to matter to him, or frighten him as it did Catherine and all the other orphans. "Can she come in?" he asked of Catherine.

Catherine was reluctant to let the girl enter.

In a creative effort to balance the assortment of punishments deemed necessary to discipline Catherine, one of the nuns casually suggested she be compelled to share the bed with Maggie, in the basement. Everyone knew that the crazy girls in the basement had been cursed. That's why they were that way. They must have been very, very bad, to have God punish them like that. Catherine was no less superstitious or fearful than the others when it came to this, and the nuns exploited that fear to gain a little obedience, which Catherine was always so reluctant to demonstrate. "…. Catherine. You will now (clean up this mess … stop the chatter … pay attention to the discussion … clear the table …) or you will sleep the night with Maggie."

And now the insouciant Maggie stood at the door, wondering if she, too, would get an invitation to enter. But while Catherine and her guests deliberated on whether or not to include the girl who stood grinning in the doorway, her silhouette was suddenly overtaken by three black clouds that obliterated the scant light of the single bulb.

Sister Marcella, to the left. Sister Masselin to the right. And looming behind them, the figure of Mother Superior, come to reclaim her face.

"Take Maggie back where she belongs," she ordered. Sister Marcella knew the remark was intended for her, and not Sister Masselin, though Mother Superior never wavered from her sizzling stare upon the girl who had brought her down, and now lay, depleted, on the meager cot before her. Sister Marcella was relieved to be excused. She had been intercepted on her way to the kitchen by Sister Masselin, who inquired about Catherine's progress, and only with reluctance did Sister Marcella admit that the girl was now conscious.

Sister Marcella, plagued with mutinous thoughts, had decided she wanted no part of this.

With the intrusion of the nuns, Tippy and Michael moved unobserved to the seclusion of the shadows. Sister Masselin came in, leaving the frame of the Reverend Mother in the doorway, where her true size was unknowable, but huge, cloaked in black.

She stepped inside, in her hand a bamboo cane, serrated at the tip.

Catherine could hear Tippy gasp.

Mother Superior dispensed with any of the preliminaries. "Turn her over."

Sister Masselin abruptly yanked the cot so that she could hold Catherine down at the head of the bed, and Mother Superior pulled the blanket to the floor, and tore the scant bed clothes from Catherine's back, leaving her completely exposed to the impending sting of retribution.

"You little … bitch."

As Sister Masselin held her tiny wrists, Mother Superior began to beat the girl, whipping her shoulders, her back, and on her buttocks, and upon her legs. Anywhere there was flesh. She didn't even see the girl—she saw only the moment of her own humiliation on the stage. Her momentum began to build, each stroke more violent, more vengeful, than the one that preceded it, the rage feeding on its own fire. And then, suddenly, halfway through an undelivered stroke, Mother Superior stopped.

Why was there no sound? No cries of pain, and no movement?

"Is she *dead*?" she asked in horror.

"... No ..." But even the simple answer contained its own horror. The young girl was staring at Sister Masselin with eyes that felt no pain. Not only had she learned to summon her friends, in the relentless proffering of violence and crises, to come to her aid, she had learned to take her fantasy one step further.

She could become one of them.

She could *be* Tippy. She could be Karen. She could be anyone of them she liked and avoid the brutality that had no other possible escape but death.

The girl turned her head over her shoulder to an absolutely astonished Mother Superior. Those vacant eyes. She now lashed at her impervious victim with fear and disbelief, though with no less fury than her anger-driven rage, and still, the face registered no pain.

For Catherine was not there. Catherine was in the pineapple fields, monkey rain spilling all around her, with Tippy. Free. Escaped. Beyond pain.

Michael, brave Michael, had chosen to take the beating for her.

Chapter Twenty-One

Catherine drifted for several days upon her cot, a raft in the dark waters of her cell. Sleep was only slightly more merciful than the nuns, spilling upon her in very small droplets from the damp pipes above that eventually found their way to the sewer. She could not lay upon her back, for several of the lashes from a frantic Mother Superior had broken the skin, which seemed to heal only with the greatest of reluctance, sandpapered raw again if she tried to position herself in any way but upon her stomach.

Sister Marcella would make frequent visits and would personally see to the food that was prepared for Catherine. She had done Catherine no harm, yet every time she opened the door, and the light from the hallway would sever the darkness, Catherine would cringe in anticipation of another beating. It would be almost a full week before she could differentiate between Sister Marcella and the nuns who had been so black and so white.

Sister Marcella entered the stale cell with a tray of rice, and chicken, and hot tea with the surprising inclusion of honey and milk. She justified it all to the kitchen staff by saying it was necessary in order to restore Catherine's health, not wishing to draw attention to her interest in the girl. Sister Marcella believed, long before there was Catherine, that it was virtuous to feel compassion for the poor, and the downtrodden, and the abused. It was, in fact, her better explanation to herself of why she had become a nun. Was it betrayal to feel benevolence for one so clearly condemned by all the other sisters of her faith? No incantation of her vows prepared her for such a dilemma.

As Sister Marcella, closer in age to Catherine than she was to either Sister Masselin or any of the other sisters for that matter, provided nourishment and comfort to Catherine, she began to feel a kinship which the sisterhood never provided, and which she so desperately sought. She had even submitted to the brutal desires of Sister Beatrice, when all she really wanted was to be held, the way she wanted to hold Catherine, the way she held Catherine, now.

She helped Catherine sit up and spoon-fed the girl. All the bruises seemed to be healing, and the open sores on her back, Mother Superior's personal contribution towards Catherine's education, had scabbed over. Sister Marcella had seen to it, with deft ability, that they had not become infected.

Catherine had become puzzled by Sister Marcella's interest in her. "Why are you helping me?" she asked, unable to conceal the suspicion in her voice.

Sister Marcella was not yet sure how to answer. She honestly did not know. Not yet anyway. And so, she gave the safest answer, which she hoped might turn out to be the truthful one. "Because this is what God wants me to do."

It did not satisfy Catherine, but it seemed to satisfy Sister Marcella, who was delighted to see Catherine eating the forbidden chicken and see her transformed when she sipped the tea and discovered it had been sweetened with milk and honey. It pleased her to think that her offering might bring a little joy into Catherine's dismal life.

Something truly remarkable was happening to Sister Marcella, and she had no one with whom to share the revelation that was now urging her reevaluation of her life and her purpose—Mother Superior was not an infallible agent of God.

This insight placed upon Sister Marcella a terrible burden. How could she convince God that her faith in him was unshaken while her faith in Mother Superior was eroding even more quickly than her respect for her? True, she still had fear of Catherine, but the fear was vacillating and no longer inspired by Mother Superior's condemnation of the girl.

As Sister Marcella had been returning on that awful day after Mother Superior and Sister Masselin had done their duty and were just vacating the cell, they seemed oblivious to her and she had to step out of the way of the nuns, who were shaking their heads in disbelief and contempt, and mumbling to themselves, leaving the aftermath of their tirade to her.

When Sister Marcella herself entered the little storage room, seeing Catherine, motionless, passive, indifferent to the newest rash of agony inflicted upon her, she could no longer accept that their victim deserved the punishment that Mother Superior felt too much delight in meting out.

She disbelieved, ultimately, that Catherine was possessed, as Mother Superior had said. She disbelieved that Catherine was the incarnation of evil, as Mother Superior had said. But mostly she disbelieved Mother Superior's parting words to Catherine, overheard as she was passed brusquely in the halls after that terrible caning. Mother Superior was wringing her hands with residue violence, as over her shoulder, justifying everything they had done to her, she said, spitting the words into the cell, "It's for your own good."

It was the fallacy of that one, simple statement, that made everything else unravel for Sister Marcella. It is what every child is told who is beaten. It is what she remembered being told by her very proper English parents. Sister Marcella believed them. Hearing these same words spill like acid or lye from Mother Superior brought to her the helpless moments of her own childhood, the spankings that somehow got out of control and became beatings. All, she was told, for her own good.

She could not even remember what she had done to inspire such wrath in her father, or such indifference from her mother, but the beatings administered by her father and endorsed (either encouraged, or ignored, she couldn't remember) by her mother seemed almost civil in comparison to what Catherine was enduring, all for her own good.

She was still frightened by Catherine, not because she feared a new eruption of violence (she was far too depleted to be a threat) but because she could hear Catherine, at times, talking in the darkness before she would enter with food, to inhabitants who seemed to populate the spirit world.

And yet, if Catherine were truly possessed, as Mother Superior had so adamantly declared, why was it that she herself could not feel the presence of evil as she cared for her flesh, the body that had suffered so much brutality, whose resilience was at last waning? Here was just a little girl on a cot. Clear distinctions between good and evil were becoming blurred and threatening the fragile order to her life.

She decided to keep these feelings very, very secret, until God Himself would show her some way out. She would administer to Catherine, with genuine affection, and pretend to her Mother Superior and to those sisters whose devotion had now become circumspect that she did it only as a matter of duty, and with no real passion. She would cunningly delete from her confessions any reference to this deceit, but in fairness to God would compensate him in the way he had come to expect from her—with aggressive and sincere self-flagellation, the way of the nuns.

And to the God that she had not yet come to doubt, in mutinous defiance to those on earth she had sworn to obey, she made a very private vow, and swore a very secret oath. Never, she resolved, never would she let the sisters, or even Mother Superior, beat her patient again ...

Sadly, the momentum of her determination did not carry her very far, as she rightly assessed how powerless she was to act upon her resolution and realized that the best she could do was to give some comfort, and maybe—covertly—even a little love.

Marcella, Sister Marcella of the Holy Order of the Infant Jesus had yet to find courage. But she had found compassion, and it was a good start ...

Chapter Twenty-Two

Sister Masselin herself would deliver the news to her old friend Sarafina about the brutal way Catherine had provoked and attacked the nuns, feeling that a letter alone could not fully express the dismay they all felt for Catherine's demonic behavior. Poor Sarafina. Disappointed by her own sons, and now this. Was there no end to the woman's suffering?

She found on the familiar verandah not Sarafina, but Joseph and Eric, smoking cigarettes in the shade of the zinc roof. Eric's first instinct, at her approach, was to toss his cigarette aside. But, then again, it was only Sister Masselin. He was quite comfortable where he sat, in his mother's rocker. Nevertheless, he stood as she neared the house. It was the polite thing to do, and though he could not part with his freshly lit cigarette, he held it discreetly off to the side.

"Good morning, Sister," he said, only slightly irritated by her visit.

"Good morning to you, Eric ... and to you, Joseph."

Hearing his name spoken required a little courtesy in response, and Joseph tossed his cigarette into the roses and stood, rising from the stoop that had recently become his territory. "And a good morning to you," he mumbled, coughing a bit as the words became entangled in the smoke he exhaled.

"And where is Kamille?" inquired the Sister.

The boys looked awkwardly at each other. Didn't she know? Apparently not. Eric volunteered, "Kamille ... isn't with us anymore." He realized as he spoke the words that what he said sounded like he was explaining someone's death, and he quickly clarified what he had been embarrassed to confess. "She doesn't work for us anymore."

Sister Masselin looked puzzled. She studied the boys. Boys. Grown men. Were they not yet thirty? At least. She had known them since their births, attended their confirmations. She took a few steps back. An idle broom was propped up against the banister, and it occurred to her that the long drive always so meticulously raked and free of leaves and fallen branches had somehow been neglected.

"And where is your mother?" she asked. The house behind them was without movement, or breath, or sound.

"She's gone to the kampong, with Joyce." It was probably Eric who answered, but Sister Masselin couldn't really distinguish which of them had spoken, distracted as she was by the haunting nature of the house before her, with its two ghosts in a cloud of smoke in attendance.

"Market day?"

"Oh, no. The wife of Pak Sarkia is sick. Very ill. Maybe dying. They came for Mother again this morning. She's been there almost every day this week. That's where you'll find her."

Eric asked nothing about his daughters, Fin or Catherine. Sister Masselin wondered if he even thought about them, or if he still carried with him the sense of shame to have fathered them with the Iban woman he should never have retrieved from the jungle. There was no point in telling Eric anything about his daughter's outrageously disrespectful behavior. It was Sarafina she had come to see, and Sarafina who would decide what Eric was entitled to know. As she bid them good day and headed for the kampong in search of their mother, she doubted that Eric even cared. He seemed content to ignore their existence.

As she parted, Eric pulled his cigarette from its hiding place at his side and drew in deeply. Joseph followed the telltale trail of smoke coming from the roses to see if his own cigarette was still salvageable.

Every encounter with Sister Masselin was something of a trial, the Sister sitting in perpetual judgment, Eric perpetually accused. She would do her subtle best to show just the slightest bit of contempt for him, and he would do his subtle best to conceal his contempt for her. This morning had been no different.

He had not forgotten his daughters, nor was he beyond caring. He had simply learned that whenever Sister Masselin or his mother had something to say about Catherine, it was something bad. His mother had never forgiven him for bringing Miri back from Borneo as the War concluded, and as Catherine grew up, she was the only one of their children with the indomitable spirit of their mother, whose will was so strong and independent that even Sarafina D'Cruz, a Madrigal, a woman of aristocratic lineage, could make her neither obedient nor subservient. Catherine was just like her mother, and as she approached womanhood, still perhaps a few years away, she began to resemble the woman who had inspired his passion and his mother's wrath, who undeniably created so much havoc when he returned with her, innocently proud of himself, more than fifteen years ago to the very porch where he now sucked a little pleasure out of a dying cigarette.

How wrong Sister Masselin had been to think he had forgotten his daughters. Eric remembered everything.

He had won the War. At least, he had done his duty, played his part in it bravely, and had even survived being captured by the enemy. His return would be triumphant, magnificent. He had left as a boy and would be coming home a man, the ordinary phenomenon of war common to so many and yet so distinctly individual, personal and profound. And he even had found a bride, a beautiful girl to present to his mother, who would surely welcome her in and teach her the more refined ways of the West. Even in his sleep, on the deck of the steamer with Miri under a blanket and her head nestled upon his chest, he would dream of the reunion, and the approach of his finest day. He would return a hero.

"Are you coming?" Joseph stood and turned to his brother.

"Yes," said Eric, his speech impoverished, tired. "But you go ahead. I'll join you in a few minutes."

Joseph nodded and shrugged his shoulders and trudged down the drive to find his father in the fields that now had been reduced to a few acres. Eric watched his departure and decided that his reverie was deserving of another cigarette, and a few more minutes, his father be damned.

It was so easy to float away, in the smoke. In the smoke, he could leave the exhausting idleness of the present, and both invigorate and manipulate the past. He could undo the moments and events that seemed to him now to have so clearly led him to his fate. The gambling? Yes. How god-like it would have been to undo that, never to have even started. But money-less and with nothing left of any consequence, it was an innocuous vice, now. Where once it had been a passion, and a great excitement, it was now only a distraction, entertainment. It could do no more harm. There was nothing left to squander, except of course, his time. And that had very little value to anyone.

Would he have undone everything about the woman from Borneo, mother of his half-wanted children? He doubted that. The pleasure was too great, and still had power even as a memory, as a recreated event, vicarious, enjoyed by the younger self he could see through the smoke. But in confessions to his cigarette, he wished that he had been more forceful or more shrewd where his mother was concerned, and defended his claim to the woman of his choice, asserted that right of manhood.

How did his father do it? His mother ruled everything and everyone, except for his father, who seemed indifferent to her power, and she adored him for it. Eric would never be as strong as his perfect father, in body or in will. If he did not know this consciously, he at least knew this particular truth about himself instinctively.

Eric's fate, to which he had become resigned only after confronting years of compiled evidence, was to disappoint three generations—his mother and father, his peers, and his bride, and now, currently, his own children. Everyone must disappoint at least one generation, but the other two offer chances at redemption. To disappoint one of the three is cause for regret. Two of the three is cause for shame. To have failed all three was cause for despair. His trinity was not the Father, Son and Holy Ghost, but Regret, and Shame, and Despair.

He served his self-imposed exile upon the vacant verandah of the plantation house, sharing it with his siblings whose crimes and punishments were similar to his own. But while they considered themselves victims of circumstances, and their conversations invariably got around to the unfairness of *their* suffering, Eric knew better. Everything, meaning the demise of his family, was *not*, as his mother still insisted, the fault of that jungle woman.

A very gentle rain fell upon the house, making a sound upon the steeply sloping zinc roof like grains of rice drumming upon tautly stretched rice paper. A drum-role of God that preceded the execution of yet another morning of false hopes and memories. Even the smoke from his cigarette would not venture from under the protection of the porch, and as the water dripped in rivulets from the edge of the roof, it further eroded his willpower to get back to work.

For a man with no reasonable expectations of absolution, only the present is a blur. The future becomes predictable, and the past more distinct, as looking through a telescope excludes all things peripheral. Eric could recall the events leading to the day of his return from the War with a clarity that eluded him then, could see his mother standing where now he stood, as he returned with Joseph and his beautiful, half-wild woman who was as bold as he was timid.

Not rushing to see them, to put her arms around them, grateful they had been spared. Waiting, almost strategically, for the three of them to approach her. Letting, forcing, her boys to make the first displays of affection and devotion. Until that moment had betrayed his youthful expectations, how proud he had been. On the long boat ride home from Kuching he envisioned a different homecoming, over and over again, eager to tell of his exploits to a father who had been so reluctant to let him go, eager to show off his new bride to his mother, as evidence of his transformation.

The journey home had been exhausting. It had been his intention, and indeed, his only option upon leaving the Iban and Jon the Poet, to find his regiment. Remnants of it, at least, might be found in the outskirts of the town Miri, and he would leave his bride-to-be in the town itself, until after the War. Upon reaching the coast together, it was decided that Eric and Joseph would remain in hiding while Miri went into town as if going to market, to see what she could find out about the location of the British commandos.

She returned in less than a day with the astonishing news that the War was over. No longer fearing retaliation, the locals slaughtered the Japanese unfortunate enough to have been in Miri before they could be evacuated. British troops had come out from the jungle and were now a presence in the town.

The hour was late, and the trio slept by an open campfire on the beach, their first sampling of freedom, banishing their fears and mosquitoes. Several hours into the next morning they entered the delta town, their presence as they walked through the wet markets drawing no particular attention. It was not long before they encountered others in uniform and were directed to the field office once again occupied by the British.

There would be a few days of very light duty, and a brief, official inquiry about why the two of them had been so long in the jungle. But Miri's presence at the interview gave it all immediate plausibility, and Eric's explanation was acceptable. He did not waver, nor did Joseph, to the grim stares of the officers of the tribunal, who had somehow managed to find a typed report that corroborated their simple but incredible story. They were given a chit to present to the quartermaster and were given an immediate discharge. Looking at their tattered clothes, one of the judges casually added, "Keep the uniforms, if you like."

As luck would have it, a convoy that had originated in Jesselton to the east was making its way to Kuching, and the three of them were able to fit themselves in the back of a lorry. Their journey home had begun.

The coast fell upon the South China Sea like a blotter, soaking up the water into endless mangrove swamps that forced the road inland from the shore as much as twenty miles. It was a trip that never would have been attempted by land during the monsoons, when the weight of the trucks and their spinning tires would churn the road into butter during merciless hours of unsympathetic rainfall.

There were enough trucks in the convoy to assure at least one breakdown per day, and for this the trio of Miri, Joseph and Eric were extremely grateful, an intermission in the relentless bucking in the back of the lorry, the fare of passage. They would gather fruit while the mechanics swore and defiant trucks would hiss and spit, and demand yet again the changing of a tire.

And sometimes, in spite of the exhaustion, Eric and Miri would leave a disgruntled and knowing Joseph with the caravan and steal off into a soft alcove of trees and wring passion and pleasure from their tired bodies. It was all so savage, so primitive, so carnal to Eric. He could not envision the simple, refined Malay girls of the kampong capable of such vigor. Years of deprivation and the inevitable self-doubt it imposed were making this woman's offering highly addictive to him. She was a fearless lover.

This, too, had a place in his thoughts as he sat out his exile upon the verandah. It did not seem fair to him that his cigarette was almost at an end. It had become his way, of late, to tell time. Time never ran out, only, his cigarette would expire.

He closed his eyes once more, drawing gently upon his cigarette in an attempt to slow time. Miri had been so beautiful. Her skin perfect, her flesh firm and undamaged by either age or circumstance or the children he would put in her belly.

It was five laborious days to Kuching. It had been preeminent on the coast before anyone knew how much oil was to be had in the fields of Miri and Brunei to the immediate east, and it seemed reasonable that it would be the dominant port on the coast, once again, with the War over. Kuching was something that the town of Miri had pretended at for the last few years but had yet to become: a municipality. Electricity, plumbing, a few hotels, a wharf. The necessities and rewards of civilization. No one who had ever made the trip could remember it taking so long.

After several days in Kuching, which hardly showed the effects of the War, they were able to find passage on one of the overloaded steamers headed for Singapore. Competition for space was intense, but Eric had the inspiration to pass a note through one of the mates to the captain, who would have to be Filipino, the boat's home port legible on the transom in spite of years of mutinous neglect and the defection of paint: Mindanoa.

Upon reading the note, (Eric could see him up on the catwalk), the captain quite callously bumped a few of the passengers to make room for Eric and his companions. He personally saw to it that they were escorted, ushered, aboard, though there were no accommodations to offer other than deck space. For this he apologized profusely, rolling down his singlet in their presence to be a bit more presentable before he shuffled back up to the deck house.

Both Joseph and Miri were baffled. "What did it say?"

Feeling a bit cocky, Eric answered, "I simply asked him to extend all courtesies." It amused him to sustain the intrigue.

"Is that it? Is that all you had to do?"

A deafening blare from the whistle adjacent to the wheel house announced their departure, and barefoot men on the docks slipped the worn hemp lines from the pilings forward and aft, and let them fall into the water, hauled in through the haws holes by the deck crew.

"Well," confessed Eric, pausing quite theatrically, "that's it ... and ... I signed my name."

"Amazing," responded his dumbfounded brother.

Joseph still didn't get it. Eric thought it best to explain his cleverness. "I signed the note Eric *Madrigal*."

It took a few moments for Joseph to comprehend. Eric explained it for Miri, who of course, would have no reason to understand. "Our mother is a Madrigal. That doesn't mean much here or back home anymore, but *her* family, the one in the Philippines, is very, very rich, the ones who stayed there. And they're powerful, too. They own just about everything. But mostly what they own is the shipping lines. If they don't own this ship, they probably once did, before it became so run down. The captain would know who they are."

It still didn't make much sense to Miri, although she was impressed that Eric had gotten them on board when there were so many who had been waiting so much longer, even having slept the night before on the splintery planks of the wharf to get a place on the ship.

"It's like this," he continued, "the captain might not know if I'm bluffing. I mean, if I am who I say I am. But it's true. I am a Madrigal. And soon, you will be, too. The Madrigals in the Philippines could have his job. They could have his ship and all his children, if they wanted it."

Miri still did not understand. Corruption. Power. Influence. Wealth. They really were such abstract concepts to her. Eric explained in step-by-step detail that the captain was afraid that if he did not grant passage to a Madrigal, there would be some eventual punishment, because the Madrigals were important people. Jon the Poet was an important person, but she could draw no parallel to help in her understanding of what Eric had accomplished, and how. Her father never used his position as chief to hurt or punish anybody. When he spoke or when he acted, it was for the tribe, and never for his selfish interests. All she was really able to grasp was that the man she had chosen to rescue had deftly gotten them on board when so many had been denied.

The scent of machinery and coal concocted in the volcanic hold of the engine room steamed through a stack in the center of the deck like a charred trunk of a branchless tree, still smoldering though flameless. It was nothing short of magical for Miri, who had only seen such ships at a distance, when they occasionally came to moor in the deep water offshore from the mouth of the delta down the coast. It was all very exciting to her. All her adventures in the jungle seemed so ordinary in comparison. Within a few hours, at a rate of eight knots, respectable for a ship so overladen with passengers, the overwhelming green of Borneo faded into gray, and the features became indistinct.

This was *real* adventure, with so much water all around them, and soon to lose sight of land altogether. Could such a large and strong ship possibly sink? How exhilarating. It was for this that she was born, and she clung appreciatively to the man who towered above her, who leaned upon the rail and watched Borneo and the War disappear into what would become the first pages of a vague memory ...

But the railing upon which Eric now leaned was the one that he was told months before to whitewash. It certainly was in need of it. He'd get around to it when he could find the time ...

The rain had stopped. It never rained for very long, the monsoons had yet to be upon them. And his cigarette was smokeless. Nothing to hold him. No excuse, real or imagined. He vacated the porch with a nameless despair to join his father and his brother. There were no longer any coolies. No point in keeping them after he had lost the fields, he and his brother, and of course, no way to pay for their labor. He and his brother always thought of themselves as nothing more than coolies in the eyes of their perfect father. But now, with everything lost, the demotion seemed formal, as his father depended upon them to help in the fields. When the family had money for coolies, their father worked his sons hard anyway, to teach them humility. What it taught was humiliation.

Eric walked the long drive, and upon reaching the gate he turned to gaze very privately upon the house in which he was raised. Strange to see it so empty, and so lifeless. How easy to imagine it on the day he returned from the War ...

They made Singapore in just over two days from Kuching, arriving at a very confused port. The War had not been so benign here, and the wharfs and shipyards had been the first casualties. Resentment for the British to have let the city fall so easily had all but vanished, as they were back with money to spend to begin reconstruction of what had been their most significant port in the region.

Bumboats slithered over the crowded water with the same kind of arrogance and disregard for others in their path as the hordes of people on the overcrowded streets, miraculously avoiding any major collisions as the Chinese began to compete for the British trade. They swarmed upon every new vessel that dropped a hook, looking for commerce. One such round-bottomed boat pitched and rolled them more than their two days across the South China Sea, but successfully ferried them ashore.

A city.

How absolutely exciting it was to Miri. Eric seemed so adept at knowing his way around, asking directions only sparingly. They were eager to find a money changer, for Eric had won a phenomenal hundred and thirty thousand rupiahs playing poker on the ship and was luckier still to get off the ship alive with that kind of money. It was enough to get fresh clothes for Miri, a night or two in a hotel, and train passage to Kuala Lumpur, if the line was running, with plenty of money to spare.

They were easily accommodated in Change Alley, appropriately named, where the rupiahs were converted to British pounds, the only currency that seemed to have credibility and value. They lost quite a bit more money in the exchange than expected, but it hardly mattered. They were jubilant and they were safe. And that was the prevailing mood in the streets, as well.

It was then straight to the makan stalls, where Miri had never seen such a variety of foods, served by vendors of assorted nationalities. She had no idea that people came in so many different colors, or food in so many different varieties. Steamed rice, packaged neatly in banana leaves and generously topped with Dahl curry was the long-awaited meal of the two returning soldiers. The sweet taste of lychee water to wash it all down. Miri herself sampled a dozen different foods, it seemed, from vendors of competing nationalities, who came around to the tables with carts on uncertain wheels or with wicker baskets displaying their wares. And never had she seen so many people. Along the waterfront they were mostly shoulder-to-shoulder, and everyone seemed to be carrying something bulky. There were displaced refugees returning home with their bundles, like themselves, or laborers shouldering crushing sacks of rice or meal, either pilfered or genuinely on its way from the bumboats to the row-shops. Hawkers and barterers were everywhere, and if they had no shop, anywhere on the street would do, preferably someplace where their presence would further restrict the flow of pedestrians who were beginning to have a little money in their pockets.

In a demonstration of confidence in the future, fanned by the euphoria of a war ended, Eric, Joseph and Miri did the unthinkable—they departed with food still left on the table, which swarms of children attacked as soon as the trio stood to leave, and before they had even turned their backs.

Miri clutched Eric's arm, to keep from being separated in the turbulence of human endeavor. So many people. The thought recurring over and over again, as they did their best to compete for a little passageway between buildings that stood too close together. Beggars, amputees squatting with their shoulders pasted to the stucco of the colonial style buildings erected by the British before the War. Occasional fistfights over the usual things. Constant offerings of opium and cigarettes, and if these were refused, the same vendor would offer something as innocuous as condensed milk, stolen undoubtedly from British surplus along with Darkey-Toothpaste, an imported commodity scarce during the war but insinuating itself back in a predominantly Chinese culture.

The three of them stumbled on to Bugis Street, where a trade of a different kind flourished. Eric had given Joseph some of his winnings, and soon it became apparent that here was where most of the money would find its way back into the local economy. Eric did his embarrassed best to explain to Miri what all those women did who looked upon him so aggressively, and who shuttled his younger brother deeper into the obscurity of the back alleys where he seemed so willing to follow.

Unable to fight the flow of the crowd, Miri and Eric found themselves at an intersection at the precise moment an elderly Chinese woman of distinction was vacating a tri-sha, and Eric quickly climbed in while she was settling her fare, hauling Miri inside before she could be carried off by the rapid current of pedestrians. Another first for Miri in this adventure that seemed without end, the adventure for which she had willingly paid full price—exile from the clan of Jon the Poet, forever.

"A hotel," ordered Eric.

"You dream." The demand for a tri-sha was so extreme in that freshly liberated city that the driver could display an arrogance normally suppressed by what Eric considered a very humble profession.

"None?" asked Eric.

"No. There is nothing. I don't even know of a boarding house. He sized up his passenger, and could see that he already had a woman. "You want some opium?"

"No, no," said Eric. It had not yet become one of his vices. "We just want some place to stay for the night."

Normally this would have been an excellent opportunity for the driver to make a little extra money, depositing them in one of the many houses that always thanked him in the conventional way. But everything, everything, was full. He shrugged his shoulders. "I don't know of anything." It didn't occur to him that Eric, in an extremely worn uniform that he was determined to wear until he could show his father, actually had enough money for a legitimate, first-class hotel. There was nothing first class about the tri-sha driver, but to conclude the conversation and get the fare on the way he posited, "The Raffles?"

"Of course. Why not." His father's very dark Portuguese skin in combination with his mother's Asian features left Eric looking almost like a Malay, or even Indian, and of course everyone knew they had no money, at least in Singapore.

Impostor, thought the driver. "Well then, the Raffles it is." He started in motion, blowing a whistle that looked conspicuously military to advise the throng in front of him that he was about to run them down. They could get out of the way, if they liked. He stopped, suddenly. "You can pay?"

Chief among Eric's flaws was an inescapable willingness to impress the wrong people. He pulled out his entire winnings, converted to British money, and flashed it haughtily at the driver, who nodded and turned his head quickly, certain that his intent could be easily read as he blushed at the sight of so much money.

He began to pedal again but found it difficult to navigate in such heavy traffic and formulate a plan at the same time. The list of people he knew who would kill for half that much money was endless. Unfortunately, they all seemed to prey upon their victims in the very quarter of the city they were leaving.

Then it occurred to him. They would find no room at the Raffles. He had just been making conversation. He would deposit them there, collect some money, and wait as they failed to get a room. Even if there was space, he doubted they would take him in, especially with the barefoot woman whose primal origins were not even vaguely disguised in her fresh sarong and blouse.

Hiyough. She still carried an Iban backpack with the handle of a parang protruding through the cinching at the top. And he was an Indian bugger. He would simply wait, he assured himself, look surprised to see them again, and then offer his apologies for forgetting that he knew a place on Bugis Street that might be able to put them up. He could have them robbed properly there by several of his trusted constituents and split the take with them later over warm beer in the evening. He smiled at his luck and pedaled good-heartedly. It appeared as if it would be a very profitable day.

It was just past noon, as he pulled up to the curb of the Raffles. The hotel staff had recently excavated a number of tin-clad crates that had been hastily buried with all the silverware and best crystal the day the Japanese invaded the island, and gardeners were busy tending the newly planted lawns.

The Raffles itself was an island, a bit of England in an Asian sea, and it became apparent as Eric stepped from the cab with his bride-to-be that upon this island, they were both foreigners. The natives all had chalky white skin and that nasal accent when they spoke. Nevertheless, Eric was still intent on finding a room. He was in uniform, such as it was, and surely this entitled him to admission into the hotel lobby. After all, he reasoned, he had helped these very white people win back their little bit of Asia.

The driver waited patiently, refusing to give up his berth on the curb, and even refusing a fare from the hotel itself, a proper English gentleman. He held steadfastly to his intuitive plan. And of course, he was correct. Within a few moments a rather discouraged Eric came from the lobby, a bit surprised to see the driver still there.

"All full," he lamented. He was bewildered and pondered his next move.

"Too bad." The driver did his best to share Eric's sense of disappointment. With self-effacing sympathy, he said, "Might I suggest," catching Eric's attention, "there could be a pension house back the way we came?" He paused to study Eric's reaction. "You see, it was before noon when I took you as my fare. It is afternoon now. Past check-out time."

In the glorious chaos of those post-war days in Singapore, Eric was easily duped. It was hard to argue with such simple logic. If Eric suspected anything, it was only that the driver was guilty of milking the fare. But it seemed reasonable enough. This time he ushered Miri into the chassis before him, and off they went.

"You know," he told Miri, "the last tiger in Singapore was shot from the bar in the Raffles Hotel. It wandered into the courtyard. But that was a long time ago. Maybe fifteen years."

"Tigers? Here?" She found it hard to believe. Still, she continued to be impressed with how worldly Eric was, how knowledgeable about events even though he was not a direct participant. In her world, what a man knows is what occurs in his own life, and the legends that were preserved mostly by her father and told at night before sleeping. How could he know such things?

They made their way back along the waterfront, a stretch of the island city distinct for its fringe of sand, rather than silt and mangrove, and facing the notorious Straights of Singapore and a cluster of insignificant islands with a heritage of piracy. In the shallow water of the beach, tight meshed nets were cast for the smaller fish that were sun-dried and salted, to be fried with peanuts and eaten with steaming rice. Smaller sampans were beached and launched, almost all of them fishing boats. Commerce seemed to confine itself to the functioning quays that fronted the deep water of the port, and the financial district that was doing its best to resurrect itself now that the Japanese were no more.

"It's just as well we're going back," said Eric, a thought spoken aloud. "I really don't know if Joseph was listening to me when I told him where to find us in the morning."

Miri nodded in agreement, but she would have nodded in agreement if Eric had told her the sun was blue and the sky was yellow. As they approached the quarter of the city they had left not an hour earlier, they were once again emulsified in human traffic. Eric enjoyed the instant status that came from riding in a tri-sha, distinguishing himself from those who could not afford the luxury.

Miri did not understand what status was and for her there was only the exhilaration of movement in their carriage, a sensation that was no less a part of the moment than the feel of Eric's arm around her shoulder, or the sound of hawkers, or the all-pervading scent of the makan stalls.

They were soon right back from where they had started. The driver had been privately speculating as to how much money Eric was actually carrying. He could almost taste the warm beer at Newton Circus.

"Stop the cab," said Eric, with impassioned impulse.

The driver spilled his beer. "What? What *is* it?"

"Stop the *cab*," repeated Eric, who fumbled in his trousers to find the fare, pulling out what he thought appeared to be the amount he had paid for the trip one-way and perhaps a little bit more, a tip, an extravagance to perpetuate the illusion of wealth that winnings from gambling always seemed to give him. He took Miri abruptly by the hand, and quickly alighted, half turning to the driver. "*Cumsiah*," he said in his best Chinese, "thank you" being about the extent of his Mandarin, and he crushed paper and coin into the betrayed palm of the bewildered driver, who looked at his money and his modest tip, and was heartbroken. *So close. How unfair.*

Eric scrambled down the passageway eclipsed in shade by buildings unthinkably three stories high, almost losing Miri in his exuberance. He had seen someone, now lost in a turn down an even more constricting alley. Eric did his best to work through the human obstacles that shifted before him, some getting out of his way, by intent or accident, some getting in his way oblivious to his urgency. He rounded the corner, Miri still in hand, and the alley opened up into yet another square that had become an *ad hoc* wet market, and was slightly less congested than the alley.

Fortunately, the man he pursued was, like Eric, a head taller than those who swarmed all around him. "Sergeant Major," Eric cried out, his voice insufficient to be heard above the cacophonous squabbling of several hundred grunting people negotiating the price of their daily makan. The subject of his pursuit was about to be swallowed into the toothless jaws of yet another alleyway that gnawed on people like beetle-nut and spit them out the other side. "Sergeant-Major!" he called again, this time his voice finding a breach in the din, successfully stopping the man in his tracks.

He looked about him, not really able to locate the direction from which he had been hailed, the clatter of the marketplace buffeting all sounds against each other. But swimming through the crowd was a man in British issued fatigues, grinning at him in obvious recognition though he himself could not quite place him.

"Sergeant Major," said Eric, beaming proudly, having made his way through a sea of hawkers, beggars and marketers. He halted the impulse to extend his hand, opting to salute, standing comically at attention until knocked off balance by an old woman unimpressed with their reunion and anxious to get home with her less-than-fresh vegetables and slightly less-than-dead chicken. He caught his balance. The sergeant major raised his hand over his brow as he squinted in the sun that burned through the open space of the marketplace, and Eric perceived the gesture as his salute being returned, snapped his wrist nattily and extended his hand.

The puzzled expression of the sergeant major evaporated as he recognized Eric, remembering the face but forgetting the name, if he ever knew it. "Oh, yes, yes, yes. Good fellow. How are you?" he said, with genuine enthusiasm. "We thought you were dead. However did you manage?"

"Oh, no. Quite alive. I assure you." They shook hands vigorously, while Miri looked rather coyly from behind her soldier. "Remember this one?" Eric sidestepped, introducing Miri.

"Why, no?" What the sergeant major had seen on the night of Eric's escape was a half-naked Iban. What stood before him was an undistinguished local girl, in a sarong and acceptable blouse.

"She's the one who *saved* us."

The sergeant major stared in wide-eyed disbelief. *This flake of a girl?* "Amazing," he said, genuinely astonished. He smiled upon her pretty face, and with a suggestion of apology in his voice said, "I honestly didn't recognize you." Quickly, turning to Eric, he asked, "Does she understand English?"

"Yes, yes. Of course. A little, anyway."

They stepped under a tarp supported by bamboo, avoiding a very light and brief sprinkle of rain, signature of the tropics. They each nodded consent when a vendor offered them a table and lychee water, and the veteran soldier was spellbound for half an hour as Eric detailed his escape, and life with the head-hunters, while Miri was content to meander within sight among the stalls and vendors, many of whom had spread their wares on grass mats before them, squatting in the center like a bird in a nest. From time-to-time Eric's former officer would gaze out incredulously at Miri, who looked so ... docile, so incapable of such manly courage.

"Well, actually," he injected at the appropriate spot in Eric's narrative, "it might be argued that you took a casualty. Because of you they shot him on the spot, when they found he'd been asleep at his post and you and your brother had escaped. Funny thing is, he knew his cap was missing before he noticed *you* were missing. Nice touch, by the way. Whatever did you do with his cap? A souvenir?"

... *Shot him on the spot,* Eric thought to himself, his final recollection for the day.

He swung closed the iron gate to the estate, and when the latch didn't catch, he made no effort to secure it.

Thoughts of the chaotic, war-less first days in Singapore provided an unfailing tranquility, and would see him through one more day of dull pain. It was better than opium.

Eric slunk down the road, becoming imperceptibly smaller with each step as he inevitably approached his laboring father, who at last was aging, having no more passions to keep him youthful and vigorous. A few moments more, by the gate, and he would have relived the day of his return, the day that his mother and his bride first squared off, usurping him of what was to be his finest hour.

He could not have known it at the time, but his finest hour was the two days in Singapore, waiting for a train, sleeping on a station floor with everyone for whom he had won the War, with his bride tucked safely under his arm ...

About the time Eric had traveled the several hundred miles from the verandah to the fields directly behind the house, a journey of some fifteen years, Sister Masselin had found her way through the kampong to the house of Pak Sarkia. Grief had made it easy to find, with many outside preparing to mourn.

They had seen her before. Some knew her by name. But it was a bad sign she was coming. A Christian. A Catholic, at that. At the time of death. Had she come to claim the soul of a dying woman on behalf of Jesus? She was not one of them, and their women belonged to Allah. They stood in her way at the door, politely, but resolute.

From his place from the side of the bed, Sarkia could see the approach of Sister Masselin. "It's all right," he said. "Let her in." He assumed she had come to help him in his grief, at the invitation of Sarafina D'Cruz, who was deeply focused on her work. Sister Masselin removed her sandals and entered the house.

Isana's bed had been placed in the parlor to allow more of the family to be with her as her time approached. Sister Masselin said nothing, even to Sarafina, perceiving her old friend was in the trance of a healer, which she had seen before. Sarafina was kneeling on the floor beside the bed, moving her knowledgeable hands over the ravaged form of Isana, reluctant to part with this life, still, though clearly very close to death.

Joyce was beside her mother, and, as instructed, was cooling Isana's fever with cloth and with water. She acknowledged the presence of Sister Masselin with a nod, but she, too, was focused on her task and did not want to be the first to break her mother's concentration.

Sister Masselin found an inconspicuous corner.

Sarafina's hands kept exploring the contours of Isana's back, having maneuvered her on her side. Her strong hands had not yet found the place where the illness had concentrated itself, and it stubbornly continued to steal the life from the woman that Sarafina had come to bring back from the shores of death.

Isana had recurring malaria. Having survived it as a child, her body had somehow lost its immunity, and with her advanced age recovery was unlikely. But still, perhaps lone among them, Sarafina had not given up hope. It was not that she needed to believe that Isana was immortal, as her family desperately wanted to believe, but that she was truly confident in her own abilities. She intuited that all she had to do was break the fever, and undo the effects, the disastrous effects of the diarrhea, which had left Isana depleted and coaxed her into delirium, the first flirtations that death whispers to seduce the living.

Pak Sarkia sat upon a small stool at the side of his wife, holding her hand when not wiping away a tear. A sister, or niece, one of the many relatives who had gathered, brought tea for Sister Masselin, and a chair.

The flow of life within Isana was in disarray, turbulent, and disease was taking over her body as surely as jungle reclaims untended fields. But slowly, Sarafina's hands found a trail. She could feel where the flow of life had been constricted, feel the subtle currents under the skin.

"Mmmn ..." Sarafina murmured to herself, having discovered another blockage of the Chi, as her strong fingers coaxed the flow once more. Upon her patient's chest and then upon her back Sarafina applied once again the strong liniment she had been three days preparing, concocted from nearly a hundred different roots and herbs she had sent the children to fetch to her kitchen. Those obscure plants that they did not know were found by Joyce, reluctant apprentice to her mother in the ways of healing.

The ointment penetrated the skin and sucked out poison, and one of its first results, accomplished over the next half an hour with the encouragement of massage, was to make it easier to breathe. Sarafina competently rolled Isana on her back now, and displaced Joyce at the head of the bed. Intuitively, she applied pressure to the base of the skull and at various points of the forehead, in an effort to diminish the symptoms, the pain and the fever. After some time she looked up without expression and nodded to Sister Masselin, acknowledging her presence for the first time in the hour she had been there.

And then, with her hands upon Isana's temples, Sarafina went deeper into her healing trance.

Isana began to tremble and sweat profusely, while Sarafina remained motionless, except for the rocking of her head, and a frightening rolling of her eyes. Now had come the moment of risk and of bravery, as Sarafina entered, alone, the world of the spirit and the body of the woman before her. Her fingers bloodlessly penetrated the skin and the flesh of the woman on the bed, hunting fearlessly for the demon pain, and walking through the fire of Isana's body until she found its lair, and leeched herself upon the beast, pulling it slowly from Isana's all but surrendered body into her own.

Obliviously Sarafina began to moan. No one spoke, out of respect and for very private reasons as they coveted their impending grief, but now no one spoke because of their communal sense of fear to be in the presence of such a transformation, a metamorphosis that was truly frightening to the uninitiated. Even Pak Sarkia moved back to sit with Sister Masselin who held his hand. Joyce quietly ushered the children from the room. Young cousins and children from the kampong whose place of vigil was the open window outside the parlor saw what they saw and ran off.

Then Sarafina's wrists began to quiver, and then her forearms, as the fever and remaining poison vacated Isana's body to enter Sarafina, who had lured and then grappled it from its place of entrenchment. A few moments later, Sarafina herself was sweating, and her shoulders and upper body began to quake, just as Isana's trembling dissipated. Sarafina swayed erratically, but held on, knowing her work was not yet complete.

She rocked violently at the head of the bed but refused to let go. Her own brow became hot with fever, the fire she had extracted from Isana. Sarafina gasped for breath deeply, suffocating in the smoke that no others could see, nor could taste nor even smell. But Sarafina could taste the smoke, and now she grit her teeth, sealed her lips and refused to breathe, refused to give the fire within her air, resolute, until she became so dizzy that she collapsed.

Her imminent fall had been anticipated by Sister Masselin, who had witnessed Sarafina the healer several times before, and both she and Pak Sarkia caught her and eased her to the floor, and with Joyce's help they ushered her into a wicker chair with a high, reclining back, and they elevated her feet. She was aroused from her trance with great agony, for she now was the host to the fever and all the symptoms she had successfully absorbed from Isana, who was now in restful sleep.

Joyce brought her mother tea and awaited further instructions. Pak Sarkia returned to his stool and held once again the hand of his wife.

Sarafina was in great pain. But she was confident—and correct—that it would quickly pass, exhaustion being its only lingering trace. The sickness had no business in her body, which was strong and healthy. It was like a wild animal lured to a pen. The gate snaps shut behind it, and then, discovering it has been trapped, takes a running leap at the lowest rail in the fence.

Sarafina drank the tea to warm her chest, and exhaled forcefully and repetitively over the next hour, allowing the disoriented illness an avenue of escape.

Her work was done.

"Pak Sarkia," she said, when after some time she could bring herself to speak, and with a peculiar arrogance out of place in one who had been given such extraordinary gifts, "your wife is going to die ... but not today, or any time soon."

She instructed the family to change the sheets once more and to burn them in the evening as a warning to future demons if they dared to intrude. She ended every healing with fire. Fire was the language of the Devil, and Sarafina was fluent in its tongue.

When Isana awakened, she was to be given very soft rice, its substance fortified over the course of several modest feedings with broth and then chicken and a few vegetables.

Sarafina's own fever and symptoms were passing as she had predicted, and she accepted more tea as she recovered her equilibrium, having surrendered her sense of balance to journey through the spirit world. She could hear whispers outside the window, which was crowded once again with those earlier frightened off. The fear evaporated very slowly. This she could sense among those in the house as well. Her trance and her power had left everyone afraid of her, and yet at the same time grateful to her that Isana lived.

Sarafina never perceived herself as one of them, though she lived her entire life on the same soil, separated only by the wall to the estate. She could not share, nor did it occur to her to share, in the joy they waited to express to one another only after her departure. But her reputation as *bomoh*, as the medicine woman, was intact. And this, more than the actual fact that Isana would recover, is what pleased Sarafina Madrigal D'Cruz. Better to be feared than loved.

And now there was something to temper the rumors and gossip about her sons having gambled away her fortune in recent months. She had saved Isana's life. Isana had saved Sarafina's face.

She left her daughter with the family, as Sister Masselin helped her to her feet, and extended her arm. Sarafina leaned heavily on her old friend, and before leaving gazed upon the tranquil face of Isana, whose care could now be relinquished safely to Joyce and to Pak Sarkia's endless family.

Sarafina, for a very brief moment, felt accidental envy for the woman she had just saved, who had no extraordinary powers, and yet was loved and respected by so many, all competing for a chance to help care for her now. She quickly and decisively exorcised it from her thoughts, but not without first becoming impulsively aware that none of these people had ever looked into her eyes before, except of course for Sister Masselin.

When they addressed her, it would be with a head slightly bowed in acknowledgment of her higher position, and eye contact was only for minimal orientation, or even an accident.

And this thought was not so easily banished, for as she was leaving, Pak Sarkia, who had returned to the side of the bed, looked up to thank her, and thank her again. He could do this only by breaching tradition, by looking fully into her eyes, that she might see his heart. This one, authentic gesture, she did not want to see, preferring the gulf that had been in place all her life between the Madrigals and those whose purpose in life was to serve them in the fields.

She bid good day to Pak Sarkia and his family and stepped from the house, squinting in the strong shadows and bright sun of a late afternoon. She was pleased that Sister Masselin had come, as moving was arduous for her now. She ambled very slowly through the crowd that had assembled, that grew in size as the word began to spread that Isana would live. The pending visitation of death that had drawn so many had frightened equal numbers away, though they cared very much for Isana. There was no ambivalence, however, about coming to celebrate her recovery. Like Chi, movement within the kampong began to flow in the direction of the house where the miracle had taken place.

Sarafina assumed that the people had come to see the woman inside the parlor, on the bed, assuring themselves that it was true, that she would survive. This was only a partial truth. It did not occur to her then, nor would she ever be aware that they had come to see her, the healer, the woman who so bravely emigrated to the other side to retrieve their beloved Isana. She was genuinely oblivious to anything they may have felt, having adroitly deflected any exchange of humanity with those she considered indentured to the Madrigals since her childhood. No matter that the fields in which they labored were now owned by a Chinese family. They would never be anything more than servants to her. Sister Masselin, alone, was her friend, and equal.

She staggered a bit, and took smaller, deliberate steps as Sister Masselin steadied her. The ground was not yet entirely below her feet.

Sister Masselin had seen all this before, several times in fact had she escorted Sarafina on her healings. Sarafina in her trance, either invoking help from the spirit world, or doing their work. It never failed to mystify her, though she never really discussed it. It was too hard to reconcile with her conservative, Catholic beliefs, and was made palatable only because the animist who performed these pagan rituals professed to be a Catholic herself. The work must somehow, circuitously at least, be an expression of the power of God whose first declaration was to demand of His creations fidelity to Himself, and disavow the possibility of co-existing supernatural forces or entities. She could stray from this mandate neither in principle nor in practice, in spite of her Chinese heritage, which allowed for multiple explanations for existence or phenomena.

But to wear the black and white there could be no gray, and Sister Masselin was first, and foremost, a nun.

The Malays were far less rigid. Allah, whose skin was like their own, made the same demand upon them that Sister Masselin's deity made upon her. But they could be disobedient without necessarily being disrespectful. A little well-intended deceit was acceptable if its reason was to avoid discord and assure harmony, which was, after all *their* god's greater purpose.

Those who were the most devout could visualize Allah as one of them, and who therefore could be sympathetic to their values. Allah was the one and true god. It would be disrespectful to tell him something other than what he wanted to hear. And surely, he would not want to hear of Sarafina's magic, and their infidelitous acceptance of it, or the hundred other rituals that Allah himself had not ordained but that nevertheless shaped their day to day existence. They had a pious obligation to deceive him, and spare him from the awareness that they supplemented their exclusive faith in him with belief in spirits of stone, or of river, or of trees, or of beast, or of Che' Wan and the Disappearing Ones.

It was a long walk through the kampong, back to the shrinking estate that now consisted of a single pineapple field, and, of course, the plantation house itself. The two graying women stopped to rest in the shade of a triangle of coconut trees, sitting on a defunct cart, abandoned rather than repaired, that had served as a public bench for several seasons.

"I need to tell you about Catherine," said Sister Masselin. She paused before continuing, hoping Sarafina had in reserve the stamina to begin what would be a trying conversation. The woman was impassive, and hard to read. Sister Masselin went on, "We've had trouble at the Convent ... with Catherine."

And this was enough to uncover a cache of animosity that revitalized Sarafina, in spite of her exhausting ordeal. "Tell me more," she said, swiftly, and as hard as ulin.

Sister Masselin then recited the facts as accurately as she could. For no apparent reason and without provocation or cause, Catherine went *amok* at the assembly and attacked several of the nuns, including Mother Superior, who was in frail health even before the incident. Your granddaughter, Sister Masselin informed her, had run through the halls shouting obscenities and had somehow produced a knife with which she killed my pet cat, Sa'ang Hitam, and the gardener's watchdog, and would have killed one of us if she hadn't been disarmed. The enraged gardeners beat her, almost to death, before they could be stopped, and though she was given private care her recovery had been very slow. And so on.

Sister Masselin was very convincing. The facts had disintegrated many times to be fastidiously reassembled by the nuns until the truth was at last fashioned properly, exonerating the virtuous. Sister Masselin ignored no detail, believing the mutation she had helped to fictionalize. She related, but more cautiously and with no superfluous embellishment, Catherine's bizarre behavior when Mother Superior had come to give the disciplinary whipping, which was, of course, to be expected and certainly not out of line. Certainly, consistent with what Sarafina herself would have done.

Sarafina nodded in approval, sympathetic to Mother Superior's outrage, and then sharing her dear friend Sister Masselin's sense of frustration at the failure of judicious violence to correct those spiritually deviant, to repair a morally damaged soul. She herself had diligently beaten Catherine with even the slightest suggestion that she was being disrespectful, and still the girl defied her authority. At first the canings had been purely altruistic, beating her for her own good, but as Catherine got older and began to resemble her mother, the beatings became a surrogate for the pain Sarafina was entitled to administer to Catherine's mother, but never could, deprived by one who would never submit to such a thing. Revenge. The beatings became revenge for the sins of the mother, and yet continued under the guise of moral education. With the mother's unavailability, the plethora of undelivered wrath and contempt traveled downstream, to the daughter, Catherine.

"You did the right thing," she assured the nun. "I blame the mother. She brought those spirits with her from those savages. It's in her blood, and it's in that demon child, too." She paused, thinking over her options. "Do you think the whipping did any good? Do you think you beat it out of her?"

"It's too soon to tell. She's been very weak. We took a chance, but only because she is *your* granddaughter and moved her out of the cellar into the infirmary. It appears she's suffering from rheumatism, now, and all her joints are aching. So she claims. It is as if she is refusing to get well, in spite of our efforts, just to defy us."

Sarafina was seething, almost snarling. She could not think about Catherine without thinking about the nefarious daughter-in-law, from whose womb this child had come. The Iban had driven her sons mad with ungodly lust, causing them to defy their mother. Causing them to drink, and to gamble, and to smoke opium. Causing them to lose the wealth it had taken several generations to acquire, over the course of a single, reckless evening of gambling with the Chinese who were so much more cunning at the card table.

"There is more," said Sister Masselin, who saved the most ominous telling for last, once she was certain that Sarafina was clearly sided with the nuns.

"Tell me," insisted Sarafina, her anger now having a fierce momentum, and hungry to consume all the facts which could be lacerated and bled to conform to *her* claim that the heathen Iban had imported poison into the family, with her primitive and adulterous ways. Catherine, the incarnation of the mother long banished from the family. Catherine, still capable, perhaps, of redemption.

Sister Masselin was just as eager to provide the facts as a completely invigorated Sarafina was to hear them, each woman only barely able to sustain the shared illusion that their concern was for Catherine's well-being.

"She speaks ... in many voices."

This confirmed it. Sarafina stilled her friend with her hand extended upon her lap, as she absorbed it all. Sarafina knew exactly what she meant and asked for no further details. This, she had seen herself in Catherine. It appeared at first to be an innocent predisposition of childhood, Catherine pretending to have friends who weren't really there. But it was more than that.

Catherine's true voice would be displaced and these imaginary 'friends' would speak to Catherine, or *for* Catherine. And always they would come when she, Sarafina, would be trying to impart an important lesson to Catherine. Always they would come and undermine those well-intended reprimands and canings. And they made Sarafina feel something completely disdainful and rare, something that no other could make her feel, except for Catherine's mother.

They made her feel powerless.

The more she tried to strangle the voices emanating from within her granddaughter, the more deeply they seemed to breathe life. Ultimately, she had hoped that in the saturation of godliness that the convent provided, the affliction would just go away.

But it was clear now, confirmed by Sister Masselin, that these demons were more deeply entrenched than ever. Several distinct voices were using her granddaughter's body as a conduit to escape from the darker side of the spirit world. Several voices, chanting the same song, in defiance to Sarafina. Several voices, chanting the identical words through the singular vessel of her granddaughter, mocking Sarafina, singing more sweetly for the choir-master whose baton was a serrated cane evoking their melody from a bleeding child, that sung of her salvation. Like an unaccompanied vocal composition, one song written to be sung by several voices in simple harmony.

A madrigal.

Chapter Twenty-three

Mother Superior was alone in her very private office, when late in the day she heard the knock upon her door of the fledgling, Sister Marcella. Undoubtedly, she had heard the footsteps, too, that preceded the very light tapping. "Come in," she said. She looked up from her broad desk, expecting to see Sister Masselin, her personal secretary, sent to fetch afternoon tea. "Oh, it's you?" she said, rather surprised, though not unpleasantly. "Come in, dear, won't you?"

Sister Marcella had wondered if her knock had been too timid.

The Mother Superior closed an accountant's ledger where she had tallied up expenses for the crop of street children most recently assimilated into the orphanage and returned her pen to its ink well.

"Am I disturbing you, Reverent Mother?" Sister Marcella half hoped to be dismissed.

"Oh, no. Not at all. Just finishing up anyway. *Do* come in ... and leave the door ajar, would you, dear? Unless, of course, you are here on a private matter?"

Sister Marcella turned and closed the door just slightly, as requested, and turned back demurely. "No, Mother. It's not at all private." A private matter implied a self, and Marcella preferred to think that she was without one and was just an altruistic though faltering extension of God. She was still at an age where she was lost in the paradox that viewed selflessness as a virtue, and not just an occasional phenomenon, random and generally indiscriminate. The *self* enhanced by selfless acts. All references to a self, such as greed and desire, or even assertion, by those more devout than she, like Sisters Beatrice or St. John, genuinely perplexed her.

"While you're up, please get that window, too." Sister Marcella proceeded to carry out instructions. "No, no ... the one behind me. The draft, you know."

Performing the small duties served to make Sister Marcella feel a bit more comfortable.

"Please." Victoria, the Mother Superior, opened her palm and gestured to one of the two tufted chairs on the brilliant red and blue carpet directly before her desk, which was richly lacquered, dark and dustless. A bouquet of pink roses from the garden directly beneath her second story window bloomed generously in a crystal vase on the corner of the desk, centered on a doily embroidered in their own sewing shop. "They're lovely, aren't they?"

Of course, they were. One of Sister Marcella's duties was to see that flowers were kept fresh daily in the office and private quarters of Mother Superior. During the recently waning monsoons, which proved to be too much even for the sturdiest of roses, there was an almost limitless selection from the convent's extensive greenhouse. It was an odd British import, which served to kept excessive water out rather than trap humidity within, an accidental success.

"Yes, Mother, quite lovely," said Marcella, who had taken one of the chairs, but sat quite erect, resisting the seduction of its inviting comfort. The room itself was spacious and entirely pleasant. It was a promontory, of sorts, from the main building, with expansive windows on three sides, and supported on stone arches rising from the flagstone entryway to the formal reception hall. It had a commanding view, a *commander's* view, of almost half the compound, and the high jungle held at bay by the formidable walls that surrounded the grounds.

In spite of her apprehensions, Sister Marcella had little to fear from the old woman in the high-backed leather chair on the opposite side of the expansive mahogany desk. Sister Marcella was adored by all, including Mother Superior. She had a genuine sweetness that everyone found endearing, and, of course, that youthful innocence. Mother Superior was neither youthful nor innocent, but in the presence of the young nun from England, she could pretend at both these things, if only vicariously.

"I understand you have a good head for figures," she said, affectionately, pushing aside the oversized ledger, as an unconscious demonstration that she was giving Sister Marcella her full attention.

"Well, yes. Thank you," the girl replied awkwardly, not expecting such flattery. "Math was always my favorite subject."

"Mine too," said Mother Victoria, as if this discovery constituted a real bond or something significant that they shared in common. It was, in fact, herself that she flattered, believing that the near- perfect way in which she lived served as an example for the youngest in her fold. "And tell me ... What can I do for you today?"

Is this the woman she had come to doubt? thought Sister Marcella? "It's about Catherine," she began, with tentative optimism.

"Oh. That one." The old nun stiffened. Her smile, genuine though it had been by the visit of the only Sister still in blossom retracted like snail to salt. Marcella had not been present in the auditorium during the outburst that had so humiliated her, so shamed her. Sister Marcella had not seen her without power or control. And so, she could not fully comprehend the inexhaustible bile that choked her Mother Superior with each mention of Catherine's name. "Yes ... What about Catherine?"

"Well, she ... she doesn't appear to be getting much better." She decided not to mention the bruises at all, which were fairly-well healed. "She's very, very weak. She can't hold down food for very long." As the Sister spoke, Mother Superior emitted no signs of concern, and remained very hard, forced, now, by this inexperienced initiate to relive the events of that horrid day when she had lost her face. Sister Marcella continued to list the ailments, but kept it brief, cautiously avoiding embellishing details.

"She may be developing rheumatism." Teeth could be heard grinding. "She cannot walk or even stand." Hands that had been relaxed and dangled over the arms of the chair became claws. "Movement in her joints is difficult." Knuckles turned white, as she clamped the comfort out of her throne.

Sister Marcella could see these changes, and when at last she said, "She is in a lot of pain," she could swear that she heard Mother Superior, who she knew said nothing, say, "That's good."

Steps could be heard from down the hallway. The sound seemed to break Mother Superior's self-absorbing trance, and color made meager attempts to retreat to her face. "Ahh...that must be Sister Masselin. Would you care to join us in some tea, my dear?"

"Oh, well ... I ..."

Sister Masselin had arrived, backing in with a tray to open the door, turning and radiating some surprise to find little Sister Marcella in *her* seat.

"Ahh, Sister Masselin. Sister Marcella has come for a visit and would love to join us in tea. What? Only two cups? Yes, of course. Sister, be so kind as to pour us tea and go back to the dining hall for another cup and saucer for yourself?"

"Oh, no, Mother," said Sister Marcella. "I really should be going, thank you."

Sister Masselin set down the tray at its usual place on the credenza against the wall, under a portrait of the son of everyone's shared husband. Sister Marcella turned awkwardly in her chair to address Sister Masselin apologetically, but Sister Masselin was not about to turn around, and poured tea as instructed, *her* tea.

"No, no," insisted Mother Superior. Sister Masselin won't mind at all. And you undoubtedly have so much more to tell me about Catherine." But what Sister

Marcella really heard was, "Don't you *dare* talk any more about that little waif." It is also what Sister Masselin heard, who had been the Mother Superior's secretary all these years and knew her very well. She stirred sugar into the tea and waited to see how Sister Marcella was going to handle all of this. *Stupid woman.*

"Well, ah ..." Sister Marcella tried to get her footing. "Thank you for the tea, really, but I'm afraid I do have to go. The child ..." an intuitive inspiration kept her from using Catherine's name, "... is really quite ill. I shouldn't leave her unattended for too very long. In fact, I was here to request that she be transferred to the infirmary." There. She said it.

At that moment, Sister Masselin turned with the tea she had prepared for the Mother Superior, the ultimate disposition of the second cup still in question.

"Well, Sister," said Mother Superior to her secretary as she accepted her tea, "What do *you* think?"

Before she could comment, Sister Marcella interjected, pleading her case for Catherine, "It's terribly dark and unhealthy down there. Very damp. And such stale air."

"Yes, it must be difficult for you," said Sister Masselin, the kind of comment that is well accepted but gives no commitment or suggests anything subject to dispute. "How ever do you manage?" she added, with a mock sincerity that was almost pious. "It must be a trial."

"Indeed, it must be." said Mother Superior, seizing an opportunity to reconcile her conflicting agenda. To punish, to torture Catherine, and yet accommodate the most feminine, the most coveted, of her apprentices. "We really did not intend for you to have been confined with her for this long, in that horrible cellar. It must be dreadful for you."

Sister Marcella was astonished. She was there to negotiate for *Catherine*, who was in desperate need of better care, and not there to complain about the conditions for herself. Before she could say another word, the compassionate Mother Victoria said, insisted, "You are quite right in bringing this to our attention. Bring the girl up to the infirmary at once and continue to care for her there."

Sister Masselin added two lumps to her tea.

For a moment nothing more was said, and the benevolent smile of one who was all-knowing hung once again on that plaster wall of a face. Sister Marcella realized that the audience was over, stood, genuflected modestly, and bid them each good day. Sister Masselin nodded politely and had retrieved her chair before Sister Marcella had even left the room. She stirred her tea.

Sister Marcella walked more forcefully down the hallway than when she had approached, the sound of each step slapping her into a new wakefulness. She was angered that her motives were understood to be a selfish request to have her station relocated out of the basement. She was certain that her motive had been the correct one, to improve the conditions for her patient. And they just assumed her motives were corrupt. They would also have to conclude that she was *deceitful* as well, using Catherine's misery as a ploy. And then, thinking these things, they were not at all condemning of her, but *accommodating*.

This was all very confusing to her. But her will was not strong enough to sustain her anger, and began to degenerate into a sense of shame. Before she turned down the end of the long hallway, acid guilt began rendering her helpless once again, etching its pattern into her will as it had all her life. She was *supposed* to be obedient. She was supposed to be respectful. Why was God showing her things about Mother Superior that undermined all that? What could be His purpose? Surely? ... No ... It must be some flaw in her own character to make her doubt the one she was sworn never to question. She could only hope that Mother Superior could not see the brooding treason in her heart.

Catherine needed her without detour or delay, but she herself urgently needed to pray. Not in the chapel, not at the altar. Better in the privacy of her room, where the sincerity of her remorse for such seditious thinking could be authenticated by God, where she could offer Him her flesh, her pain, in exchange for His forgiveness. Her mother, offering her flesh and her pain to her father, to appease him. In her own room, her habit pulled down to her waste, bent down on her knees by the side of her bed. Like her mother, bent down on her knees before her husband, while they thought Marcella was sleeping. In her room, where now, under her bed, she kept the stiff leather instrument of her penance, the crop.

Chapter Twenty-four

"Antoinette said you were dead."

Catherine held up her tray to the nun dolling out porridge. "No, Fin. I'm *never* gonna die." She was certain that the nun who pretended not to hear would repeat the words to Sister Masselin, who in turn would relay the information to Mother Superior. A challenge.

And the challenge was met. A scant two weeks after she was permitted to reclaim her cot in the dormitory, she was sentenced to another month of confinement in the catacombs, for reasons she could not remember, if she ever knew them, for that was three years ago.

Catherine surfaced from the basement yet another time, after another long disappearance. The charges always different; the punishment always the same. This time the latest infraction was sabotage. Guilty, of course, though she was frustrated that the accusation had not been sufficiently proven, in spite of being true. But in the courtroom mind of an adult, suspicion carried the same veracity as proof. Bobbins from the machines in the sewing room had been found by the gardeners among the roses trying so desperately to be perfect, only to be dismantled a petal at a time after an unfairly short bloom. Without the bobbins, not only were the machines unproductive, but orphans as well became idle, and in the absence of structure the nuns had real difficulty managing the girls.

Someone had removed the bobbins from every machine and tossed them in the garden. Someone had plucked the roses clean of their petals, making them unfit for the vase atop the credenza in Mother Superior's office. It had to have been Catherine. It could only be Catherine. Her audacity eclipsed that of Antoinette, and Catherine had become the suspect of choice for every crime and every misdemeanor that required stealth and cunning to perpetrate.

Catherine sat down for lunch in her spot, a place of honor at the center of the table that no other girl would dare now to take, even when Catherine vacationed in the cellar. "Catherine? Did you really do it?" asked Fin.

"Of course not."

"Then who?"

Catherine put down her spoon and looked at her sister. "Fin. It doesn't really matter, does it? Just eat your makan."

It had indeed been Catherine, but there had been no evidence, no confession, nothing incriminating. And certainly, no informers. Catherine, both ruthless and compassionate, had inspired, had earned, remarkable loyalty among the orphans, at least, those not still indentured to Antoinette. She was like no other. For her, they would go hungry. For her, they would starve. Those who at one time during her tenure in the orphanage would have sold her for as little as a smile from a nun would not even think of doing so now, not even Antoinette's minons. There would be no more frivolous betrayals, and treason could not be coerced or even bribed. Catherine had managed to accumulate what the nuns could never hope to acquire—respect, and even admiration. This accidental success infuriated her tutors.

Catherine ate quickly, expecting Sister St. John to come storming in at any moment.

"Liar." The nun was her usual shade of furious, and Catherine gulped down the food as quickly as she could.

Sister St. John slapped the bowl from under her and took Catherine by the ear. She marched her off and Catherine hardly struggled. She had been in confinement in her little room in the cellar for almost a month, this time, and when she heard Sister St. John in the hallway had somehow managed to convince her that she needed to go straight to the chapel to talk to Jesus and confess. "Fine. I will accompany you."

"Of course, Sister." Catherine had no firm plan, until she noticed how filthy the month in confinement had left her.

"Sister, will you help me in the washroom? I cannot speak to Jesus looking so dirty."

The Sister looked down upon the girl. Yes. Filthy. "Well, all right then. But you're old enough to wash yourself. Look at you. You are almost up to my shoulders, now." She changed course and walked down the hall that led to the washroom. "Now. Get yourself cleaned up. I'll wait for you here." Catherine kept her contrite demeanor. "Not more than five minutes, mind you. I'll be waiting."

Five minutes became ten, and the washroom had a rear window. Sister St. John hunted her down, and once again Catherine found herself in the little storage room in the basement. Home. A place she so frequently visited the nuns no longer used it for storage.

"You'll stay here until we get that confession." Sister St. John slammed the door and turned the key. *But that girl needs more than a confession,* she fumed. Catherine waited until she heard the nun climb the stairs before she pulled out the slice of bread she had smuggled from the cafeteria.

Catherine felt rather pleased with herself, though she knew the nun, sooner or later, would be back. Though Mother Superior had been reluctant to prescribe overt violence herself, ever since the episode now three years behind them, when she herself had seen the very strong link Catherine had with the Devil, Mother Superior closed one eye to both Sister St. John's and Sister Masselin's admonitions about Catherine. *That girl's body is a flu from Hell,* she reasoned. Better to keep it congested with the teachings of Christ, or better still, constricted, choked, with acts of penance and starvation and beatings. And a confession of wrong doing, of her own free will, might actually render her unsuitable as a conduit for the demons of the spirit world.

And so, it was decided that Catherine would remain in the storage room in the cellar this time until a confession was forthcoming. To encourage her to do the correct thing, she would be given water and a single slice of toast, with jam, with each passing day. When a full week had passed and salvation seemed no closer at hand, the jam was stricken from the menu.

"Mother Superior," Sister Masselin had said, "it is best that *I* tend to Catherine. Young Sister Marcella has developed feelings for the girl which may conflict with her duties."

"Relieve her of her burden, Sister."

The face of a nun, seen once daily and then only as a silhouette against the punishing, stark light bulb, was that of the nun who never felt sufficiently avenged for the murder of her beloved Sa'ang Hitam.

"Well, my dear. That was very naughty what you did today. So, it seems you won't be needing your supper tonight." She looked for some sign of pain, but Catherine only smiled. "Have you anything to tell us, today, my dear? About the sewing machines?"

"Allah O Akbah." A Muslim response that rippled with disguised insult. God is great. The Muslim's god.

And so, it went for another fortnight. Catherine mysteriously strong, losing no weight, confessing no sins. The nuns were baffled, their superstitions nurtured. She *must* be in league with the Devil. Still so strong.

Tippy was not baffled. Neither was Michael. Or Karen and Angelica. They knew Catherine's secret. They had been with her during the discovery.

She had found that by prying the heavy ulin boards, each about a meter long and as thick as Michael's forearm from the channel in her stone floor cell she could access the drainage ditch that took the overload of rainwater from the courtyard.

It was fully four feet deep, and she could straddle the accumulated sludge built up on the bottom and along the tubular sides of the ditch by stiffening her legs across the expanse and hunching forward on her hands. After several yards of this, she could arch her back and raise the boards on the opposite side of the storeroom and into the basement proper. She had been such a frequent tenant, that now, even in the dark, she knew the lay of the basement. But there was that beacon light at the top of the stairway, and the task became simple.

A comb smuggled mercifully to her by Sister Marcella before she was replaced by Sister Masselin could slide between the imperfect union of the heavy door and jamb until it caught and lifted the latch, and she could reverse the procedure upon her return. The comb also unlocked a side door to the kitchen as well, always the first stop. Skills she had brought with her from home now served her very well, and she was able to discriminately steal more food than even the regular diet before her incarceration in the basement. She would peel back the slightly crusted rice from the surface of the pot on the stove, and skim enough from underneath to fill a bowl. A scoop of cooked vegetables was hard to inventory, as was an occasional chunk of pork. Good little guest, she washed and dried her bowl, and cleaned up every trace of her presence.

What the nuns had unwittingly accomplished was to provide Catherine a foolproof alibi for this as well as unlimited larceny and vandalism. Laundry left on the line would be found trampled in the mud, and Catherine would be asleep in her cell in the morning. Cow dung from the garden would materialize in a teacher's desk drawer, discovered during the middle of lessons. So bold as to be reckless, and always the alibi. Found, each morning, in her cell, taking secret delight in the nun's baffled expressions to find their prime suspect still there.

"I have nothing to confess because I have done no wrong. If I confess to something that I did not do, it would be a lie. God does not want me to lie, does He?" She would ask this innocently of Sister Masselin, whose only hope was that time would break her. But Catherine's remorseful look was only feigned. Something learned. To show arrogance might substantiate their suspicions. She was far too shrewd, too cunning, to be betrayed by a facial expression or emotion that would not serve her well. There was no emotion that she could not falsify, the gamut of her feelings at her disposal like blow-darts in a quiver. She had become the consummate actress. She would *act* afraid. She would *act* intimidated. She would act the things that she had learned would be most likely to deflect suspicion, for no one as confidant as she truly was could get away with the escalating volume of her crimes and expressions of loathing and disdain.

And the nuns were never the wiser. The prospect of crawling through a drainage ditch and becoming unclean was so abhorrent to them that they simply could not allow that even Catherine would do that, and it never even occurred to them as an explanation for the plethora of vandalism that transpired every time Catherine ended up in confinement. Perversely, in ways that everything within those walls was perverse, the nuns even started to think that Catherine had somehow managed to keep the other girls under control, and without her presence, structure was undermined, and anarchy blossomed.

One remarkable evening, two weeks into this marathon, Catherine dispersed the rats in her passageway to freedom, and emerged from the ditch without really having a knowable objective in mind. But her thoughts had been focused upon Mother Superior, and she persuaded herself that the Mother had never really paid for the beating she had inflicted upon her, now, three years ago.

She had never been in the private office of Mother Superior. It was time to pay it a visit.

Hallways that had been so confusing, even frightening in her early days were now commonplace, familiar. She had been where no other children had been, though always surreptitiously, always at night, departing either from the dormitory or from the cell. Catherine was fearless. Her fearlessness, compass-like, would guide her to that plush office of the Reverend Mother. Her eyes had become cat-like. She could see in the dark. And what she could not see, she could sense. She glided, effortlessly, even artistically, like a dancer, spinning down unlit hallways and up awkward stairways to the forbidden territory of the sleeping nuns, and to the office of Mother Superior.

The door ... was not even locked. She entered the office of the able administrator. Moonlight, which also had no business being there, had jimmied the locks on the windows and found its way inside. A co-conspirator.

The first impulse, of course, was to feel anger. This was far too comfortable for a woman who had condemned Catherine to sleep on a cot in a rheumatic cell that listed Death within the pages of its registry. In the office of the Mother Superior an animal, a beast of burden, had died to give its skin for the high backed chair, the throne, which glorified the nun who had risen through the ranks of the holy to run this place. Flowers had been conscripted to surrender their beauty and elegance, to sacrifice their perfect fragrance, to mask the vile scent of the woman in the animated death mask.

There was no austerity in the room, where vows of poverty had been negotiated, compromised. A chalice of silver, a paper weight studded with stones of color that had to be jewels. A decanter of cognac. A floor, polished into obedience, and upon it, an island of carpet, plush, and a vulgar red and blue. A candelabrum. It, too, silver, jewels broken out upon its skin like acne, a gift from a visiting bishop. A portrait, of course, of the Son of God, blissful and oblivious.

And on the credenza, underneath that smiling, almost erotic face of Jesus, Catherine saw a package. This required a little investigation.

The package had been torn open, at least, its outer wrappings. Coarse string had been cut and left fallen at its sides, and the brown paper, so it appeared, had been clawed at either with some urgency or else disregard for its worth. It was clearly a package that had come through the mail. But sent by whom?

From instinct, Catherine looked about herself routinely, confirming that she was alone, and she approached the credenza. In the litter of paper, she uncovered a tin, Jacobi's Salt Crackers, or so it said. But the Jacobi tins were coveted for their capacity to be re-used, and often held something entirely different. And this proved to be the case.

Catherine pried open the lid, and clearly had not been the first to do so, for a layer of discarded wrappers, most of them crumpled, buried the last of the treasure at the bottom of the tin. She filtered through the papers until she felt the unmistakable sensation of a cookie between her fingers and retrieved it from the bottom.

Delicious. In fact, very much like the cookies her Aunty Joyce made, which in more generous moments she would share with Catherine, Fin, and Beni, though they clearly were intended for Nestor and Marta.

It suddenly occurred to Catherine that they were exactly like the cookies she remembered from home. She lit the small lamp on the credenza, moonlight not sufficient to confirm her suspicions. Yes, a Jacobi tin of crackers, just like home. She tried to re-construct the paper torn and in disarray on the credenza, impervious to fear that the light could possibly be seen escaping down the hallway from under the closed door to the office. This was too important to be inhibited by fear. She had to know.

The shredded paper had left the return address unreadable, except for "D6- Fifth Mile". That was enough. That was the plantation. And something else, on a scrap of paper, though its place in the mosaic of torn pieces indeterminable. "For Cathe … "

And so, she knew. For whatever reasons, perhaps falsifying genuine concern to sustain the illusion that they cared for Catherine's well-being, Grandma or Aunty Joyce had decided to send her cookies, and the parcel never made it past the office of Mother Superior. Catherine's rage and her instincts for self-preservation wrestled with this new hurt, this new frustration, and though she wanted very much to scream, or break something, she broke nothing, said nothing, desecrated nothing, but left the office with the scavenged tin of cookies back down to the basement, into the drainage ditch which she sealed behind her, and back to the unlikely sanctuary of the chamber that had been the very arena of so much persecution.

She could not return to her cot. It was not safe enough, or distant enough. It was too exposed. Instead, she took herself to the darkest of the dark corners of the cell, blanket in hand, with the tin under her arm. She drew her knees to her chest, tangled, not really covered, by the damp blanket, making herself very small as she awaited the approach of demons, clutching the blanket and the canister. Something that was hers.

The night was without momentum, stalled. The crush of darkness thickened the air of the cell, so that even apparitions had no room to dance. Her fearlessness was broken down, made lame by the isolation and this new hurt. And when she called, and when she whimpered for Tippy, even Tippy would not materialize, breaking the promise she had made to Catherine that she would never let her be alone there. And for this, Catherine wept.

It was a few tears, only, at first. But her spirit had been punctured, like a spear through the ribcage of Christ, and in the anonymity, the intimacy of darkness, she cried without restraint, copious tears that softened her face.

Beatings and humiliation had never produced these kinds of tears. But holding the tin of cookies against her, knowing she had such little significance that the nuns would steal even this acknowledgement that she had a family, had at last made her vulnerable. Her tears lubricated the night, which at last began crawling, slipping, into morning.

And when there were no more tears left, and her spirit was again hard and dry, what remained was anger. It had been incubating all night, maturing. And now, with the first evidence of dawn, sounds of muffled footsteps on the floor above, the anger could be contained within the stone cell no more.

She broke down the door from within, ramming the latch with an ulin plank from over the drainage ditch, which she would use for passage no more. She tucked the evidence of the nun's thievery under her arm and marched to the steps that led to the dining hall, becoming more powerful with each step, becoming her mother, becoming Jon the Poet, becoming Iban, becoming a warrior, becoming unstoppable. Becoming herself.

She thrust herself into the dining hall, where the nuns had come to feed on the children. The bursting of the door against the wall announced her presence, the trifling resistance of the latch no match for her fury. All sound was crushed by the force of the concussion, all breath in the room, for a moment, abruptly halted, and all fearful eyes, those of children, those of nuns, were locked upon her in the paralysis of terror.

Framed by the doorway to Hell behind her, Catherine lifted the Jacobi tin above her head, making her even taller, and when she first spoke, her words seemed to fill out her entire body, making her stronger. "THESE were supposed to be for *me*. Do you think I don't even exist? I *am* somebody." No one knew quite what she was talking about, except for Mother Superior, at the head of the table, and Sister Masselin, to her right.

"No." said Sister Masselin. "You are *nobody*. Even your own *family* doesn't want you. Why do you think you're *here*?"

The tin took on the weight and dimensions of a boulder, and Catherine seemed poised to launch it upon her oppressors, who had consumed half her irreplaceable childhood, and had greedily consumed half the delicacies within the Jacobi tin she steadied over her head. To crush their skulls.

Sister Masselin clenched her fist under the table. Everyone in the room was mesmerized by the stunning metamorphosis taking place before them, as an adult emerged from within Catherine, the child. Catherine's motion had the hypnotic rhythm that entranced the room, as she stalked forward to the table of the nuns, so full, so abundant, so bloated, so superfluous with food. And yet all that food to which *they* were entitled but the children were *not*, was not enough, not enough food to satisfy their gluttony. They had stolen *her* food and given her dry bread, a slice for each day.

Catherine overcame the impulse to crash the boulder upon the head of Mother Victoria, who sat without expression, remembering that the girl approaching her was three years younger when she had done such violence before, killing the dog, and invoking demons. She was now three years meaner and physically much larger, stronger. It tempered Mother Superior's reactions. And when Catherine spoke now, it was somehow a man's voice. And when Catherine now spoke, it was clear it was not to the room in general, not an indiscriminate protest. She was speaking directly to Mother Superior. She whispered the same words that had a moment before heralded her entrance so boldly. "These were supposed to be for me. I am somebody." And *somebody* terrified the old woman.

And then, roaring once again, with a voice that was both man and woman, but certainly not child, Catherine strutted belligerently around the table, the tin high over her head, turning to everyone. "These were supposed to be for me. My family made this for *me*, sent this to *me*. And you. You stole it." She had worked her way to the head of the table once more, and brought the tin to her chest, clutching it possessively for a moment. In rage she pulled the lid and let it fall to the floor and hoisted the container over her head one last time, and Mother Superior reflexively lifted her arm before her head and flinched, her first motion since Catherine entered the room, but Catherine turned the canister upside down, and crumpled papers and the remaining cache of cookies and pastries were heaped upon the table. She flung the empty tin against the wall, the way a nun might fling a child, then sprang, tiger-like, upon the table, bellowing the words, "These were *mine*."

There was still no resistance to the force of her will. She squatted down on the table, and scattered what remained from the tin around the room. A few orphans picked up the cookies, but most were too astonished by what they were witnessing to harvest the unexpected windfall.

Sister Beatrice, closest to Catherine, was about to make her move. Catherine, animal, Iban, could sense it spontaneously, and turned, flared at her. "And you ... don't you dare." It was enough to stop Sister Beatrice from action. "You whore." And so, she knew, at last, from life in the convent, what a whore was. "I *know* what you do at night. I *know* what you do at night. I know what you did to *Luka*. I saw you. And I *know* what you do to my sister." Fin, six years out of the nursery and in the company of older orphans, was in awe of her sister's bravery. "*All* of us know."

Suddenly under scrutiny, found out, Sister Beatrice was defused as an immediate threat, but Sister Masselin ignited to launch the attack, before other untrue accusations might be spoken. *Blasphemy.* She stood righteously and sprightly and lunged for Catherine, only to get a foot in the face, woefully missing her eye, but bloodying her lip. She rolled on the floor and Sister St. John grabbed Catherine from behind, but before she could pull her off balance, a charge of orphans, led by none other than Antoinette, assaulted the nuns from all sides, and the insurrection was upon them. The nun was pulled down herself, was pummeled and kicked. A cascade of children delirious with revenge, for themselves, for Luka, holding her down under the flood waters of their pain, making *her* grasp for breath.

"Let *this* be a lesson to you." Antoinette, repeating the words the nun herself had spoken in the washroom.

Mother Superior could do nothing but clutch at her breast, as if it contained a heart, as those nuns who could stand surrounded her and thrashed at the children. Some of the children ran screaming. Others by reflex went straight for the food at the table of the nuns. Others sought out their persecutors, and in the safety of overwhelming numbers, kicked, or bit, or punched them. A nun escaped the fray and ran to find the gardeners, and their ... but there was no dog.

The eruption of bodies jolted the table upon which she was still standing, a pinnacle of the mayhem, and Catherine fell. Sister Masselin had recovered and broke from the pack surrounding their queen, seizing an opportunity to strike at the fallen rebel. She had instinctively taken a cane from the corner of the room, left there to instill good table manners, and came forcefully towards Catherine, not yet recovered from her own fall, and unable to get a footing on the table still swaying with violence and liberation, agitated like a wok over an open flame.

Sister Masselin was swearing and foaming, making ugly words more hideous, frothed in the blood of her bleeding lips, as they escaped her mouth. She lifted the cane, wishing it were an axe, high above her head. "You're going to *die*." This she said to amplify the sense of pleasure, the exhilaration she had begun to feel, knowing that she could at last beat the girl to death with impunity while she was momentarily helpless on her back upon the table.

But Sister Masselin would never deliver the blow. As the wide arch of destruction sprung into descent, its seemingly inevitable path was halted, and in one, very swift movement, the grip upon the cane was broken, and Sister Masselin herself crumbled into the floor in outrageous pain, holding her wrist, twisted and snapped, limp, rendered useless, crippled forever, never to inflict another beating upon Catherine, or upon anyone.

Sister Marcella, the very timid, the very humble Sister Marcella, had found her courage.

Defiance, book two of the *Courtesans of God*, reveals the potential for joy and abundance of the human spirit when unfettered by guilt or fear or violence.

Having failed to crush Catherine's spirit, the nuns condemn her to the street. Despondent, she remembers vaguely the words of Che' Wan spoken half her life ago: "Catherine. This much I promise you. I will see you again ... In seven-years-time, you will find your way to the temple, and I *will* see you again."

The prophesy is fulfilled, and Catherine is taken in and nurtured by the *Bida Devi*, mystics so ethereal of spirit they leave no footprint where they tread. Under the tutelage of Che' Wan she learns the healing arts and masters their liberating sexual rituals. She discovers her true destiny while fending off the advances of a nefarious king as she is groomed to take the place of the old woman who had foreseen her coming.

Unknown to her, her grandmother and Sister Masselin, bent on revenge, have been scouring the countryside to find her.

They are unprepared for what they discover.

A word about

A Word with You Press

Editors and Advocates of Fine Stories in the Digital Age

A Word with You Press is a passionate consortium of writers, editors, and graphic designers drawn to the notion that nothing is more beautiful or powerful than a story well told. For more than a decade, writers such as yourself have leveraged our award-winning professional editing, book design, and publishing management services to become successful authors. After all your labors, nothing compares to the feel of your new-born book in your hands.

Our mission is to partner with you to make that happen.

Bring us your story, work with us, and together we will make it a compelling page-turner. When your manuscript is the best it can be, we will guide you through the publishing process and find your readers.

Here's a direct line to the Editor-in-Chief: thorn@awordwithyoupress.com What's your story?

Then, the world beckoned...

Why I am an Editor.

I was the skinny kid with glasses who held the jacket when somebody with more balls than me had had enough and was going to punch somebody's lights out in the playground after school. I observed the passions—sometimes volatile passions—of life's real participants, from the safety of the sidelines.

I lived my adventures for the longest time vicariously, a type b, lower case, ten-point font, in a world intimidated by type A's, bold, maybe even italicized and underlined, Franklin Gothic Heavy.

Then, the world beckoned, and I dabbled in high risk, exposing first myself and eventually my family to unconscionable danger (such as paying a smuggler to get us across the Straights of Malacca in a sampan at two in the morning after the gunboats passed).

One day while shaving I saw the first lines penciling across my forehead, and then I knew it; I wasn't holding somebody else's jacket anymore, and somewhere along the line I stopped living my life like a turtle crossing a highway.

Though retelling my (mis)adventures can hold anybody's attention for a half an hour at a dinner party, I know the best stories are the ones that take place under the skin.

Tell me a story about climbing Mount Everest, and I am already bored. I know what it's all about. You climb. There is risk. You almost die. You have an epiphany. You come down off the mountain. You write a book about it.

BUT ... tell me how you screwed up your marriage(s). Tell me what went wrong, what you did wrong. Tell me how your youngest daughter ended up in prison, and why it should be you in her place. Tell me of the insurrections that you yourself led with every relationship that ever meant anything to you, who you wanted to murder, and why. Who wanted to murder you, and why. Tell me of sabotage and heresy and destruction and betrayal and mutiny, redemption and infinite "second" chances and of pain and of pleasure and fury, and the joy you carved out for yourself in spite of it all. Tell me these things, and you have my attention, and I will hold your jacket after school in the playground. Old habits die hard.

I became an editor because you have a story, yet to be told.

I'm listening.

Thornton Sully
Editor-in-Chief
A Word with You Press
Hroznová 51/11, České Budějovice 370 01
thorn@awordwithyoupress.com
+420 608 988 551

Send up to 30 pages of your work, Times New Roman, double spaced for a *pro-bono* evaluation. Visit www.awordwithyoupress.com for a full listing of services and endorsements.

Thornton Sully has Jack-Londoned his way across the globe sleeping with whatever country would have him and picking up stray stories along the way. A litter of dog-eared passports that have taken up residence in his sock drawer are a constant temptation, but, as the founder in 2009 of *A Word with You Press*, dedicated to helping you tell your story persuasively and with passion, it's not likely he will stray too far from the towers that are *A Word with You Press*, now located in the Bohemian township of České Budějovice in the Czech Republic, except, perhaps, for an occasional swim in the Aegean or ziplining in Montenegro. Authors who have sought his advice have won major awards, including the Pulitzer Prize, the Isabel Allende Miraposa Award for new fiction, and the Best Poetry Award from San Diego Writers' Awards.

"I arise in the morning torn between a desire to improve the world and a desire to enjoy the world. This makes it hard to plan the day."

Thornton Sully, plagiarizing E.B. White

Made in the USA
Las Vegas, NV
06 January 2023

65119233R00136